A DEATH AT RAVEN'S ROOST

EMILY ORGAN

Ebook ISBN: 978-1-83700-325-9
Paperback ISBN: 978-1-83700-327-3

Cover design: Ghost
Cover images: Adobe Stock, Shutterstock

Published by Storm Publishing.
For further information, visit:
www.stormpublishing.co

ALSO BY EMILY ORGAN

Emma Langley Victorian Mysteries

The Whitechapel Widow

The Poison Puzzle

Murder in the Soho Graveyard

The Clockmaker's Murder

Penny Green Series

Limelight

The Rookery

The Maid's Secret

The Inventor

Curse of the Poppy

The Bermondsey Poisoner

An Unwelcome Guest

Death at the Workhouse

The Gang of St Bride's

Murder in Ratcliffe

The Egyptian Mystery

The Camden Spiritualist

Augusta Peel Series

Death in Soho

Murder in the Air

The Bloomsbury Murder

The Tower Bridge Murder

Death in Westminster

Murder on the Thames

The Baker Street Murders

Death in Kensington

Churchill & Pemberley Series

Tragedy at Piddleton Hotel

Murder in Cold Mud

Puzzle in Poppleford Wood

Trouble in the Churchyard

Wheels of Peril

The Poisoned Peer

Fiasco at the Jam Factory

Disaster at the Christmas Dinner

Christmas Calamity at the Vicarage (novella)

Writing as Martha Bond

Lottie Sprigg Travels Mystery Series

Murder in Venice

Murder in Paris

Murder in Cairo

Murder in Monaco

Murder in Vienna

Lottie Sprigg Country House Mystery Series

Murder in the Library

Murder in the Grotto

Murder in the Maze

Murder in the Bay

ONE

December 1888

The first mouthful of beer tasted good.

The second spilled a little down Archie Mitchell's chin when his neighbour elbowed him in the ribs. 'Watch out, Archie. Seamus is in here.'

'Where?' A sudden twinge of anxiety tightened in his chest. From his seat at the crowded table, Archie glanced around the busy room. It was difficult to distinguish Seamus from the others. Everyone looked much the same in their shabby work jackets and frayed trousers: labourers and dockhands with roughened hands and dirt-streaked faces. They jostled shoulder to shoulder, their shouts and laughter mingling with a lively tune from the fiddler in the corner. The air was thick with pipe smoke. The day's toil was over and the rest of the evening would be filled with beer and song.

But Archie was uneasy. The heat of the room felt suffocating and the smoke made his eyes smart. Every burst of laughter seemed too loud, the men around him too close. He took another swallow of beer to steady himself, but his hand trembled slightly as he set the tankard down. Somewhere in this haze of noise and smoke, Seamus Byrne was watching.

He drew in a breath, trying to instil some courage.

'Seamus won't do anything,' he said, forcing confidence into his voice. 'He's all talk.'

But his neighbour was already deep in another conversation. Archie risked another glance around. Still no sign of Seamus. Perhaps he'd found someone else to bother.

And while everyone was distracted, Archie had an opportunity.

He slipped his hand into his jacket pocket and closed his fingers around the small bundle hidden there. Casually, he lifted it out, keeping it hidden in his palm. Another quick look around told him no one was watching.

Bending low, he ducked his head beneath the table. With his free hand he fidgeted with his laces, while in the gloom beneath the seat he spotted the wooden panel he had knocked loose on a previous visit. He'd realised it would make an excellent hiding place.

Now was his moment. The blood rushed to his head as he worked quickly, pressing the small bundle in behind the loosened board. The panel didn't fit back properly, the corner still jutted out. But this was his regular seat in The Tiger Tavern. He sat here most nights. No one else would notice.

Straightening, Archie blinked at the sudden light and steadied himself, feeling a little light-headed.

'All right there, Archie?' asked his companion, noticing him shifting about.

'Just tied up my lace,' he said lightly, lifting his tankard and taking a long gulp.

It was hidden. And his secret was safe. For now.

The night air felt cool and fresh as Archie stepped out onto the cobbles in front of The Tiger Tavern later that evening. Everything was quiet now the fight was over. He felt something crunch under his boot. He moved his foot to look down and saw a broken piece of clay pipe. There was spilled beer and a splash of blood too. He felt a queasy flutter in his chest and moved on.

He pulled his folded cap from his pocket and fitted it onto his head. Ahead, orange lights glimmered from the windows beyond the Tower of London's wall. They gave off a slow, mysterious glow. What went on inside that great old place, he wondered, then shook his head a little at himself; he was tipsy from the evening's beer.

To his right, the river lay black and wide. He could smell its salt-edged dankness and hear the low puff of a steamboat some-where upriver. He hiccoughed loudly and sniggered as his feet slipped on the uneven cobbles. How many beers had he drunk in the end? Perhaps it was more than he remembered.

A nearby gas lamp threw a circle of light onto the little building marking the entrance to the Tower Subway. His route home. All he had to do was cross the short tunnel beneath the river, and he'd be back at his lodgings and his bed.

Something small landed at his feet with a clatter. He stopped and looked down. A stone. Perhaps he'd kicked it without noticing. As he moved on, another hit his right boot with a dull, stinging tap.

Someone was throwing them.

'Oi!' he called, more surprised than angry. 'Watch it!'

A figure moved to his right, disappearing into the darkness near the path which led to the river. Archie heard a quick peal of laughter.

'Oi!' he called again, louder. Why was someone pelting stones at him?

A third missile struck his shin. A sharp pain flared, but the beer dulled it quickly.

'Come here!' he shouted, staggering after the figure now lost in the dark. 'Come here now!'

If someone wanted a fight he might as well give it to them. He'd show them what he was made of. They wouldn't dare throw stones at Archie Mitchell again.

He reached the riverside where a line of gas lamps marked the embankment. In the darkness beyond them stood the new bridge he was helping to build. He couldn't see it now but he knew it was there. A vast structure which would become one of London's finest bridges. In six short hours he'd be back there, riveting steel beams into place.

But before then, there was a problem to deal with.

'Oi!' he called into the dark, his voice loud with ale and bravado. 'Think you're brave throwing stones at me? Come on then... Come on if you dare!'

Up ahead, he could see a figure walking away from him.

'Oi!' he called out again, stumbling on the cobbles of the riverside path. 'Trying to get away now, are you? I'll teach you to throw stones at me!'

He hurried on, but his legs wouldn't move as well as he'd like. It seemed the drink had taken more of a hold over him than he'd realised.

And now there was no sign of the person. He spun round, wondering if he'd missed them. Where had they gone?

'Archie.'

He let out a nervous laugh when he heard the voice. It was one he knew well.

'Throwing stones at me, were you?' he called, his eyes straining through the gloom. A gas lamp flickered ahead, casting a weak glow.

'Where are you?'

'Here.' The figure stepped out of the shadows.

'What's this about?' he asked, his voice tight, his heart beating fast in his chest. 'Why did you...' His words caught in his throat as he saw the faint light glinting on something metallic.

A gun.

Archie froze. Time seemed to stand still. His legs wouldn't move. He tried to scream but no sound came as the figure raised the gun.

TWO

'I can't say I'm getting on very well with "Für Elise",' said Mrs Solomon as she sat on the piano stool, her shoulders slumped. 'It's all the jumping around with the fingers that I don't like.'

'The arpeggios?'

'The what?'

Emma suppressed a sigh. She'd explained arpeggios to her landlady the previous week. She glanced at the shaggy cat who watched them from the most comfortable chair in the room. Surprisingly, he seemed to enjoy his mistress playing the piano.

She turned back to Mrs Solomon. 'Perhaps we can learn a different piece instead?'

'I like the idea of playing Beethoven though, it sounds impressive when you tell people you play a bit of Beethoven. Does he have any easier ones?'

'We could try his nineteenth sonata, that might be a little easier.'

'Nineteen? Why can't we just start at one?'

Emma pulled a grimace. 'That one's a lot harder.'

Mrs Solomon gave a cheeky wink. 'I was just pulling your leg, Mrs Langley.' She sighed. 'I'm not a very good student, am I? I thought that because I'd played the piano as a girl I would find it very straightforward. It's not though, is it? There's a lot of thinking involved.'

'Daily practice helps,' said Emma. She'd not heard her landlady practise since the last lesson. 'Just ten minutes a day is enough at the beginning. It helps your fingers learn the patterns.'

'Ah yes.' Mrs Solomon scratched behind her ear again. 'There's always so much to do and I have so little time. But I suppose there wouldn't be any harm in finding a few minutes each day to practise.'

'Ten minutes.'

'Ten?'

'At the very least. Otherwise there's...' Emma stopped herself from saying there was little point in bothering at all. Her landlady had enthusiasm for playing and she didn't want to dampen it. She fixed a smile on her face and continued, 'Try doing the practice at the same time every day. And once you've done it for a few days... a week even... it feels like a habit you can continue with.'

Mrs Solomon nodded. 'Very well. I won't give up on Elise just yet. Who was she?'

'I don't think anyone knows for sure,' said Emma.

The sound of the doorbell interrupted them.

'I'll go and see who that is,' said the landlady, getting up from the piano stool. She left the room and returned moments later with a small envelope. 'A telegram for you, Mrs Langley.'

Emma opened it and saw it was from Penny Blakely:

Can you call on us at 5pm? An inspector from
Scotland Yard is visiting.

'Well, I wonder what that could be all about?' said Mrs Solomon, reading the telegram over Emma's shoulder.

Emma stepped away from her, a little surprised by the extent of her nosiness. 'I don't know,' she replied. 'But it sounds intriguing.'

THREE

As she travelled to St John's Wood Road station on the Metropolitan Railway, Emma wondered why an inspector from Scotland Yard wished to meet them. Was he a colleague of Penny's husband, James?

Perhaps the meeting concerned a case Emma and Penny had worked on in the past. Some news about the murder of Mrs Melbourne or – heaven forbid – Emma's late husband, William. She shuddered, hoping his name wouldn't be mentioned. After learning about his lies and deception while investigating his murder, she'd been trying her hardest to put the past behind her.

She could hear Florence crying as she knocked on the Blakely family's door. Penny answered with the baby in her arms, looking a little weary. 'I'm sorry about the noise,' she said as she led Emma to the sitting room. 'Florence is hungry. James is going to give the children their tea while we speak to Detective Inspector Simpson. Hopefully we'll have a bit of peace while we speak to him.'

'What does he want?' Emma asked. But her question was drowned by the baby's cries as they stepped into the front room. There, Penny and James's three-year-old son, Thomas, was showing the inspector his toy train.

James and the inspector got to their feet. The detective

inspector was a long-faced man with greying muttonchop whiskers. 'Mrs Langley,' he said. 'It's a pleasure to meet you. I've heard all about you.'

Emma glanced anxiously at Penny then James, wondering what they'd told the inspector. 'Is that right?' she said.

'Very much so.' He gave her a firm smile and she hoped she had nothing to worry about.

Penny handed Florence to James who'd already rolled up his shirtsleeves for the task ahead of him. He then left the room with the children and Emma moved some toy soldiers from a chair before sitting down.

Inspector Simpson hitched his trousers at the knee and made himself comfortable in James's armchair. 'I've had a good chat with Inspector Blakely about this and he agrees the pair of you will be able to help me,' he began. 'I've heard all about your excellent sleuthing skills and I'm beginning to believe the fairer sex have some advantages over chaps when it comes to detection methods.' He paused to smile at them both, but Emma felt impatient for him to continue.

'I must say... as I regard the pair of you now, I'm impressed that two genteel ladies of such demure nature have achieved so much. After all, investigating crimes is a grisly business and not for the faint-hearted. There are countless men of sturdy constitution who would quail at the details of some cases—'

'My husband was fatally stabbed in Whitechapel,' Emma interrupted, her patience almost gone. 'I felt forced to investigate his murder because the police were slow to do anything about it.'

'I see.' He gave an awkward cough.

'And I was a news reporter on Fleet Street for ten years,' added Penny. 'Having reported on the wide spectrum of human nature, there's little which surprises me these days.'

'Indeed.' He coughed again. 'Which is exactly why I think your help would be invaluable.'

'What do you actually want us to do?' asked Penny.

'Well, there's an unsolved case which puzzles us,' he said. His condescending smile had vanished now. 'Archie Mitchell. He was murdered close to the Tower of London in December last year.'

'How awful,' said Penny. 'What happened?'

Emma leaned forward a little, keen to hear what the inspector had to say.

FOUR

'Archie Mitchell was twenty-eight years old and a labourer on the Tower Bridge which is currently under construction,' said Detective Inspector Simpson. 'He was found injured by Traitors' Gate on the riverside embankment next to the Tower of London. It was late in the evening on Friday the fourteenth of December and he was unconscious when he was discovered. He'd suffered a gunshot to the leg and an injury to his head from the fall to the ground. He never regained consciousness after the attack and died two days later in the London Hospital in Whitechapel. His death was caused by the head injury and loss of blood from his leg wound.'

Emma winced. 'How horrible,' she said. 'Who found him?'

'A young lady called Miss Sarah Lyford,' replied the inspector. 'She works as a barmaid at The Tiger Tavern on Tower Hill. At the time of the attack on Mr Mitchell, she was outside the public house sluicing the pavement after a brawl. Brawls are not uncommon at The Tiger Tavern; beer and blood are spilled there quite often I'm afraid...' He paused and cleared his throat. 'Anyway, Miss Lyford heard the gunshot and immediately ran to the scene. She tried to rouse Mr Mitchell but to no avail. Within minutes, several others had arrived at the scene and a doctor was found. Mr Mitchell was then transported to the hospital.'

'So the culprit fled the scene,' said Penny. 'Did anyone see them running away?'

'After the gunshot, a witness saw someone running in the direction of St Katharine Docks. We don't know if that person was the culprit, but it would be quite easy to hide in the wharves at that time of night. The area is poorly lit with plenty of hiding places.'

'How did Archie Mitchell spend his evening?' asked Emma. 'And what was he doing by Traitors' Gate?'

'He spent his evening at The Tiger Tavern,' replied the inspector. 'As he did every evening. It's a popular place with the bridge labourers and sailors from the docks. He left the public house at half past ten to return to his lodgings in Bermondsey. I don't know how familiar you are with that part of London, but the entrance to the Tower Subway is outside The Tiger Tavern. His usual route was to walk through the subway beneath the river to Bermondsey on the southern side. For some reason that evening, Mr Mitchell walked past the Tower Subway entrance and a short distance east to Traitors' Gate.'

'So he met someone at Traitors' Gate,' said Penny. 'Did he mention he'd arranged to meet anyone that evening?'

The inspector shook his head. 'No. And no one saw him with anyone. The last sighting of him was when he left the public house.'

'Presumably robbery has been ruled out as a motive,' said Penny.

'Absolutely. Mr Mitchell's pocket watch and wallet were still with him. A spent bullet casing was found at the scene which suggests the revolver was a Webley. It's possible the weapon was Webley's British Bull Dog revolver which is small enough to be carried in a pocket. It could explain why no one saw anyone with a revolver in their possession either before or after the attack.'

'Have you got any idea what the motive for the attack could have been?' Penny asked.

'No,' replied the inspector. 'Inquiries were made about

disagreements Mitchell may have had, but nothing untoward was found. He had no obvious enemies.'

'You mentioned the barmaid was cleaning the pavement outside The Tiger Tavern after a brawl,' said Emma. 'Was Mr Mitchell involved in that at all?'

The inspector shook his head. 'Archie Mitchell doesn't appear to have been the pugnacious type. By all accounts, he was a quiet chap. Mild-mannered and averse to confrontation.'

'He had no enemies?'

'No obvious ones, no. However, people we spoke to did mention Mr Mitchell's mood had changed shortly before his death. His manner was usually easy-going and he was always ready with a joke. But apparently something changed. He became more serious and seemed troubled by something.'

'Had something happened?' asked Penny.

'That's the mystery. There was no bereavement anyone knew about. But friends noticed he'd started drinking more. And he was late for work a few times, which was unlike him.'

'Financial problems?' Emma suggested.

'Some guessed that, but there's no evidence,' said the inspector. 'He had steady employment and was earning a decent wage for a labourer. They pay them well on that bridge. There were no debts that we know of. No evidence of gambling his money away. His landlady said he always paid his rent on time.'

'But something happened to him which changed his mood,' Penny said. 'Perhaps it wasn't obvious to others and he kept quiet about it.'

'So this happened in December,' said Emma, sitting back in her chair. 'And Scotland Yard have made no progress at all?'

'Neither has H Division,' said the inspector quickly, clearly keen to disperse the blame. 'Although one could argue they've been rather occupied by the Jack the Ripper investigation. It's important to remember the timing of Mr Mitchell's murder, it occurred only a month or so after the last known attack by the Whitechapel murderer.'

Emma gave a bitter nod. 'I know how H Division and the Yard were struggling at the time,' she said. 'My husband was murdered in Whitechapel last November.'

'Luckily we caught the person responsible,' said Detective Inspector Simpson.

'With our help,' chipped in Penny.

'Indeed.' He put on his condescending smile again. 'Which is why I'm calling on you today. I think you can help with this case too.'

'But how?' asked Emma. 'What can we do which your men can't?'

'I'm pleased you've asked me that because that's what I wish to discuss with you next. I'm rather suspicious of the barmaid, Sarah Lyford.'

'Why?' asked Penny.

The inspector gave a thoughtful pause. 'Her manner is evasive,' he said. 'And that presents two possibilities, in my view. First, she may have seen who shot Archie Mitchell. Maybe she arrived just as the assailant was fleeing. And maybe that person saw her too. If she's scared, it's understandable. She could be protecting herself. Perhaps she was even warned to keep silent.'

'And the second possibility?' asked Emma.

'She's guilty,' the inspector said simply. 'And silence is her best defence. Fear can be real, but it can also be feigned. It's possible she orchestrated the attack on Mitchell. Lured him to Traitors' Gate under false pretences, shot him, and concocted a convenient story.'

'You told us Archie Mitchell usually entered the Tower Subway when he left the public house,' said Penny. 'Are you suggesting Sarah Lyford persuaded him to walk with her along the riverside until they reached Traitors' Gate?'

'Yes, that's one theory.'

'So Mr Mitchell and Miss Lyford knew each other?'

'I believe so. Although she denies it. She says she knew who he was but didn't know him well. Mr Mitchell was a regular drinker in the public house in which she worked so I think it's likely they knew each other. Perhaps there was a love affair... Who can say? I can't persuade her to tell me.'

'The only reason you suspect Miss Lyford is because she found Mr Mitchell after he was fatally injured, is that right?'

'Yes. But I think it's no coincidence she left The Tiger Tavern shortly after he did that evening. And if the weapon was a British Bull Dog revolver, then it would have been very easy for her to conceal it on her person. Perhaps beneath her apron or dress... In a garter perhaps.' He gave a polite cough, embarrassed at having mentioned the item. 'Anyway, there's a belief that Sarah Lyford might speak more freely to someone outside the police. Someone she doesn't see as a threat. Someone who's... well, a lady.'

'You think she might talk to Emma and me?' Penny said.

The inspector nodded. 'I hope so. She might be more at ease in a conversation which doesn't feel like an interrogation. And you both have a way of encouraging people to open up. Of course, you don't have to say yes. But,' he continued, 'we're at a dead end at the moment. And if there's any chance you might help us find a way out, I think it's worth a try.'

Emma and Penny exchanged a glance. The case intrigued Emma, but she wasn't sure how much help she could be.

'We'll need to discuss it between us before we can make a decision,' Penny said to the inspector.

'Of course.' He gave a polite nod. 'Take all the time you need. But I do hope you'll agree to it.'

FIVE

'If Sarah Lyford doesn't want to tell the police what she knows, then I don't see why she'd confide in us,' Emma said once the Scotland Yard inspector had left.

'That's a good point.' Penny nodded. 'But it's worth a try, don't you think?'

'It's definitely worth a try,' agreed James, who'd returned to the sitting room with the children.

Emma didn't feel so sure. 'What if Sarah Lyford refuses to talk to us? What then? It will be a struggle to know what to do next. I don't like the idea of committing ourselves to something that we may not be able to solve.'

'There's no shame in failing,' said Penny. 'After all, the Yard haven't had any success yet with this case, have they? And besides, perhaps Sarah Lyford will talk to us. There's only one way to find out isn't there?'

'You're right. I suppose I feel the need to do a good job. I want to be able to solve this and if we can't... then I'm worried we'll be wasting everyone's time. In fact we might even make things worse. If we upset Sarah Lyford then we could ruin the chances of her speaking to anyone about the case ever again.'

Penny smiled. 'You need to have a little more confidence in your abilities, Emma.'

'Penny's right,' added James as he bounced baby Florence on his knee.

Their compliments made Emma blush a little. 'Abilities?' she said. She'd worked on a few cases with Penny, but only because she'd been pulled into them. She had helped as best as she could and there had been some luck involved too. 'I'm a piano teacher,' she added. 'Not a detective.'

'A piano teacher with some good investigative skills,' said James. 'I wouldn't have suggested you and Penny to Detective Inspector Simpson if I didn't think you were capable of solving Archie Mitchell's case. And Inspector Simpson's a good chap,' added James. 'He used to work with my father. You won't have any problems with him.'

'That's reassuring.' Penny turned to Emma. 'I want to know what happened to Archie Mitchell. Don't you?'

'Yes,' said Emma. 'And I'll be happy to help you if you need it, Penny.'

'Good. I can't do this without you.'

SIX

Two days later, Emma and Penny walked down Great Tower Hill towards The Tiger Tavern. The fortress walls of the Tower of London rose to their left and ahead of them the River Thames was busy with ships and barges. Clouds whipped past the sun in the late afternoon sky. The two women had timed their visit before the labourers on the new bridge finished their work for the day. Hopefully the public house would be quiet.

The Tiger Tavern was on their right between a warehouse and a carman's business. It was a broad, four-storey structure with sash windows and a large lantern which hung from a bracket over the door.

Inside, the tavern was dark and close, the air thick with the smell of hops and pipe smoke. There were a few labourers inside, dressed in well-worn shirts, stained trousers, and heavy boots. Conversation slowed and heads turned. This wasn't the sort of establishment where women, especially well-dressed ones, were expected to appear.

Emma felt her cheeks burn. She felt acutely aware of the stares, of her gloves, her hat, her neatly pressed skirt.

'Try to ignore the stares,' murmured Penny beside her. 'All that matters is finding Miss Lyford.'

Penny, as ever, carried herself with quiet assurance. Emma admired the way her friend held her head high, as though she had every right to be there. She'd clearly walked into places like this before.

Behind the bar, a broad-shouldered man with thick forearms and a grubby apron gave them a cautious look, drying a glass with a rag.

'Good afternoon,' said Penny, her voice calm and clear. 'Could you please tell us where we might find Miss Lyford?'

He raised a thick brow and called over his shoulder, 'Sarah! You've got company. Two gentlewomen want a word.'

A woman emerged from a door behind the bar. She was fair-haired with regular features and sharp cheekbones, but the fine lines around her mouth and eyes spoke of long, hard days. Emma thought that in finer clothes and easier circumstances, Miss Lyford would be considered a beauty.

Miss Lyford's eyes narrowed with suspicion. 'What is it?' she asked. Her tone had a defensive edge.

'My name is Mrs Blakely, and this is my friend Mrs Langley,' Penny said. 'We'd like to speak with you somewhere quiet, if that's possible.'

Miss Lyford folded her arms. 'Not unless you tell me what this is about. Are you from the school board? Because I've been sending them every morning. I don't need another warning letter.'

'We're not with the school board,' said Penny. 'We're lady detectives.'

The phrase sounded oddly official to Emma. Professional, even. She wasn't sure she'd have used the description herself, but she liked it.

Miss Lyford sighed and rolled her eyes. 'I can give you two minutes. But I don't like detectives – lady or otherwise.' Without waiting for a reply, she stepped out from behind the bar and brushed past them, disappearing through a side door.

As they followed, a sharp-eyed, wiry man caught Emma's eye. He was young with scruffy hair which looked like it had never seen a comb. He watched them from a table where he sat alone with a tankard of beer. There was something in his gaze which unnerved her a little. She quickly glanced away and went on her way.

Miss Lyford led them up a narrow, creaking staircase and into a small room above the bar. Through the grimy window, Emma could see the Tower of London's stark grey walls.

The room appeared to be a living space. A battered armchair sat by the window and there was a wooden stool by the fireplace. An iron-framed bed with a faded quilt was pushed against the wall.

Miss Lyford didn't offer them seats so they remained standing, the three of them forming an awkward triangle in the centre of the room.

'Well?' said the barmaid, folding her arms. 'What do you want to talk about?'

'Archie Mitchell's murder,' said Penny, her voice calm but firm.

Miss Lyford's expression hardened. 'I'm not talking about him.'

'Why not?'

'Because I've said all I have to say.'

'But his murder's still unsolved,' said Penny. 'Don't you want to help catch whoever did it? They're clearly dangerous.'

The barmaid gave a sharp shake of her head. 'I told you. I'm not talking about it. Are you working for the police?'

'We work for ourselves,' said Penny, carefully avoiding the directness of the question. 'I was a news reporter for ten years. I've investigated several murder cases. Mrs Langley here solved her husband's murder.'

Miss Lyford's eyebrows lifted, her expression softening a little. 'Your husband was murdered?' she asked Emma.

Emma nodded. 'Yes. And while I was investigating the case, I discovered he'd been keeping secrets from me. A lot of them.'

Miss Lyford gave a dry laugh. 'Like most men, then.'

'Have you had a similar experience?' Penny asked.

Miss Lyford glanced away. 'Let's just say I've known a few with secrets. But they're rarely clever enough to keep them hidden for long. Anyway, I'm afraid I can't help you with Archie Mitchell. I spoke to the police at the time and I've got nothing new to say.'

'I apologise if we're asking you to repeat yourself,' Emma said. 'We're not familiar with the details. He was killed nearby, wasn't he?'

'Down by the riverside,' she replied. 'By the Tower.'

'And this was last December?'

The barmaid nodded. 'Archie had been drinking here as he did every evening after work.' Emma noticed she used his first name, as if she'd been familiar with him. 'There was a fight outside that night and I had to wash down the pavement afterwards. Archie must have left shortly before or after, I didn't see him leave. But I did see him in the pub before the fight happened.'

'Was he involved in the fight?'

'No. Archie wasn't the fighting type. I heard the gunshot while I was washing the pavement. Obviously I had no idea Archie was involved at that point. I ran along the river path to see what had happened and nearly tripped over him. I could only just see him in the light of the gas lamp. He was just lying there where he'd fallen.'

'Weren't you frightened?' asked Penny.

Miss Lyford shrugged. 'Not really... I suppose I didn't stop to think about it. I just wanted to know what had happened. When you work in a place like this, you get used to fights and trouble of that sort. And there was no sign of the attacker when I got there. He'd run off.' She paused, her voice quieter now. 'I crouched beside him. It was dark and I couldn't see him very well. But he was out cold. I thought then he was dead. It turned out he wasn't but he died a few days later.' She lowered her gaze to the floorboards and hugged her folded arms a little tighter.

'You called for help?' asked Emma.

'Yes.' She lifted her head and met Emma's gaze. 'People came running and then a policeman arrived. Since then, I've answered every question people have asked. Over and over.'

'Did you see anyone who appeared to be loitering by the tavern?'

'Not when I was sluicing, there was no one about then. The old blind soldier had been out there singing but he'd left earlier that evening. He must have got enough pennies in his tin. And there were a few women waiting for their men like they do. Sometimes they come in and drag them out if they're feeling brave enough.'

'Would any of them have seen anything suspicious, do you think?'

'Well, not the blind old soldier, that's for sure.' Sarah laughed nervously. 'But the women? I don't know. I'm sure the police asked them if they saw anything.'

'Did you know Archie Mitchell well?' Penny asked.

'He was a regular. Like plenty of others. I saw him most days.'

'So you knew him quite well?' Emma said.

Miss Lyford pushed her lips together. 'He was just another labourer who came in for a drink. That's all. He worked on the new bridge. There's a dozen like him in here every night.'

'Did he ever speak to you about his life?' Penny asked.

'No. He was polite. Quiet. Nothing unusual.'

'We've heard his mood changed shortly before his death,' said Penny. 'Did you notice anything?'

'I wouldn't know.' She glanced at the door. 'I should be going. I've already told you I didn't want to discuss this.'

But somehow they had got her talking – Emma felt a quiet sense of achievement about this.

'Do you live here?' Penny asked as Miss Lyford stepped over to the door.

'No. Nearby.'

'And you have children?' Emma asked, recalling her mention of the school board.

'Yes. We live with my mother and she watches them while I'm working.'

'How old?' asked Penny.

'Five and seven.'

'A little older than mine,' said Penny. 'They're hard work when they're young, aren't they?'

The barmaid gave a weary smile. 'They're hard work at every age. But I'd do anything for them. I just wish I didn't have to work in a place like this to keep them fed. But that's the way it is.'

'You're lucky to have your mother's help,' said Penny. 'It must be a comfort to know they're in good hands.'

Miss Lyford gave a quiet nod as she opened the door. 'It is.' Then she paused and gave Emma a curious look. 'What secrets did your husband keep from you? If you don't mind me asking.'

Emma welcomed the question. It was a sign Sarah Lyford didn't mind talking to them, despite her protestations.

'I discovered he had a love affair,' Emma replied.

Miss Lyford pulled a grimace. 'I'm sorry to hear it. A lot of men get up to that sort of thing.'

'He also stole the money I inherited from my family,' Emma said.

'He stole from you?' Her eyes widened. 'That's bad. I'm truly sorry to hear it.'

Emma hesitated, then added, 'I found out he only married me for the inheritance. He didn't love me. He never did.'

The barmaid's mouth dropped open. 'That's awful! He completely fooled you?'

Emma nodded, her voice quieter now. 'I was naïve.'

Miss Lyford shook her head firmly. 'No, you weren't, Mrs Langley. You mustn't say that. I've known men like him and they can fool anyone. It's not my place to say, but I'll say it anyway – you're better off without him. And you said he was murdered?'

'By someone who didn't want him around any longer,' replied Emma. 'You say you've known men like him?'

Miss Lyford let out a breath, as if deciding whether or not to speak. 'Yes. Not quite the same as yours, but bad enough. He was a drinker. Might still be. I've no idea where he is. When the children ask about him, I say he walked out one day and never came back.

It's not nice for them to hear, but it's the truth. I won't lie to make him sound like something he wasn't.'

'You speak like someone who's been let down more than once,' ventured Penny.

The barmaid gave a crooked smile. 'You don't need to hear the details, it won't do much for my reputation. What little I've got left of it, I'd rather keep.' She turned back to Emma. 'I hope you find someone who treats you well, Mrs Langley.'

'Thank you,' Emma said. 'And I hope the same for you.'

'Maybe I have found someone.' She gave a small shrug. 'Or maybe not. You never really know with men, do you?'

'Why not?'

Miss Lyford scratched at her neck. 'He's a busy man. Here one week, gone the next. But when he's around, he can be very good to me...' She paused and Emma noticed Sarah rub her hands together nervously. 'Sometimes.'

'Sometimes?'

'Johnny's not known for his...'

'Johnny?'

The barmaid shook her head. 'I've said too much. Besides, you don't know who he is.'

'Maybe we do,' said Penny. 'What's his surname?'

'If you know him, you know him. Everyone around here knows he who is.'

She stepped through the door, ending the conversation.

They were outsiders and Sarah Lyford had just reminded them of that.

SEVEN

As Emma and Penny left The Tiger Tavern, the fresh breeze from the river cleared Emma's head of the reek of tobacco smoke and stale beer.

'So Sarah Lyford was here sluicing down the pavement when she heard the gunshot,' said Penny. 'Shall we see how far it is to the riverside?'

'Good idea,' said Emma. They walked along the cobbles, passing the kiosk for the Tower Subway entrance, and headed for the river.

'I wonder who Johnny is?' said Penny. 'Miss Lyford seemed keen to inform us he's well known locally. Well known for what, I wonder?'

'It's telling that she didn't elaborate,' said Emma. 'She could have said he runs a business, works in the docks, or does something respectable – but she didn't.'

'That sort of vagueness usually means someone doesn't want to say too much.'

'Because it might be criminal?'

'Quite possibly.'

They followed the cobbled path along the Thames with the weathered stone of the Tower of London to their left. A line of trees had been planted alongside the path, softening the effect of the ancient fortress. Emma had read about the Tower's macabre history, of the imprisonments, murders and executions there. But she'd also heard about the famous menagerie which had once been housed within its walls: lions, elephants and polar bears.

The sky was turning grey in the east and large clouds were rolling in along the river, bringing with them a threat of rain.

Ahead, two towers rose from the middle of the river. They were constructed from steel girders and stood on two enormous stone piers which had been built on the riverbed. Long steel sections connected the piers to the north and south riverbanks. The new Tower Bridge was taking shape.

'Doesn't it look ugly?' said Penny as they paused for a moment.

Emma agreed. 'It doesn't look like the drawings I've seen in the newspaper.' She recalled stone arches, mullioned windows and decorative turrets and spires. The structure in the river looked very different. 'From what I hear, the entire structure is steel and they're going to clad it in stone.'

Penny smiled. 'To make it look as old as the Tower of London? That would be clever indeed. It's difficult to imagine at the moment, but I'm looking forward to seeing it when it's finished.'

They continued on their way until the low arch of Traitors' Gate came into view. Built into the Tower's wall, the gate sat lower than the raised embankment path. Moss coated the damp stone, and the steps leading down to the water had long since darkened with age.

Pausing, they glanced around. 'We're quite a way from The Tiger Tavern,' said Emma. 'Two hundred yards, at least.'

Penny nodded. 'Which makes it all the more curious that Sarah Lyford was first on the scene when Archie Mitchell was shot. You'd think someone closer would have heard the shot and reached him before she did.'

'I suppose we don't know exactly where he was on this path when he was attacked,' said Emma. 'It's possible it was a little closer to the public house.'

'Even so, The Tiger Tavern is out of sight,' said Penny. 'I'm beginning to understand why Detective Inspector Simpson considers Miss Lyford to be a suspect. Although I think she spoke fairly honestly with us, I sensed some reticence when we asked her how well she'd known Archie Mitchell.'

'I agree,' said Emma. 'I think she was trying hard to pretend she hadn't known him very well.'

Penny glanced up and down the embankment. 'The assailant had two ways to run,' she said. 'And Inspector Simpson said they ran that way.' She pointed in the direction of the new bridge. 'East, towards St Katharine Docks.' Emma followed her gaze to the wharves beyond the new bridge where tall-masted ships were moored by the warehouses and cranes.

'I can imagine there are a lot of hiding places there, especially at night.'

She imagined the scene under the cloak of a winter evening. The wind sharper, the river black. Mist and fog. 'It might not have been as dark as people assume,' she said. 'Look, there's a gas lamp over there.'

'That makes sense,' said Penny. 'Mr Mitchell's assailant had to have been able to see something to be able to point a gun at him.'

A chill wind picked up from the river and the dark clouds which had loomed on the horizon earlier were now overhead. The temperature dipped and Emma felt a prickle on the back of her neck.

She and Penny were standing close to where a man had been fatally injured. Had it been an ambush or an arranged meeting? She imagined Archie Mitchell leaving the tavern that evening, his mood lifted by the beer he'd drunk with his fellow labourers. As he'd stepped out into the night air, he'd had no idea his life was close to its end...

Or had he? Inspector Simpson had told them he'd seemed troubled by something shortly before his death. Perhaps he had known he was in danger...

A sudden cawing noise startled her, like a harsh gravelly laugh.

Heart pounding, she looked up into the grey sky in time to see a large black bird rise up from beyond the Tower walls and swoop down again.

'A raven,' said Penny, her tone ominous. 'The harbinger of death.'

EIGHT

Sarah arrived home that evening to the warming scent of stew. 'I've boiled the chicken carcass,' said her mother, stirring the pot on the stove. 'I put the oats in which I got from Mrs Henderson, they'll give you a bit of strength.' She turned on her stool and looked her daughter up and down. 'You're getting thin.'

'I'm not.' Sarah pulled her shawl around her.

'They overwork you in that place.'

'It pays our way.' She stepped over to her children who were waiting patiently at the little table for their food. She bent and kissed their heads and gave each one a hug.

'You've got to go back there later, haven't you?' asked her mother.

'Yes, but I get a day off tomorrow.'

Her mother tutted in reply. 'First day off in... how long? It's little more than slavery.'

Sarah sat at the table with her children. 'It's not slavery, Ma. I receive a wage. And it means we can keep this roof over our heads.'

Her mother glanced up at the mildewed ceiling. 'Some roof. And he's been making a noise up there all day.'

'Doing what?'

'I don't know, I've not been up there and asked him.' Her

mother paused for a moment, scrutinising her face. 'What's wrong?' she asked. 'You look as pale as milk.'

Sarah sighed. Her mother could always tell when something was bothering her. She ushered the children into the other room. 'Just for a moment,' she explained. 'I need to talk to Grandma about something.'

Her mother planted her hands on her knees and gave Sarah an expectant look.

'Two lady detectives came to speak to me today,' said Sarah, sitting back at the table.

'Detectives? Don't tell me they asked you about that dead man.'

'Archie Mitchell. Yes.'

'And what did they want to know?'

'Everything I told the police months ago. I told them I didn't want to talk about it. I've done my bit.'

'Yes, you have.' Her mother turned to the pot again and gave it another stir. 'Archie Mitchell,' she repeated. 'Whatever mess he got into, it was his own doing. There was always something odd about the whole thing. Why are the two ladies interested, anyway? It's not the sort of thing they should be troubling themselves about. Lady detectives...' She shook her head in amusement. 'Sounds like they're ladies with too much time on their hands to me. This is ready now, get out the bowls and spoons, would you?'

Sarah obliged. But as she did so, she heard heavy footsteps on the wooden staircase which led to their rooms. She froze for a moment, heart pounding. She'd recognise those footsteps anywhere.

For a moment, she and her mother held each other's gaze, an understanding passing between them.

Sarah straightened herself as the door flung open.

'Guess who?' said Johnny Cooper with a roguish grin. His frame filled the doorway. He removed his cap with a casual flourish and laughed. His eyes held a glint of amusement which made

Sarah's heart beat faster, even when she wished it didn't. She felt relieved the children were out of sight.

'Well then,' he said, stretching out his arms. 'Where's my warm welcome?'

Sarah smiled, aware of her mother's disapproving glare. She stepped forward and gave him a quick embrace. He reeked of alcohol and tobacco.

'I'm glad you're back,' she said.

He pulled off his overcoat and handed it to her. It was heavy, lined and expensive for someone of Johnny's means. She hung it on the nail by the door. The coat had cost good money but she doubted he'd paid for it.

He rolled up his sleeves and sank into one of the chairs the children had occupied. 'Smells like heaven in here. Where's mine?'

Sarah's mother pressed her lips into a thin line. Then she picked up a bowl, ladled some stew into it and placed it in front of him.

'There,' she said. 'Don't say I never feed you.'

'It's barely enough for a child,' he said, peering into the bowl. 'I need a proper meal. I've got things to do tonight.'

'Such as what?' Sarah asked.

Johnny gave her a crooked grin. 'Just a few errands. You don't need to worry about it.'

Sarah always worried. About where he went, who he met and what trouble he might be walking into.

'I hope you're not dragging my daughter into anything foolish,' her mother said sharply.

Johnny responded calmly, 'I wouldn't dream of it, Mrs Lyford. Sarah's the best thing in my life. I know that.'

But Sarah wasn't sure she believed him.

He ate hungrily, wiping stew from his mouth and chin with the back of his hand. Sarah thought of her hungry children in the neighbouring room. She would make sure they ate once Johnny had finished and left.

'So what have I missed?' he asked between mouthfuls. 'You

were both talking before I arrived and now it's gone quiet. What were you talking about?'

'Nothing much,' said Sarah. But like her mother, Johnny was good at reading her face.

He pointed his spoon at her. 'Nothing much?' he said. 'You're lying. Tell me what's happened.'

Sarah cast a glance at her mother, seeking reassurance. But her mother's expression was merely one of disapproval at Johnny's eating habits.

There was a possibility Johnny would find out about the two ladies' visit and she knew he'd be angry if he thought she'd hidden it from him. 'A pair of lady detectives called on me today asking about Archie Mitchell,' she said trying to keep her voice steady.

He chewed over a mouthful, his eyes fixed on hers. 'Lady detectives?' he said after a pause. 'Who were they?'

'Mrs Blakely and Mrs Langley.'

'Never heard of them. What did they say?'

'They just asked me the same questions the police did.'

'And you told them to go away, I hope.'

'I told them I didn't want to talk to them.' It was only half the truth, but she hoped this answer would satisfy him.

'Good.' He picked up his bowl and drained the rest of the stew into his mouth. Then he dropped the bowl onto the table and wiped his mouth on his sleeve. 'Well, that will keep me going for an hour or two.'

He got up from his chair and looked down at her, hands on hips.

'If they come again,' he said, 'you say nothing. Do you understand?'

Sarah nodded. She didn't protest. She never did when he was like this.

He took his coat from the nail and jammed his cap onto his head. He glanced at her once more, his eyes unreadable.

'Where are you going?' she asked.

'To sort out a few things.'

Then he was gone, the door banging shut behind him.

The room remained silent for a while. Sarah felt some tension leave her shoulders.

Then her mother spoke, her voice low and grim. 'He's nothing but trouble,' she said. 'You need to be rid of that man, Sarah.'

Sarah said nothing. She knew her mother was right, but she wasn't brave enough to tell her she was frightened of him.

If she tried to be rid of him, who knew what he might do?

'Let's feed the children,' she said, her voice quavering.

NINE

'Johnny?' said the desk sergeant at Leman Street police station. 'Do you know his surname?'

'No,' replied Penny. 'But apparently everyone around here knows who he is. That makes me think he could be a man of business or a man of criminal character.'

Emma and Penny had made the short walk from the Tower of London to Leman Street in Whitechapel. It was the first time Emma had returned to the area since her husband's murder. She felt a little uneasy – it was a place which held uncomfortable memories for her.

The desk sergeant folded his arms. 'Why are you asking about him?'

'The Yard has asked us to look into the murder of Archie Mitchell—'

'Mitchell?' the officer interrupted. 'That's one of the cases Detective Inspector Harmsworth has been working on. The Yard has asked you to investigate, you say?'

'Yes. My husband, Detective Inspector Blakely, works at the Yard.'

'Does he now? I suppose that explains it then. I don't know how Harmsworth will feel about this.'

'I also worked as a news reporter on Fleet Street,' added Penny. 'Just in case you thought we'd been asked to help only because I'm married to an inspector.'

The desk sergeant scratched his cheek, his fingertips rasping on his whiskers. 'No, I wasn't thinking that, Mrs Blakely.' He gave Emma a curious glance, as if wondering what she was doing there.

'I solved my husband's murder,' she said, holding his gaze. 'With Mrs Blakely's help.'

He raised an eyebrow. 'Well, it will still be interesting to see what Harmsworth—'

'Let's forget about him for the moment,' said Penny. 'We're asking about a local man called Johnny. If you're doing your job properly then you'll know this area well, sergeant. You must know who Johnny is. Apparently everyone does.'

He scratched his cheek again. 'Well, I suppose it would be Johnny Cooper. And you're quite right, Mrs Blakely. He is well known.'

'For what, exactly?' asked Emma.

'He has an aversion to honest work and a talent for imaginative ways to make money. He's known to steal from warehouses and fence the goods. And, for a time, he was running a team of shoplifters.'

'He's been arrested?' Penny asked.

He nodded. 'Several times. He's served short spells in prison over the years, but never for long. Before you know it, he's up to his old tricks again.'

'What do you know about Sarah Lyford, the woman he keeps company with?'

He narrowed his eyes a little as he thought. 'I know who you mean now, she's a barmaid at The Tiger Tavern. She had something to do with Mitchell... That's right... I believe she was the one who found him. As far as I know she's never been in trouble. Seems an honest, hard-working woman like many around here. She could do better than keep company with Cooper, but some women seem drawn to men with that kind of reputation. I hope she fares better than the last one... She drowned after falling off London Bridge.'

Emma startled at this horrifying revelation. 'Who was she?'

'The young woman Cooper was keeping company with at the time. Harriet Barnes I believe she was called.'

'When did this happen?'

'Late last year. Shortly before Archie Mitchell's murder as I recall.'

'And it was an accident?' Penny asked.

'Yes, the coroner ruled her death as accidental. She and Cooper had both been drinking. Cooper claimed she was trying to walk along the wall on the bridge, showing off. He said he warned her, but she lost her balance and fell in.'

'That was his version of what happened?' said Penny.

'Yes, and no one could prove otherwise. And truthfully, Miss Barnes was known to drink heavily. It wasn't hard to imagine her doing something reckless.'

'So there was no reason to suspect foul play?'

'Absolutely not. The inquest was thorough and heard before a jury and coroner. There is no need for the verdict to be questioned.'

'No need for the verdict to be questioned...' muttered Penny as they stepped out of the police station. 'I've heard that before.'

Emma smiled. 'They said the same about Lord Harpole, didn't they?'

Penny nodded. 'Yes, we've learned that mistakes can be made at inquests. It's possible we're looking into two murders now instead of one. Let's look up the inquest reports and see if we can find any more clues.'

TEN

The following afternoon, Emma and Penny stepped into the quiet newspaper reading room of the British Museum. It smelled of polished wood and old paper. Around them, the soft rustle of pages and an occasional cough echoed beneath the high ceiling.

'The sergeant at H Division said it happened late last year,' Penny whispered. 'Let's start with the *Morning Express* editions from then and see what they say.'

They each took a stack of bound volumes to a desk and began turning the pages with care. Emma noticed with sadness that there had been a number of accidental drowning cases. She checked the names in each report, looking for a mention of Harriet Barnes. It was sombre work.

'Here,' whispered Penny after a while. 'I've found a report. It was written in early December by your Harry Wright?'

Emma immediately felt her face flush. 'My Mr Wright? He's not mine! And besides, I haven't seen him for a few weeks.'

Penny gave her a knowing look and returned to the article. 'It happened on the night of the fifth of December. Harriet Barnes fell from London Bridge at around quarter past eleven. She had been on the bridge with Johnny Cooper. He said she climbed onto the wall because she wanted to walk along it. He urged her to get down, but she wouldn't listen. Moments later, she slipped and fell into the river.'

Emma winced. 'Were there any witnesses?'

'I'm not sure...' Penny continued reading through the report. 'Cooper said he shouted for help and ran to the north bank of the river to raise the alarm. The river police searched for hours, but they couldn't find Miss Barnes. Her body was recovered the following day, downriver at Hammersmith.'

'How tragic.'

'The landlord of The Rose and Crown public house on the south bank of the river testified that Cooper and Barnes had been drinking a lot that evening. He asked them to leave because they were intoxicated and bothering the other customers.'

'But we don't know whether she slipped off that wall or if Cooper pushed her,' said Emma.

'Indeed. The report says a few other people were on the bridge at the time, but none were close enough to see clearly. It was late, dark and only a few gas lamps were lit. They heard Cooper calling for help, but no one saw Barnes on the wall.'

'It's an odd thing to do,' said Emma.

'Not so odd if she'd been drinking,' said Penny. Then she gasped. 'Look at this!'

Emma leaned in. 'What is it?'

Penny pointed at a paragraph. 'Look at the name of one of the witnesses!'

Emma caught her breath. 'My goodness,' she said. 'Archie Mitchell.'

ELEVEN

After leaving the British Museum, Emma and Penny walked to Fleet Street. A fresh April breeze stirred the trees in Lincoln's Inn Fields and the sun made a brief appearance before hiding behind the clouds again.

'So it seems Archie Mitchell gave evidence at the inquest into Harriet Barnes' death,' said Penny. 'And a week later, he was murdered. Could the two incidents be connected?'

'I think they could be,' said Emma. 'Johnny Cooper could have pushed Harriet Barnes off the bridge wall. And he could have shot Archie Mitchell the following week.'

'But what could his motive for murdering Mr Mitchell have been?'

'Archie Mitchell may have seen more than he stated at the inquest. Perhaps he saw Cooper push Harriet Barnes.'

'And was too scared of Cooper to tell the truth?' Penny gave this some thought. 'But if Mitchell lied about what he saw... why would Cooper then murder him?'

'That's a good question. It will be interesting to find out what Harry Wright makes of it all. After all, he attended the inquest.'

. . .

In the scruffy newsroom of the *Morning Express* offices, they found the editor, Edgar Fish, and his colleague, Frederick Potter. Penny had worked with the pair of them for many years during her time as a reporter for the newspaper. To Emma's disappointment, there was no sign of Harry Wright.

Edgar grinned as they stepped into the room. 'Mrs Blakely! And Mrs Langley. How nice to see you again. I was just telling Potter here that his latest report needs to be a thousand words.'

Frederick sat slumped in his chair, arms folded, like a sulking schoolboy. 'What else am I supposed to say about the parliament vote?' he grumbled. 'Scraping together six hundred words was difficult enough.'

'You've been writing for this paper a long time,' Edgar replied. 'You should be able to find another four hundred words in your sleep.'

'I could find them,' said Potter, stretching his legs out under the desk, 'but they'd be four hundred words of twaddle. I don't think it's fair to give our readers twaddle.'

'I don't think it's fair either which is why I'm asking you for four hundred informative words, Potter. Give the readers some background to the vote. Most of them will have forgotten what it was all about.'

'I wrote about it in yesterday's edition!'

'Exactly! They've all forgotten about it since then.' He turned to Emma and Penny. 'How can we help, ladies?'

'We came here to see Mr Wright,' said Penny.

'Not us?' replied Edgar, his face falling.

Penny opened her mouth to reply when the door swung open and Harry Wright stepped into the room. Emma felt a flutter in her stomach. He had an easy confidence about him and a warm smile as he greeted them all.

'They're here to see you, Wright,' Edgar muttered.

'Me?' Harry looked a little coy. 'Golly. What can I do for you, ladies?'

'We'd like to speak to you about the inquest into the death of

Harriet Barnes,' said Penny. 'You reported on it last December. She fell from London Bridge.'

His brow furrowed. 'Oh yes. That was very sad indeed. I recall it well. Miss Barnes had been drinking and apparently decided to walk along the bridge wall. She lost her balance and fell into the river. Her body was recovered the next day at Hammersmith.'

'That was Johnny Cooper's account of events, wasn't it?' Emma asked. She felt her face flush as Harry's eyes moved to her.

'Yes, he was the chap she was keeping company with at the time,' he replied.

'What did you make of him?'

'He appeared genuinely distraught about her death. The poor fellow had tried his best to persuade her to get off the wall and yet she'd considered it to be some sort of joke. She had no fear at all, she'd been emboldened by the drink. And then tragedy struck.'

'Did you believe him?' Emma asked.

Harry paused, considering. 'His upset seemed genuine, but... I couldn't be certain whether or not he was telling the truth.'

'We've discovered he's a man of criminal character,' said Penny.

'Yes, I understand he is. That doesn't mean he lied about what happened that night, though. And besides, there were witnesses. They didn't see exactly what happened because it was too dark. But they'd been on the bridge at the time and heard Mr Cooper's cries for help.'

'One of the witnesses on the bridge was Archie Mitchell,' said Penny. 'Do you recall him?'

Harry thought for a moment. 'Yes... a young, quietly spoken man. A labourer, I think. He said he'd realised there wasn't a lot he could do once he learned she was in the water. It was too dark to see anything properly, when he looked over the wall of the bridge the river was just black.' He shook his head. 'Poor Miss Barnes stood no chance at all.'

'Did you know Archie Mitchell was murdered nine days later?' Penny asked.

Harry's jaw dropped. 'Really?'

'He was fatally shot on the riverside path by the Tower of London.'

'That was him? The same man?' He ran a hand through his hair. 'How did I not notice that? I reported on that death too, although I didn't attend the inquest. I believe that was you, Potter.'

'Me?' Frederick blinked as if he'd just been woken up.

'You attended Archie Mitchell's inquest,' said Harry. 'The chap who was shot near the Tower of London.'

'Yes, I remember. They didn't know who'd done it.'

'They still don't,' said Penny. 'Scotland Yard has asked us to help.'

All three men regarded her with interest. 'You?' said Edgar.

'Both of us,' said Penny, taking Emma's arm.

'Goodness. They really don't know what to do about the case, do they?'

Penny frowned. 'Are you suggesting the Yard has called on us as a last resort?'

'Yes...' said Edgar, shifting awkwardly from one foot to the other. 'However, I mean it as a compliment. Who can the Yard turn to when a case remains unsolved? You and Mrs Langley!' He gave them a broad, appeasing smile.

'I think it's wonderful,' said Harry Wright, catching Emma's eye. 'I'm sure you'll find the culprit.'

'Do you think so?' said Emma, feeling unsure.

He nodded. 'You've got the detective skills, I'm sure of it.'

Emma felt heat rush into her face. She looked down at the floor, embarrassed by her reaction.

'We have a theory at the moment,' said Penny. Her tone was calm and measured, something Emma was grateful for as she tried to combat her bashfulness. 'We think Johnny Cooper deliberately pushed Harriet Barnes off London Bridge and Archie Mitchell witnessed it. We think Mitchell could have lied at the inquest to support Cooper's account that Miss Barnes fell accidentally. We think he lied because he was frightened of Cooper. And despite his lies, Cooper murdered him to keep him quiet for good. We know Mitchell's mood had changed shortly before his death, as if something was bothering him.'

Harry nodded. 'That's certainly an interesting theory.'

'And we've found a person who connects the two,' added Emma, trying to be as calm as Penny. 'A lady called Sarah Lyford. She was the person who found Archie Mitchell after he'd been shot and she keeps company these days with Johnny Cooper.'

The reporter's eyes widened. 'Is that so?' He rubbed his chin. 'So is that merely a coincidence or could there be more to it?'

'That's what we need to find out.'

Harry stepped over to his desk and looked through a pile of notebooks. After finding the one he was searching for, he leafed through it. 'These are my notes from Archie Mitchell's inquest,' he said, stepping over to Emma and Penny. They both peered over his shoulder until Emma realised everything was written in shorthand and there was no use in her looking. Penny – on the other hand – could understand what was written there.

'Robert Mitchell,' she said. 'Who's he? A relation?'

'His uncle,' replied Harry. 'I recall him saying he'd noticed a change in Archie's mood shortly before his death.'

'How interesting. Did he say anything else useful?'

'Not that I recall...' Harry continued, looking through his notes.

'Do you know where we can find him?' Emma asked.

'I haven't got a record of his address... but I know he's working on the new Tower Bridge as a diver.'

'Diver?'

'Yes, a team of divers was needed to build the piers in the river. From what I hear, it's a very skilled job.'

Penny turned to Emma. 'I think he's the person we need to speak to next.'

'I agree.'

Harry folded his notebook closed. 'Well, if you need any help, just let me know,' he said. 'At the moment, I struggle to see Johnny Cooper as a murderer. But I'll have a look in more detail at my notes from the two cases again and see if I can recall anything which might be useful.'

'All rather fascinating,' said Edgar who'd been listening intently. 'If any progress is made on the case then we want to be able to publish it first.' He turned to Penny. 'I don't suppose you've brought your latest Ladies' Column with you, have you?'

'No, I thought the deadline was Thursday.'

'It is and Thursday is fine. I wonder if we might have a quick conversation in my office before you leave?'

TWELVE

'Do please take a seat,' said Edgar as Penny arrived in his untidy office. She perched on an ink-stained chair while he seated himself behind his desk.

'I'm looking forward to reading the next Ladies' Column,' he said, moving a stack of papers from one side of his desk to the other. 'I think you've covered a range of useful topics and offered some excellent insights into motherhood and child-rearing...'

'But?' said Penny, sensing there was more to come. Edgar steepled his fingers beneath his chin and allowed a pause to settle between them.

'But...' He gave her a tight-lipped smile. 'I feel it's time for a change.'

'A change?' she repeated. 'But I've only been writing the column for four or five months. That isn't very long at all. You're not planning to end the column, are you? Because I think that would be a mistake. The *Morning Express* has gained a loyal readership of women.'

Edgar gave a placating wave of his hand. 'No, no, not at all. I'm well aware of the column's popularity and the contribution you've made to it. I have no intention of losing our female readers. Quite the opposite. I'd like to broaden the column's appeal.'

Penny raised an eyebrow.

'I'd like to change it into something more varied,' he continued. 'Shorter topics, perhaps grouped under headings such as fashion, motherhood, cookery, etiquette. A little something for everyone.'

'I see,' said Penny. 'That's an interesting idea. Although I feel most comfortable writing about motherhood. Cookery, on the other hand...'

'Yes, I'm aware you're not particularly domestic.' Edgar gave a chuckle. 'Nor do I imagine you take great delight in the daily rhythms of running a household. You're a mother, certainly, but perhaps not the sort our readers typically envision when they think of a lady at home. And that's why I've decided to bring in another writer. Someone with practical experience of managing a household.'

Penny felt her jaw tighten. 'Who?' she asked.

'My wife.'

Penny stared at him. 'Mrs Fish?'

'Yes. She's quite a marvel, you know. She oversees our home with precision and knows everything there is to know about furnishing a home, entertaining, menus, recipes, managing servants—'

'But she's not a journalist,' Penny interrupted. 'Has she written anything before?'

'No. But this new format doesn't require journalistic skill. Just good, sound advice. She can jot down a few notes and I'll give them an editorial polish.'

Penny gritted her teeth, resisting the urge to protest. She'd spent years on her craft and now she was being pushed aside for the editor's wife. She balled her fists in her lap. If she said anything untoward about Edgar's wife then there'd be little chance of writing for the newspaper again.

'I know you're disappointed, Mrs Blakely,' Edgar continued. 'And you're no doubt wondering where this leaves you now. The answer is, I have something new in mind for you.'

Penny gave a sigh and narrowed her eyes. 'What?' she asked, sceptically.

He smiled. 'A new column. One which I think is perfectly suited to your talents and experience. I call it Musings of a Lady Detective. What do you think?'

The idea surprised her. 'I'm not sure.'

'You've worked on many cases now. You've seen things most women haven't and most men for that matter. Your insights would make excellent reading. And I'd like to give the column a good amount of space in the paper. More than the Ladies' Column ever had.'

Penny felt the tension lift a little. The idea had merit.

'I like it,' she said. 'I wouldn't be able to write in detail about the current investigation, of course...'

'No, no, of course not. We'll avoid anything which risks breaching confidence. But past cases, reflections on the work, what it's like to navigate the world as a lady detective... I think our readers would be riveted.'

Penny found herself smiling. She now had a column dedicated to the work she loved. 'I like the idea,' she said. 'When you first mentioned...'

'My wife?' Edgar chuckled. 'Your face darkened like a thundercloud. But I hope this new arrangement suits you.'

'It does indeed. When would you like my first submission?'

'Give yourself a fortnight just to adapt and get some ideas together. After that, shall we say weekly?'

'Yes,' she replied. 'Perfect.'

THIRTEEN

The study at thirty-three Portland Place was panelled in mahogany and had a richly coloured oriental carpet. Gilded leather volumes filled the tall bookshelves and oil paintings of Mulholland ancestors hung next to stag heads and antler mounts. Velvet cushions and exotic animal pelts were arranged on the age-worn leather chairs while ornate gas lamps bathed the room in a comforting glow.

Sir Laurence Mulholland sat at the enormous teak desk fiddling with his pen as he listened to his estate manager update him on the St Pancras project.

They were interrupted by a knock at the door.

It was his secretary. 'Mr Pugh is here to see you, sir.'

'Very good, show him in.'

The estate manager – caught mid-sentence by the knock – gave an expression of protest.

'I'm sorry, Marshall, but this will have to wait,' said Sir Laurence, gesturing at the door. 'I'm keen to hear what this chap has to say.'

The estate manager got to his feet nursing a wounded expression. Moments later, he was replaced by the private investigator.

Sir Laurence got to his feet. 'Drink?'

'Thank you, sir.'

The investigator was a slight, sharp-faced man with a thin black moustache. He stood with his bowler hat in his hand until Sir Laurence told him to sit down. 'I can't bear it when people stand about,' he added. 'It makes the place look untidy.'

He stepped over to the whisky decanter and poured out two drinks into crystal cut glasses. He placed one of them on the desk in front of Pugh then made himself comfortable opposite.

'Well?' he asked. 'Have you found it?'

Pugh's expression remained impassive. 'I'm afraid not, sir.'

A flash of anger rose in Sir Laurence's chest. He thumped his desk with the side of his fist but Pugh didn't flinch. 'Damn it!' he exclaimed.

He took a swig of whisky, almost finishing it in one gulp.

'Damn it, I say!' He put down the glass and fixed Pugh in the eye. 'You've had months to find it. *Months*. Where can it possibly be?'

'I don't know, sir.' Pugh avoided his gaze.

'You searched the house?'

'Twice, sir.'

'You lifted floorboards, pulled out furniture, that sort of thing?'

'Yes, sir. As I reported previously, I even rented a room there for a month.'

'You looked in the attic?'

'I did.'

'So what did Mitchell do with it?'

'He didn't hide it in the house, sir.'

'The bridge...' mused Sir Laurence, drumming his fingers on his desk. 'Perhaps he strapped it to one of the beams.'

'With all due respect, sir, I don't think that would be a particularly safe location. There would certainly be a risk of someone else—'

'All right, all right, I get the idea, Pugh. Bank vault?'

'I found no evidence he had a vault at a bank, sir.'

'But that doesn't mean he didn't have access to one. A friend's vault, perhaps?'

'I've found no evidence that—'

'Look into it more, man!' Sir Laurence washed away his irritation with a final gulp of whisky. 'Find out if any of his friends or acquaintances have a vault at a bank somewhere. If it's nowhere else to be found then it must be the only answer! Don't forget I'm paying you very good money for this.'

Pugh gave a polite nod.

Sir Laurence leaned forward a little, lowering his voice. 'I'm willing to spend as much as it takes to find it. Remember that, Pugh. If you can find that locket, you'll be very richly rewarded indeed.'

<h1 align="center">FOURTEEN</h1>

The following day, Emma and Penny made their way to Tower Bridge. A new elevated section of road had been built to form the approach. They walked along it, the Tower of London on their right and the clamour of the riverside wharves on their left.

Ahead, a rough wooden fence barred their way. From beyond it, hammering rang out from the half-built towers and labourers called out to each other as cranes lifted steel beams into position.

Weak spring sunshine filtered through gaps in the overcast sky. A man in a cap stood at a gate in the fence, leaning against a post with a clay pipe in his mouth. He raised an eyebrow as the two women approached.

Penny stepped forward. 'We're looking for Robert Mitchell,' she said. 'We believe he's one of the divers.'

The man removed the pipe and squinted at them. 'Who's asking?'

'Mrs Blakely and Mrs Langley.'

He gave a sigh, opened the gate and sauntered off.

'I've no idea whether that means he's going to fetch him or not,' Penny remarked.

'I suppose we'll just have to wait here for a bit and find out,' said Emma. 'But even if he does fetch him, will Robert Mitchell want to speak to us?'

'That's a good question.'

They waited, listening to the persistent din of the construction site. A tall sail ship passed between the steel timber towers.

'Have you heard the bridge will lift to allow ships to pass?' said Penny. 'Apparently there's a railway bridge over Deptford Creek which does the same.'

'That's going to be interesting to see,' said Emma. 'I can't imagine how that's going to work at the moment.'

She noticed a figure approaching the gate: a wiry man in his forties wearing grimy labourer's clothes and heavy boots. He remained on the other side of the fence and gave them a wary look.

'Robert Mitchell,' he said. 'I understand you two ladies are asking after me.' His voice sounded a little more educated than Emma had been expecting. 'What's this about?'

'Thank you for coming,' said Penny. 'We understand you're the uncle of Archie Mitchell.'

'That's right. My brother's boy. What do you want?'

Emma noticed the stiffness in his posture and the guarded look in his eye.

Penny explained how Scotland Yard had asked them to assist with the case. As she spoke, Robert Mitchell's expression softened a little.

'So they've got two ladies on the case now, have they?' he said with a grim smile. 'Well, it's about time someone took an interest. Four months have passed and still no one knows who shot my nephew in the leg.' He shook his head. 'It's the same everywhere, isn't it? They still haven't caught Jack the Ripper. Too many crimes and not enough coppers. At least the Ripper hasn't struck again which is a small mercy. So tell me, how exactly do you plan to find the man who did this?'

'It will be a challenge,' Penny replied. 'And to begin with we're trying to learn everything we can about Archie. Anything that might help us understand what happened.'

Mr Mitchell removed his cap, opened the gate and joined them. 'He was a good lad,' he said. 'Kept himself to himself. And he worked hard.'

'He worked here on the bridge with you?'

'Not doing the same thing, but I helped him get the job. I've been here since the early days, working as a diver.' He nodded towards the bridge. 'You see those big stone piers? They had to be built on the riverbed. We were lowered in cages down to the bottom to excavate the foundations. You can't see a thing in that water, it's as thick as soup. You just feel your way around and trust the men above to keep the air coming.'

'Goodness,' said Penny. 'That sounds like dangerous work.'

'It is, but you try not to think about it. We got the job done.' He gave a small proud smile. 'Anyway, you're here to talk about Archie. What do you want to know?'

'We heard his mood changed shortly before his death,' said Penny. 'Is that something you noticed as well?'

Robert rubbed his jaw, the lines around his eyes deepening as he thought. 'Yes... he was different. Quieter. Something was weighing on him. He never said what it was, but I could tell. I know one thing that bothered him – he didn't much like being called to that inquest.'

Penny and Emma waited silently.

'It was the inquest into the death of a young woman. She'd fallen from London Bridge and Archie had been walking across the bridge that night. He said he didn't see anything but they still made him stand up in court and tell the coroner what he'd heard. I think that upset him more than he let on. He said it was dark and he heard her fall. He ran to the edge to see if he could spot her but the current pulled her under before anyone had a chance to save her. That really upset him. He wasn't comfortable talking about it.'

'Do you think it's possible he saw more than he admitted to?'

'What do you mean?'

'Perhaps Miss Barnes's death wasn't an accident. Maybe Archie knew that, but he didn't say so at the inquest because he didn't want to risk incriminating someone else. He might have been afraid of the consequences and that fear could have stayed with him.'

Robert Mitchell shook his head firmly. 'No. If Archie had thought something untoward happened on that bridge that night, he would've said so. I know he would. That fellow the girl was with... he didn't sound like much of a gentleman. He wasn't the sort to stay quiet about something like that. Is that what you're suggesting? That she was pushed and Archie saw it?'

'It was just a possibility,' said Emma. 'But you knew your nephew well and if you're certain he told the truth at the inquest then we believe you.'

Robert gave a slow nod. 'He wasn't murdered for being on the bridge that night when the young woman died. But as for who murdered him... I had a suspicion once.'

'Who?' asked Penny.

He shifted his weight, resting one hand on the gate. 'When you're building something like this bridge, you've got to trust your fellow labourers. Riveting is no job for half-measures. Everyone pulls their weight, or someone gets hurt.'

Emma and Penny exchanged a glance, wondering where this explanation would lead.

'I don't know if you ladies know much about riveting,' continued Mr Mitchell. 'Let me explain. All the steel on this bridge... beams, supports, plates... they're joined together by red-hot rivets. The rivets are heated until they glow then they're hammered into place before they cool. You've got to be quick and good with your hands. And you've got to be careful too.'

Emma and Penny nodded, listening intently.

'A labourer called Seamus Byrne burned his hand badly on one,' Mitchell continued. 'A nasty injury which damaged the muscles in his hand. He still can't work now. Or so he claims. Anyway... he claimed the accident happened because Archie distracted him and he picked up a hot rivet bare-handed. No man with any sense would ever do such a thing and I can't say I ever made sense of the full tale. After that, he blamed Archie for the injury and said he was responsible for the loss of his livelihood.'

'And you believe Seamus took his revenge?' asked Emma.

Robert nodded slowly. 'That's what I think. Seamus Byrne has a temper and he enjoys a good fight. He's a violent man and I think he could have killed Archie.'

Penny frowned. 'Did the police speak to him?'

'Yes, they knew about the accident with the rivet and the grudge Byrne bore towards Archie. They questioned him but he had an alibi for the night Archie was attacked. Some young woman he'd been with.'

'Do you know who she was?'

'No idea. But once they confirmed the alibi, the police weren't interested in him anymore.' He sighed. 'So that was that. The police didn't seem to do anything else and now it's just another case left unsolved. I hope you two ladies fare better than the police did. Someone knows what happened to Archie. He deserves justice.'

'Yes he does,' said Penny. 'He lived in Bermondsey, didn't he?'

'That's right. He rented a room in a lodging house on Shand Street. Near London Bridge station. The landlady there is Mrs Fielding.'

'It will be interesting to speak with her,' said Penny.

'I'm not sure you'll get much; Archie only lived there for about six months. I've met her once and that was when I collected the trunk of his belongings from his room.'

He paused for a moment, turned his head and glanced out over the river. Emma noticed he swallowed hard, trying to keep his emotions under control.

A few moments later he was ready to speak again.

'I wish you two ladies the best of luck,' he said. 'If you want to speak to me again about Archie, I live in Greenwich. Circus Street. Number four.'

They thanked him and he replaced his cap. 'I'd better get back to work.'

'It seems he cared for his nephew a great deal,' said Penny as they watched him walk back to the bridge.

'Or seemed to,' added Emma.

Penny turned to her. 'Why do you say that?'

'Don't we treat everyone as a suspect at this stage? Robert Mitchell has told us his version of events, but we might find something which contradicts him.'

Penny smiled. 'Spoken like a proper detective. You're absolutely right, Emma. We can't trust anyone yet.'

FIFTEEN

'Shall we call on Archie Mitchell's landlady, Mrs Fielding?' Penny asked Emma as they left Tower Bridge. 'Do you have time now?'

'Yes, my next lesson is this evening.'

'This evening?'

'Mrs Solomon, my landlady.' Emma smiled. 'And I think she's my most difficult pupil.'

Penny laughed.

'She says I don't need to pay her any rent if I'm teaching her piano, but at the moment... I think I'd rather pay rent instead.'

'Oh dear. Perhaps she'll improve soon?'

'She'll only improve if she does some practice. My younger students usually do the practice I ask them to. But ladies in their fifties can be quite set in their ways.'

'Or perhaps it's just her character,' said Penny. 'Plenty of people want to be good at something but they're not keen on putting in the hard work.'

'I agree.'

They walked along the river, past the Tower of London and the place where Archie Mitchell had been attacked. High up on the tower wall, Emma caught sight of a large black bird again. One of the ravens?

She felt as though it was watching her. She turned away and heard a gunshot in her mind. Then a cry in the dark as Archie collapsed to the ground. She imagined the stunned silence which would have followed. And then the blood... pooling and spreading between the cobbles...

'Are you all right?' Penny asked her.

Emma blinked a few times, coming to her senses. 'Yes. I'm fine. I'm just a little tired. Actually...' She decided to be honest. 'I was thinking about the attack on Archie Mitchell.'

'It happened around here somewhere, didn't it? It's hard to imagine it now.' The sunshine was a little stronger now and people strolled past, pausing to admire the Tower and the new bridge.

Emma struggled to agree with Penny's sentiment. She had little difficulty imagining what had happened. But the raven had now gone and the gloom had lifted a little. She and Penny went on their way to the hexagonal kiosk which marked the entrance to the Tower Subway.

After paying the ha'penny toll, they descended the steep steps down to the tunnel which would take them beneath the river to the south bank.

At the foot of the staircase, they began making their way through the cast-iron tube, its walls slick with moisture. A narrow wooden walkway ran through its centre and was lit with dim lighting.

Voices echoed from further along the tunnel, and a snatch of deafening laughter bounced around the enclosed space.

'I wouldn't like to walk through here regularly,' said Emma. 'And to think Archie Mitchell took this route twice a day.'

A smell of rust, damp and stagnant water lingered in the air. A few people bustled past them, seemingly keen to get out of the claustrophobic space as soon as possible.

'We'll be able to walk over the Tower Bridge when it opens,' said Penny. 'That day can't come soon enough.'

A cold drip caught Emma unexpectedly on the back of her neck. She shuddered and quickly wiped it away with her gloved hand. They walked the rest of the way in near silence, their footsteps quickening as they neared the staircase at the far end.

The exit on the south side of the river brought them out by a brewery. A heavy smell of malt accompanied Emma and Penny as they made the short walk to Shand Street.

SIXTEEN

'Archie Mitchell was a good lodger,' said Mrs Fielding. She sat at the table in her parlour, arms folded and chin held high. She was a small woman with sharp grey eyes and thick grey hair pinned into a roll at the back of her head. 'He was quiet and polite. Always thanked me for his meals.'

Emma and Penny sat opposite her in the impeccably tidy room. A lace cloth covered the table and china figurines were arranged neatly on the mantelpiece. The wallpaper had a faded lilac design and light filtered thinly through the narrow window which overlooked a yard at the back. It was a modest house but well looked after.

'I think it's dreadful the police haven't caught anyone yet,' Mrs Fielding continued, a scowl on her face. 'I know it happened late at night and no one saw anything, but you'd think they'd have got someone by now. I can't make sense of it.'

'When did you last see him?' Penny asked.

'The morning of the day he died. I cooked him breakfast, as I always did. Eggs and toast. Probably a slice of ham too although I can't recall exactly. Then he went off to work.'

'Did he seem different shortly before his death?' Emma asked. 'Some people say his mood changed.'

The landlady nodded slowly.

'Could it have been the inquest he gave evidence at?' Penny asked.

'You've heard about that, have you? He was upset by it, there's no doubt about that. Seeing a young woman fall off a bridge and drown is very upsetting. And he didn't want to speak at the inquest but he was told he had to. I could tell he didn't want to go because he didn't eat a bite of breakfast that morning.'

'How was he afterwards?' Emma asked.

Mrs Fielding scratched her chin. 'It's hard to tell really... He was relieved to have got it out of the way, I think.'

'Did his mood improve?'

'Not really. He remained quiet. But I didn't see him a great deal so it's hard to be certain. I only really saw him at mealtimes – breakfast and supper. We didn't chat much, just a few pleasantries. He was always respectful. Paid his rent on time, never caused a moment's bother.' She gave a wistful sigh. 'The men working on the bridge are well-paid, that's why I like having them here. They earn steady, honest money and – by and large – they're good men.'

'Did you meet his uncle, Robert Mitchell?' Emma asked.

'Yes, after Archie died. He came here to pick up Archie's belongings. I put them all in a trunk for him.' She gave a sad sniff.

'Can we see the room Archie stayed in?' Penny asked.

The landlady pulled a puzzled expression. 'Why? None of his belongings are there anymore. His uncle took them, as I just told you.'

'It might help us to see where he stayed,' said Penny.

'I don't see how.' Mrs Fielding gave a bemused smile. 'But if you insist on it, I've no objection. There's no one in the room at the moment so I'll take you up there.'

She got up from the table, the bunch of keys at her waist jangling as she moved.

Emma and Penny followed her up the narrow staircase, which creaked underfoot. On the third floor, the landlady took a key from the bunch and unlocked a plain wooden door.

The room beyond was barely larger than a cupboard. It had a small window and a low ceiling slanted with the pitch of the roof. The furniture consisted of an iron bedstead, a scuffed chest of drawers and a small washstand.

Mrs Fielding moved to the window and unlatched it, pushing up the sash. A draught stirred the thin curtain.

'He liked the trains,' she said, peering out. 'He said he found the sound comforting believe it or not. If you look beyond those rooftops, you can see the tracks. London Bridge station's just around the corner.'

As she spoke, a distant rumble grew louder and a train rattled past. The window trembled in its frame.

'It can be a bit noisy,' Mrs Fielding added with a laugh. 'Some of the lodgers complain, but what do they expect when you live this close to the lines?'

Emma glanced around the spartan room. There were few signs or clues to tell them more about Archie Mitchell. She didn't even know what he'd looked like. At the present time, he felt little more than a ghost.

'Thank you for showing us the room,' said Penny.

'Why you two ladies are doing the job of the police, I really don't know.' The landlady shook her head and left the room. Penny followed, as did Emma until something on the floor caught her eye. It was a small triangle of grey poking out between the floorboards.

She heard Penny ask Mrs Fielding a question about Archie Mitchell's family. Had she met anyone else other than his uncle?

While the landlady answered, Emma stooped down. It looked like a tiny piece of paper. Penny was in the doorway, blocking the landlady's view and Emma took the opportunity to lift the corner of paper by pushing the nail of her forefinger beneath it.

It looked like a visiting card, but Emma pushed it up her sleeve before the landlady could notice what she'd found. She stepped over to the door where Mrs Fielding was having to answer another question Penny had put to her.

Emma couldn't resist a brief smile; Penny had deliberately distracted the landlady to allow her to have a quick look around the room.

'Right, I'd better get on,' said Mrs Fielding. She closed the door to Archie Mitchell's former room and securely locked it.

SEVENTEEN

Emma waited until she and Penny had left Shand Street to stop and show her the calling card she'd found.

'It may be nothing,' she said. 'Or it might be very useful indeed.'

The cardstock was smooth and thick, with a subtle texture. In one corner, a gold-embossed coat of arms featured a rampant lion.

'This looks like an expensive card,' said Penny. She ran her finger over the lettering. 'Copperplate engraving.'

Emma could see the ink had been carefully etched into the surface of the card.

'And I suppose it's not surprising,' Penny continued. 'Sir Laurence Mulholland and an address on Portland Place. Has he been calling on Mrs Fielding? Or even Archie Mitchell?'

'Or someone else entirely,' said Emma. 'Other people must have rented that room since Archie was there.'

'True. But the card has been there a while. Look how dirty the corner is where it was caught on the floorboard. People have been walking on it for some time without realising it was there.'

'We could call on Sir Laurence and ask him if he knew Archie Mitchell,' said Emma. 'But I think we should find out more about Sir Laurence first.'

Penny smiled. 'Very wise. At the moment, I can't understand why someone important would have a connection to a modest lodging house in Bermondsey. It makes sense to find out more about him. And before we do that, I think we should meet with Detective Inspector Simpson to tell him what we've learned. I'll invite him to dinner seeing as he's an old family friend of James's. It's possible Simpson has heard some of the names of the people we've encountered. He might even be able to tell us more about Mulholland.'

EIGHTEEN

Jane Fielding watched the two ladies from an upstairs window. Once they reached the end of Shand Street, they disappeared from view.

It was odd that Scotland Yard had requested their help with the investigation into Archie Mitchell's death. What could two lady detectives possibly achieve that the police had failed to do?

Shaking her head with bemusement, she descended the stairs and made her way to her parlour. Once there, she locked the parlour door and retrieved a penknife from its drawer in the writing desk.

Then she knelt by the rug, lifted it and prised up the loosened corner of a floorboard with the knife. She smiled as she saw the bags nestled in the cavity beneath.

They were still there.

She pulled each bag out, its sacking cloth rough beneath her fingertips. Placing each bag on the table, she felt reassured by the soft clink of coins inside. A short while later, the bags were neatly lined up on the lace tablecloth.

Twelve bags.

She'd had eighteen once.

The sight of the diminished pile made her chest tighten.

She'd worked hard for this money but it was going to run out. She sighed as she untied the lightest bag and took out ten shillings. Then she slipped them into the purse she kept on a ribbon beneath her apron. She hated using the money. Every time she took from it, she felt like she was compromising her future.

The ten shillings would be spent in no time. Some of it would have to go on advertising for lodgers. She longed for the day when each room was occupied. For some reason, lodgers never stayed with her for long. Perhaps they didn't like the noise from the trains or maybe they didn't like her cooking.

She sat back in her chair and sighed. Running a lodging house was proving more difficult than she'd imagined. She and her husband had worked in service together, but she'd stopped enjoying the work after he'd died.

And being a widow was difficult.

She blinked away a tear. There was no use in feeling sorry for herself. She still had some money and she would find a way to earn more. Before long, the twelve bags would grow to fifteen. Then twenty... twenty-five... It was possible. She'd done it before and she could do it again.

Jane was returning the bags of money to their hiding place when a knock sounded at the front door.

She stopped. Had the two women come back?

Hurriedly, she pushed the bags back beneath the floorboard and replaced the rug. Then she got to her feet, unlocked the parlour door and made her way to the hallway.

Everything was silent except for the ticking of the clock.

A sharp rap sounded again. It wasn't the same as the women's knock. It was stronger. More insistent.

A chill ran through her. Instinct told her not to answer the door.

The room leading from the hallway at the front of the house was rented to a lodger. He was out at work so Jane took the key from her belt and unlocked the door. Quietly, she stepped inside and made her way to the window where a lace curtain offered some privacy from the street outside.

Her breath caught as she saw the carriage and pair outside. Sleek, polished and imposing.

There was only one man she knew who rode in such a conveyance.

Another knock rang out. Louder again. Then the unmistakable voice. 'Mrs Fielding?'

She shrank back from the window, heart thudding. Had he seen her?

She moved over to the bed and crouched between it and the wall. Her mouth was dry and a fine tremble crept through her limbs.

'Mrs Fielding?'

She squeezed her eyes shut. If she stayed silent and hidden, he would have to leave.

Wouldn't he?

But what if he didn't? What if one of the lodgers came home and let him in?

She held her breath and waited, each second slowly stretching in the silence.

And still he didn't leave.

NINETEEN

'I'll never forget the day James's father brought him along to the police station to have a look around,' said Detective Inspector Simpson a few days later. 'It was on his day off, of course. I was a young constable at the time and this young lad was very taken with the handcuffs and truncheon. He didn't care for the whistle, though. When I blew it, he put his hands over his ears and cried!'

He slapped the dining table in mirth and Penny joined in with his laughter. James gave a wry smile and cut a boiled potato in half.

'I recall James's father was keen to show him the cells,' continued the inspector. 'So we took him down there and his father told him he'd be locked up in one of them the next time he refused to go to bed when he was told!'

He collapsed into fits of laughter again and Emma felt torn between laughing with the inspector and sympathising with James.

'That sounds like my father,' he remarked, slicing at his steak.

Emma was keen to bring an end to the anecdotes and discuss Archie Mitchell's case. She thought it might be impolite to change the subject herself, so she tried to catch Penny's eye in the hope the hostess would do it.

She cleared her throat and Penny looked her way. After they'd exchanged a glance, Penny seemed to understand Emma's intention.

'Goodness,' she said, turning to the inspector. 'I think we could sit here all evening listening to stories of James as a boy.'

'No, I don't think we could,' said James.

'We really should get on with discussing what Emma and I have uncovered during our investigation into Archie Mitchell's murder,' said Penny.

'Ah yes.' Inspector Simpson wiped his mouth with his serviette. 'How have you been getting on?'

Penny told him about the people she and Emma had spoken to and what they'd learned. 'Seamus Byrne sounds like an interesting character,' she added. 'What do you make of him?'

'He's an uncouth Irish chap as I recall. A ne'er do well. Although he did have employment working alongside Archie Mitchell for a time. Some thought he was the culprit but he had an alibi for the evening Mr Mitchell was attacked.'

'Who provided the alibi?' Emma asked.

'A young lady.' The inspector reached into his jacket pocket and pulled out his notebook. 'I remembered to bring this with me as I thought you might ask me some questions. He licked his forefinger then leafed through the pages. 'Here we are. A young lady who goes by the name of Rosie Clark.'

'Do you know where we can find her?'

'You want to speak to her? Oh, very well...' He leafed through some more pages. 'Prince's Square in Stepney. I expect she'll tell you what she told me though. She was adamant she was with Seamus Byrne that evening and no one can prove otherwise. There's little doubt Byrne is an unpleasant character, but I don't believe he's Mitchell's murderer.'

'What about Johnny Cooper?' Penny asked.

'Another unpleasant chap,' said Inspector Simpson. 'I don't believe he and Mitchell knew each other but I understand Mitchell gave evidence at an inquest into the death of a young woman

Cooper was acquainted with. She was a drunkard and drowned in the river.'

'Or did Cooper push her?' Penny asked.

The inspector raised an eyebrow. 'As far as I'm aware, he didn't. But the pair were both under the influence of drink, so who knows what happened?'

Penny told him she and Emma had a theory Archie Mitchell had witnessed Cooper push Harriet Barnes.

The inspector scratched the back of his neck. 'I don't suppose it's impossible... but unlikely. You need to be careful not to come up with a theory then try to make the evidence fit. That sort of thing can send you down the wrong path.' Emma noticed Penny's lips thin as she listened to the inspector's condescending tone. He continued, 'I think the pair of you have done some marvellous work so far but it's a shame you haven't found anything yet which incriminates Sarah Lyford. I still consider her to be the chief suspect.'

'What about Sir Laurence Mulholland?' Penny asked. 'Have you heard of him?'

The inspector folded his arms as he thought. 'Mulholland...' he repeated. 'Yes, I think I've heard the name before. An important gentleman.'

'We found his calling card in Archie Mitchell's former room at the lodging house.'

'I doubt there's any connection. If Sir Laurence had known Mitchell then I'd have heard about it by now. And besides, what would a man of Sir Laurence's status have to do with a labourer?' He shook his head. 'I'm sorry, ladies. The calling card may appear to be an exciting clue but it's a red herring, I'm afraid.'

TWENTY

Emma and Penny travelled by horse-drawn omnibus to Stepney the following morning. Rain pattered against the windows and Penny was in a glum mood.

'A red herring,' she muttered. 'How can Inspector Simpson tell whether Sir Laurence's calling card is a red herring or not? He's just making assumptions.' She grew more animated as her anger increased. 'And wasn't he trying to lecture us on the dangers of coming up with a theory and trying to make the evidence prove it? As if we didn't know how to conduct an investigation! Has he any idea how many cases I've worked on? Ten years on Fleet Street! And he has the nerve to—'

Emma rested a hand on her arm to interrupt. 'I know, Penny. You don't have to get angry about him. He's just a bit old-fashioned—'

'But I can't help getting angry! He really annoyed me yesterday evening. I bit my lip and was polite to him because he's an old friend of James's family and a guest in our home. But if he'd been someone else...'

'Forget about him,' said Emma. 'He can have his opinions but we're in charge of what we're doing. Perhaps the calling card is a red herring... but perhaps it's not. Wouldn't it be wonderful to prove him wrong?'

Penny's shoulders relaxed a little and a smile played on her lips. 'Yes, it would be wonderful to prove him wrong.'

'So let's do it. We're on our way to speak to Rosie Clark and with a bit of luck she'll tell us something which she didn't tell Simpson.'

When the omnibus reached St George Street, they disembarked into the rainy street. Emma noticed the area was suffering from its proximity to the docks. A number of seedy establishments had been set up to service the needs of visiting sailors.

'I'm sorry for my outburst,' Penny said as she put up her umbrella. 'Florence was awake a lot in the night and she didn't want to be left with Mrs Tuttle when I left the house.' She sighed. 'I feel so incredibly guilty about leaving the children. I spend more than half my time with them and I also value the opportunity to get out and about doing things like this, but... the situation creates a lot of conflict within me. I find myself questioning what I'm doing most of the time...'

Emma gave her arm a comforting squeeze. 'You're a good mother, Penny. And you're a good writer and investigator too. It's hard to do it all, but you still manage it. We'll be out for a few hours, then you can go home this afternoon and spend time with the children again. I realise it's tiring, but would you have it any other way?'

Penny turned to her and smiled. 'Actually I wouldn't. Thank you, Emma.' She patted her hand. 'And I've completely forgotten to tell you about the new column which Edgar Fish wants me to write!' Her eyes brightened with enthusiasm. 'Musings of a Lady Detective.'

Emma laughed. 'Really? So no more Ladies' Column?'

'No. I'll be able to write about much more interesting things. Anyway, let's get on with this and show Inspector Simpson that we know exactly what we're doing.'

They reached Prince's Square which was lined with scruffy

terraced houses. Rain fell steadily, trickling from broken guttering and topping up puddles on the uneven pavement. Some of the houses were well-constructed and Emma imagined the square had once been respectable. These days, the homes in the area could probably be rented very cheaply.

Miss Clark was at home, along with her mother and a smiling, chubby baby.

'Who are you?' Rosie Clark asked them as she stood in the doorway. She looked about eighteen and was dark-haired with an attractive round face. She resembled her mother who cradled the baby. Both women were short with striking blue eyes.

Penny introduced herself and Emma. 'We're lady detectives,' she added. 'And we're investigating the murder of Archie Mitchell.'

'Oh, him.' Miss Clark gave a sigh.

'Did you know him?'

She shook her head. 'No. But I heard all about it. I had to speak to the police even though I had nothing to do with any of it.' She folded her arms and her expression grew sulky.

'Because of Seamus Byrne?' asked Emma.

'I'm not talking about him,' she said. 'He's not worth my breath.'

'You're not on good terms with him?'

'No. I've not seen him in two months and that's exactly how I want it to stay.'

Emma and Penny exchanged a glance. This was good news. If Rosie Clark had fallen out with Seamus Byrne then she had no reason to protect him.

'I think you'll be able to help us a lot,' Penny said to her.

Rosie narrowed her eyes. 'How do you mean?'

'Let's just invite the ladies in if we're going to talk some more, Rosie,' said her mother. 'They're getting soaking wet standing out there in the rain.'

The room they were shown into was small with a few pieces of simple furniture. The place smelled of damp and Emma noticed patches of it on the walls. A small fireplace doubled as a makeshift stove and a couple of pictures were propped up on the mantelpiece – the only decoration in the room. A trestle table stood in one corner, piled high with stacks of fabric.

'Take a seat,' said Mrs Clark, gesturing to a stool and a crooked rocking chair.

'But where will you sit?' Penny asked, clearly aware they were the only two seats in the room.

'We'll be all right for now.' She handed the baby to her daughter. 'I'll make some tea.' She busied herself decanting some water from a bucket into the kettle.

Penny turned to Rosie. 'You should take this seat, you're holding the baby.'

'No, I'm—'

'I insist.'

'All right then.'

Miss Clark sat on the rocking chair and the baby smiled at Penny.

'A boy or a girl?' she asked.

'Boy.'

'About six or seven months old?'

Rosie smiled. 'That's right. His name's Edward.'

'That's a lovely name.'

Tea was served in chipped mismatching cups and Penny and Mrs Clark sat on the floor, despite protestations from Emma and Rosie that they could have their seats instead. By the time everyone was as comfortable as they were likely to be, Emma felt she and Penny were establishing a good rapport with the two women.

'We've heard Seamus Byrne was questioned by the police,' Penny began. 'And you provided Mr Byrne with an alibi for the night Archie Mitchell was killed.'

'That's right.' Rosie looked down at her son and adjusted his woollen shawl over his small shoulder.

'So you were with Mr Byrne on that night?' Penny continued.

'That's what I told the police.'

'But was it true?'

Rosie hesitated, still avoiding Penny's gaze. Then she cleared her throat and fixed her eye. 'Will I get into trouble if I tell you something different to what I told the police?'

'No,' said Penny gently. 'Not at all. We're not here to accuse anyone. We're only trying to understand what happened.'

Rosie studied their faces a moment longer. 'All right,' she said at last. 'But will I get into trouble for it?'

'For what? Lying to the police?'

Rosie nodded.

'I'll make sure you won't,' said Penny. 'My husband is a detective inspector at Scotland Yard. I'll speak to him to make sure you don't get into any trouble. After all, you probably provided an alibi for Seamus because you were frightened, didn't you?'

Rosie gave a shrug, glancing away. 'Sort of. I was told what to say.'

'Exactly,' said Penny. 'You were told what to say and you were afraid of what might happen if you didn't obey. Even if you didn't feel frightened at the time, you were under pressure. When someone tells a lie because they're afraid or manipulated, it doesn't make them a criminal.'

Rosie nodded again, slowly. 'Yes. I suppose that's right. He told me to lie.'

'Seamus did?' asked Emma.

'He said the police might ask me questions and I should tell them I was with him that night.'

'So you gave him an alibi,' said Penny. 'But the truth is, you weren't with him when Archie Mitchell was killed?'

'No. I was here.'

'She was,' added her mother. 'And he wasn't. I wasn't happy about her covering for that man. I never liked him.'

Penny turned to Rosie. 'Is it true Seamus and Archie Mitchell had a disagreement?'

'Yes, Archie caused the accident which injured Seamus's hand.

He still can't work from it. The burn was so bad it went down to his bone and muscles. He can't use his hand properly.'

Despite her previous disdain for Seamus, it was clear Rosie felt sympathy for him regarding the accident.

'Some people suggested Seamus was so angry about what had happened that he shot Archie in revenge,' said Emma.

'That's right. And that's why Seamus got me to lie for him. He said he was the obvious suspect but he didn't do it. And I believe he didn't, too.'

'Do you know what he was doing on the night Archie was attacked?' Penny asked.

'I don't know, he never told me. He was probably drinking somewhere, playing cards, that sort of thing.'

'Could he have been near the Tower of London?'

Rosie gave Penny a steady look. 'He could have been. But I don't believe he's a murderer. I'm not saying he's a good man but he settles things with his fists. Never a gun. I never saw him with one and I don't think he'd even know how to shoot one.'

'When we first arrived, you mentioned you hadn't seen him for two months and didn't want to see him again,' said Emma. 'What happened between you?'

'He left.' She shrugged again. 'And that was the end of it.'

'He doesn't visit his son?'

Rosie's face instantly flushed. 'Oh no. Edward's not his son. Edward's father is dead.'

'Oh. I'm so sorry to hear it,' said Penny.

'Seamus and I courted for a few months and he left when he found out about Edward. I didn't tell him, you see. I was worried he wouldn't want to know me if he knew I had a son. And it turns out I was right...'

'You're better off without him,' said her mother. 'A proper gentleman would love your child the same as he loved you.'

Rosie sighed. 'There aren't too many proper gentlemen about though, are there?'

'No, there aren't,' agreed her mother. 'So we have to do what we can to get by.'

'Ma does slop work,' Rosie gestured to the fabric piled on the trestle table. 'She sews shirts, dresses and sometimes uniforms too. Sometimes you work all night, don't you, Ma?'

Her mother nodded. 'Three shirts for a penny. I can make a penny for a dress but they take longer, of course. It was easier when Rosie was in service but that had to come to an end.'

'Because you had a child?' Emma asked Rosie.

The young woman nodded.

'As soon as they found out she was in the family way, she was dismissed,' said Mrs Clark. 'I was angry at Rosie for getting into that condition.' She shook her head. 'I brought her up telling her not to repeat my mistakes. But as soon as little Edward was born, my mind was changed.' She smiled. 'I'd do anything for that little boy. And Rosie too. She's helping me with the sewing.'

'I'm trying. It doesn't pay as well as maid's wages but it's all we can do.'

'Where were you in service?' Penny asked Rosie. 'Was it a household near here?'

'No, it was a good household on Portland Place.'

'A very good household,' added her mother. 'She was working for the Mulholland family.'

Emma startled and exchanged a glance with Penny.

'Sir Laurence Mulholland?' Penny asked.

'The very same,' said Mrs Clark. 'A decent, respectable gentleman. The chance to work for a gentleman like him doesn't come along too often. And he has a very nice family too.' She turned to her daughter. 'It was a shame how it turned out, wasn't it, Rosie? A real shame.'

TWENTY-ONE

'Hearing you worked for Sir Laurence Mulholland is a surprise,' Penny said to Rosie Clark. 'We think Archie Mitchell may have had a connection to Sir Laurence. We found his calling card in Archie's room.'

Rosie's eyebrows lifted. 'Really?'

'Did you ever see Archie at the Mulhollands' house?'

Rosie shook her head. 'No. Never.'

'Did anyone mention him? Did any of the staff seem to know him?'

She shook her head again. 'I can't think how Archie Mitchell would have known Sir Laurence. It doesn't seem possible. Archie was just a labourer like Seamus.'

'It's possible we're mistaken,' said Emma. 'We found the calling card in the room which Archie Mitchell rented. But perhaps someone else left the card there.'

'Perhaps they did,' said Rosie. 'I never knew Archie Mitchell and I never saw him at the house on Portland Place. Everything I know about him is what I heard from Seamus. And Seamus didn't have much good to say about him because of the accident he caused.'

'What was it like working in the Mulholland household?' Penny asked.

Rosie shrugged. 'Much the same as any other large house, I suppose. It was long hours and hard work. We were up at six and finished about eight in the evening.'

'And Sir Laurence?' said Emma. 'What was he like?'

'I didn't have much to do with him. He's a busy gentleman and he mostly kept to himself. But everything had to be just so. If something wasn't right, he'd tell Lady Mulholland and she'd tell the housekeeper, and the housekeeper would take it out on us.'

'And he dismissed you when he heard you were expecting a child,' said Emma.

'Anyone else would have done the same,' said Rosie. 'I got myself into trouble and I paid the penalty for it. I'm just lucky Ma has helped me. I'd have had Edward taken off me otherwise.' She gave a sniff. 'They would've taken him away.'

Emma's thoughts turned to the home for fallen women which she and Penny had visited while investigating the murder of Mrs Melbourne in a Soho graveyard. She had witnessed herself how austere and miserable such places could be. Although it was difficult to consider Rosie's circumstances as lucky, there was little doubt her mother's support was helping her a great deal.

'You found out you were expecting a child while you were working in the Mulholland household,' said Penny. 'Did Edward's father work there too?'

Rosie scowled. 'I told you he died,' she said sharply. 'I don't want to talk about him.'

'I was just wondering if he was in service there—'

'Rosie doesn't want to talk about him,' interrupted her mother. 'And that's that.' She glanced at the pile of fabric in the corner then got to her feet. 'And if you don't mind, I've got to get back to work.'

'Of course.' Emma and Penny got to their feet. The mention of Edward's father had ended the conversation for now. Emma could understand the shame which Rosie felt, but her sudden hostility felt surprising.

Penny thanked Rosie and her mother for their time then she and Emma stood in the rainy square once again.

'I made a mistake mentioning Edward's father, didn't I?' said Penny as they put up their umbrellas.

'I don't think it was a mistake,' said Emma. 'Rosie's reaction was quite revealing.'

'That's a good point. Her mood changed completely, didn't it?' Penny glanced around them. 'I know this area reasonably well from when I investigated a murder here.'

'Goodness. What happened?'

'A young woman called Mary Steinway was poisoned. We managed to catch the killer, thank goodness. I recall St George's church is near here. Why don't we go there and examine the parish records?'

'To see if baby Edward's father is listed on a baptism record?'

Penny smiled. 'Absolutely. You're learning fast, Emma.'

Emma and Penny walked down to St George Street, a busy thoroughfare which formed part of the Ratcliffe Highway. Rain had turned the gutters into thin, rippling streams. The air was thick with the scents of fried fish, baking bread, and wet timber from the docks. To the south, loomed the dark shapes of the Western Dock warehouses. The street was lined with cramped little shops: tattooists, laundries, tailors and tobacconists. Each one serving the sailors who poured in from the ships beyond the dockyard wall.

The church of St George-in-the-East was a smart stone church with arched Romanesque windows and a prominent tower. It was tucked away behind the densely packed shops and houses. The churchyard was now an attractive public garden.

'I wonder if the Metropolitan Public Gardens Committee were involved with turning the churchyard into a park?' said Emma.

'I think they must have been,' replied Penny. 'We can ask Clara about it. Isn't it nice to see what can be achieved?' Clara had become a good friend after helping with their investigation into the murder of Mrs Melbourne. As a researcher for the Metropolitan Public Gardens Committee, Clara studied disused graveyards – an unusual vocation which Penny found endlessly fascinating.

Inside the church, they found a churchwarden who was happy

to let them examine the parish register for baptisms. In the light of a flickering candle, they turned the thick pages on which lists of baptisms were recorded in a sloping script of black ink.

'How old is Edward?' said Emma. 'Six or seven months old?'

'That's right,' said Penny. 'So he would have been born in September or October of last year.'

They turned to the relevant pages and began examining the lists. The information was ordered into neat columns: the date of the baptism, date of birth, the parents' names and the trade or profession of the father.

Emma spotted the entry first. 'Look.' She pointed to it. 'Edward Clark. Born on the twenty-third of September and baptised on the fourteenth of October. Mother's name is Rosie and... there's no mention of the father.' There was a gap where the father's name would otherwise be. And a line had been drawn through the box for the father's profession.

'His name's been omitted completely,' said Penny. 'Edward is clearly illegitimate but Rosie didn't want to record his father's name, even though he's dead.'

'Or so she says,' replied Emma.

'Exactly. Claiming the father has died is a convenient excuse, isn't it? And I can understand why Rosie would say it. She's clearly ashamed about the circumstances of her son's birth. But it makes me wonder...'

'About what?'

Penny turned to her. 'Sir Laurence Mulholland,' she said. 'Perhaps he's baby Edward's father?'

They fell quiet for a moment, pondering this possibility.

'We need to learn more about Sir Laurence, don't we?' said Emma.

'We do. It would be useful to call on him and meet him for ourselves. But before then, let's find out what we can about him. Shall we visit the reading room at the British Museum tomorrow and see what we can find out?'

TWENTY-THREE

Emma and Penny met outside the British Museum the following day. They planned to visit the reading room then meet their friend Clara Clifton for their regular lunch.

Inside the reading room, spring sunlight filtered through the high windows of the great dome. Beneath it, readers sat hunched in concentration at their desks.

'Let's look in *Debrett's Peerage*,' Penny said, her voice low. 'Sir Laurence Mulholland might be listed there.'

She led the way towards an iron spiral staircase. The metal creaked faintly underfoot as they climbed, and Emma glanced down at the desks arranged like spokes of a wheel around a central hub.

Penny strode along the gallery. 'All these volumes cover the British aristocracy,' she whispered, gesturing at a shelf of thick volumes. 'I've had to consult this section a few times before. And here we are... *Debrett's*.' She pulled out the book and opened it at the letter M. Emma peered over Penny's shoulder as she leafed through the pages.

'Here he is!' Penny whispered. 'Mulholland, Sir Laurence John. And I recognise the coat of arms with the lion, that's on his calling card. Second Baronet, son of Sir Lionel. Now where's

Lionel? Here he is listed above his son... It says he was a gunsmith and was created a baronet in 1856. That was the year the Crimean War ended. I wonder if he supplied a lot of guns for the war and was recognised for his effort.'

'Effort?' said Emma. 'Presumably he made a lot of money too.'

'Yes, I should think so,' said Penny. 'War is lucrative for gunsmiths. Let's look at Sir Laurence again... Born in 1833, educated at Eton followed by Trinity College, Cambridge. He married Lady Eugenia Featherstone in 1860 and has two sons and three daughters.'

From the corner of her eye, Emma noticed someone walking along the gallery towards them. She turned to see Francis Edwards.

He smiled as he approached and pushed his sandy hair away from his spectacles. 'How lovely to see you both,' he whispered. 'Do you need any help?'

'We're looking up Sir Laurence Mulholland,' said Penny. 'Have you heard of him?'

'Mulholland and Son?'

'What's that? A company?'

Francis nodded. 'Construction. The company has made good money from the slum clearance projects in recent years; it enjoyed a close relationship with the Metropolitan Board of Works. The MBW has just been replaced by the London County Council, of course.'

Penny raised an eyebrow. 'A close relationship?'

'I understand Sir Laurence is good at that sort of thing.'

'And his son?' asked Emma.

'I don't know much about him,' replied Francis. 'But I believe he married a young lady from a prominent family last year; I recall seeing the wedding announcement in the newspaper.'

'He must assist with the running of the company if he's mentioned in its name,' said Penny. She looked again at the entry in *Debrett's*. 'Perhaps it's his eldest son. He's named here as the Honourable Gregory Charles Mulholland, born in 1865.'

She closed the book and returned it to the shelf. 'We're trying to understand how Sir Laurence could have known a young labourer who was murdered last year close to the Tower of London,' she explained to Francis. 'At the moment, it's very puzzling.'

'And it's possible there's no connection at all,' added Emma.

Francis smiled. 'Investigations can be frustrating, can't they? If I can find some spare time, I'll see if I can find out anything more about Sir Laurence, if that helps?'

'Thank you, Francis,' said Penny. 'And if you come across any mention of Archie Mitchell. while you're looking into him, please let us know.'

'He's the labourer you mentioned? I'll keep an eye out for him.'

TWENTY-FOUR

Clara Clifton listened intently as Emma and Penny told her about the case of Archie Mitchell during lunch at the ladies' dining room in Café Monaco. Waiters moved briskly between the tables, and the clink of cutlery mingled with the soft murmur of conversation.

'That sounds like a tricky case,' she said, frowning slightly. 'And I suppose it's made more complicated by the time that's passed. The longer a murder goes unsolved, the harder it is to find reliable evidence.'

'That's right,' said Penny. 'People forget things and witnesses vanish.'

Their first course arrived: bowls of steaming onion soup. 'I wish I could be of some help,' Clara said as they ate. 'But I'm hopeless at detective work.'

'Nonsense!' said Penny. 'You're a graveyard detective.'

Clara laughed. 'That really does sound strange.'

'Yes it does, but you're gathering information and trying to make sense of it. You're identifying disused burial grounds and visiting them to assess their condition and find out who owns them.'

'True,' said Clara. 'But is that detective work? I call it research.'

'You could call it that, but I don't think it's dissimilar to what

Emma and I are doing. All three of us have curious minds, don't we? We're searching for answers.'

Clara nodded. 'That's true. And we're encountering some difficult characters along the way.'

'Are you referring to anyone in particular?' Emma asked.

'Yes.' Clara put down her spoon and began buttering the bread roll on her plate. 'I recently found a disused burial ground in St Pancras. It's very small and you wouldn't know it was there. The only way to reach it is through a narrow alleyway where the gate is locked most of the time. I managed to find a friendly shopkeeper who happened to have a key and opened it for me. He told me he looked after the key for the landlord who's just agreed to sell the leasehold for the area. The sale includes the burial ground and several buildings. Some of the buildings are in a poor state of repair and have been condemned by the borough council.' She paused from buttering the roll and gave a sigh. 'The shopkeeper told me he has to close his shop because the street is going to be demolished. He's very unhappy about it and I feel quite sorry for him. He says the repairs would be straightforward and there was no need for the council to condemn them. People live in those buildings too and they've been told to leave with only a fortnight's notice.'

'How sad,' said Penny. 'And the burial ground?'

'It will be built on if the Metropolitan Public Gardens Committee isn't quick enough to save it.'

'But surely that's illegal?' said Emma.

Clara turned to her. 'Yes, it is, it's forbidden by the Disused Burial Grounds Act which was passed five years ago. But it hasn't stopped some small burial grounds from being built on. We have to rely on the law being enforced and sometimes these places are built over before anything can be done about it. If the buildings around the graveyard in St Pancras are going to be rebuilt, then the burial ground could be used as a small public park. There's a desperate need for such places in the parts of London which are densely populated.'

'There needs to be respect for the burials,' said Penny. 'It's awful to think that some graves are now nothing more than founda-tions for the buildings above them. I can only hope the Metropolitan Public Gardens Committee can save this particular burial ground.'

'So do I,' said Clara. 'We've been meeting with the St Pancras vestry and they tell us we have nothing to worry about. I don't believe them, though. I don't think they mind if the old burial ground is covered by a new building. It's a miserable place which has been neglected for many years.'

'But surely they have a duty to stop it?' said Emma.

'Yes, I believe they do. But I'm worried they're going to deliber-ately forget about it while the construction company gets on with its work. They could claim the construction was too quick for them to be able to do anything about it.' She sighed and shook her head. 'It's a great shame.'

Emma sat back in her chair. 'This may be an odd coincidence,' she said. 'But Penny and I have just found out about a construction company which has been building in areas of London where slums have been cleared.'

'What's the name of the company?' Clara asked.

'Mulholland and Son.'

Clara nodded. 'The same company. What a funny coincidence indeed.'

Penny leaned forward, lowering her voice a little. 'Sir Laurence Mulholland,' she said. 'Have you met him?'

'No,' replied Clara. 'But I've heard a lot about him.'

'What have you heard?'

'That he's ruthless and demanding.' Clara glanced around her then lowered her voice to a whisper. 'And there are rumours that he's bribing officials to get his own way.'

Emma caught her breath. 'Goodness, that's interesting to hear.'

'He's a rich, powerful man,' continued Clara. 'A member of the aristocracy with important friends. Unfortunately, gentlemen like him usually get their own way.'

Penny shook her head. 'They do indeed. I wish more could be done about it.'

'Perhaps the company Mulholland and Son has something to do with the construction of the new Tower Bridge,' said Emma. 'Maybe that's how Archie knew him?'

'I think we shall have to ask him for ourselves,' said Penny. 'Why don't we call on him after lunch?'

The visit seemed a little too sudden for Emma; she didn't feel prepared enough for it. 'Today?'

'Why not?' said Penny. 'He doesn't live too far from here. It's just a short walk up Regent's Street, across Oxford Street and up Langham Place. Let's see what he has to say for himself.'

TWENTY-FIVE

'Are you ready?' Penny asked Emma as they approached Sir Laurence's grand home on Portland Place.

'I think so.' Emma's stomach gave an anxious turn. She was more worried than she wanted to admit. She didn't enjoy meeting difficult people and confrontation made her uncomfortable. Penny, on the other hand, seemed fairly at ease in these situations. Emma tried reassuring herself that she could rely on Penny to say and do the right thing.

A man with a jaunty gait passed by, a small wooden stool slung over his shoulder. 'Umbrella repairs!' he called out, tipping his cap with a grin. 'Fine morning for it! Ladies, do your parasols need attention?'

'We don't have them with us, I'm afraid,' Penny replied.

'No trouble at all,' he said cheerfully, continuing on his way whistling a merry tune.

Emma and Penny paused by the Mulholland home – number thirty-three. It was a smart, four-storey Georgian terrace with a wide facade and rows of large sash windows.

'Very nice,' said Emma. 'I imagine the Mulholland family have a house in the country too.'

'Of course... all these people do,' said Penny wryly as she made her way to the shiny black front door.

The brass knocker was heavy and loud. Emma winced a little as Penny sounded it. She didn't feel ready for the meeting.

A footman answered the door and Emma's and Penny's calling cards were placed on a silver platter and carried away. They stood in silence, listening to the heavy tick of a clock and glancing at the portraits of Mulholland family members on the walls.

'A gun,' whispered Penny, pointing to one displayed on the wall. 'And another over there. Wasn't Sir Laurence's father a gunsmith?'

Emma nodded. 'That's what it said in *Debrett's*.'

A sombre housekeeper in a stiff grey woollen dress approached and lifted her chin so she could look down her nose at them.

'Sir Laurence wishes to know the purpose of your visit.'

'We're lady detectives,' said Penny. 'And we're investigating the murder of Archie Mitchell, a labourer on the new Tower Bridge. We believe he and Sir Laurence knew each other.'

'A labourer?' The housekeeper winkled her nose in distaste.

'Yes, we know it sounds odd. But we believe the two men were connected in some way. We're investigating the case on behalf of Scotland Yard—'

'Scotland Yard? They've asked you?'

'Yes. I'm a former news reporter and my husband is a detective inspector. I know a bit about solving murder cases and so does my friend here, Mrs Langley.'

The housekeeper's eyes flitted between them as she attempted to take in this information. She seemed a little surprised by it. 'I see. I shall inform Sir Laurence.'

'Thank you,' said Penny. They watched the housekeeper march away again. Penny lowered her voice to a whisper. 'I can't bear it when servants act superior. Why can't she just speak to us normally instead of treating us like washerwomen from Seven Dials?'

Emma gave a quiet laugh but straightened her expression as she saw the housekeeper returning.

'He will see you,' she said. 'But not for long. He's very busy.'

They followed her along a corridor carpeted with a long oriental rug. Moments later they found themselves in a large study furnished with mahogany panels, gilded books, hunting trophies and leather chairs.

A man behind the large desk got to his feet. He wore a black velvet coat and a neatly knotted burgundy silk cravat. His dark hair was turning to grey and his handsome features were hardened with stern lines. His deep brown eyes held a slight menace and the corner of his mouth was faintly curled. He looked as intimidating as Emma had feared.

'Lady detectives?' he said, gesturing to the chairs at his desk. 'I've never met a lady detective before. And now I'm meeting two.' One side of his mouth lifted in a vaguely mocking smile.

He reached for a silver letter opener on his desk and turned it idly in his hand. 'So you wish to speak to me about a chap called Archie Mitchell,' he said. 'The name means nothing to me.'

'He was shot near the Tower of London last December,' Penny explained. 'A young man. A labourer. The case was reported in the papers.'

Sir Laurence's gaze drifted to the window. 'Ah, yes,' he said eventually. 'Now that you mention it, I may have read something about it. A tragic business, of course. A murder, was it?'

Emma nodded, watching his face for a flicker of discomfort. But his expression remained calm.

He met their gaze again. 'And you're helping the police?' He gave a chuckle. 'Now that is something. I've no doubt you're both very capable, but it's hardly conventional.'

Penny reached into her handbag and pulled out the calling card. She held it out to him. 'We found this in the room Archie Mitchell rented in Bermondsey.'

Sir Laurence raised an eyebrow. 'My calling card?' He put down the letter opener, took the card and studied it with mild interest. 'I've had hundreds printed over the years. I suppose he could have come across it somehow.'

'You never gave it to him personally?' Emma asked.

He smiled. 'I don't hand out cards to labourers. And you said he lived in Bermondsey?'

Penny nodded. 'Yes.'

He gave a faint grimace. 'I very rarely go south of the river. I believe the last time was for some dreadful charity event at Southwark Cathedral. And I never go to lodging houses. So unless Mr Mitchell plucked this from a pavement or a wastepaper basket, I've no idea how it came into his possession.'

'You're quite sure you've never met him?'

Sir Laurence set the card aside with a shrug. 'Quite sure.'

'Does your construction company, Mulholland and Son, have anything to do with the construction of the new Tower Bridge?' Emma asked. She felt a little braver now she'd asked him her first question.

Sir Laurence gave her a condescending smile. 'Not at all. My company builds homes for people.'

'I've heard you plan to build some in St Pancras,' she said.

He raised an eyebrow, clearly surprised she knew about the project. 'That's right. We're clearing some slums there and building some proper homes.'

'There are slums there?'

'Oh yes. Dreadful place. The buildings have been condemned.'

'Their condition could have been improved with some repairs.'

Sir Laurence stared at her for a moment. His gaze was unsettling but she forced herself to meet it. She couldn't look away. Not now.

His voice, when it came, was low. 'Who've you been speaking to?'

'Someone familiar with the St Pancras project.' She didn't want to give him Clara's name.

'I see.' Another pause followed.

'We met Rosie Clark yesterday,' said Penny.

'Who?' Sir Laurence frowned.

'She worked in your household as a maid.'

He shook his head and looked down at some papers on his desk. 'I don't recall her.'

'She had to leave her employment because she was expecting a child,' Penny added.

He said nothing but ran his tongue over his upper lip.

'Are you sure you don't recall her?'

He raised his head and gave Penny a sharp stare. 'No. My wife and the housekeeper deal with household matters. Now, I don't have time to answer questions from interfering women. I've got work to get on with. Can you show yourselves out, please?'

Emma felt anger in her chest as she rose from her seat. Sir Laurence was an unpleasant man, she had little doubt about that.

Out on the street, she felt able to breathe a little easier again. It was a relief to be out of the house and away from the intimidating presence of Sir Laurence Mulholland.

'So what do you make of him?' Penny asked her. 'Do you think he knew Archie Mitchell?'

'Probably,' said Emma. 'He was dismissive of our questions and showed no concern for Archie. I didn't like him at all.'

'Me neither. But let's not feel disheartened by him. He deliberately made us feel uncomfortable and that suggests we're finding out more about him than he'd like. Let's forget about him for now; we've got other suspects to consider such as Sarah Lyford and Seamus Byrne.'

'I think we need to pay Miss Lyford another visit, don't we?' said Emma.

TWENTY-SIX

Emma and Penny returned to The Tiger Tavern the following day. Emma didn't like the place. It was dingy and the air was close and stale.

She noticed the sharp-eyed, wiry man who'd caught her eye on their previous visit. He sat alone again with a tankard of beer. Emma avoided his gaze but she could feel him watching her and Penny.

Sarah Lyford glanced in their direction, then turned away, her shoulders stiffening. The message was clear enough – she had no interest in another conversation.

But they had to speak to her. Emma mustered some courage, approached the bar and called out to her.

Eventually, the barmaid came over, her lips pressed into a hard line. 'I've said all I've got to say,' she said. 'There's nothing more I can tell you.'

'I disagree,' said Penny. 'We've discovered a connection between Johnny Cooper and Archie Mitchell.'

Sarah scowled. 'I'm not talking about it. I've told you that already.'

'Johnny Cooper gave evidence at an inquest four months ago, didn't he?' Penny continued. 'A young woman, Harriet Barnes, fell from London Bridge and drowned in the Thames. Archie Mitchell was there that night too, wasn't he?'

Sarah glanced around the tavern, as if hoping to be interrupted. She bit at a nail clearly uneasy. 'So I heard,' she muttered at last. 'But I wasn't there. I don't know anything more about it.'

Penny nodded. 'You're courting Johnny Cooper now, aren't you?'

Sarah's voice rose in pitch. 'I didn't know him when Harriet died! And he's never spoken to me about it.'

'But don't you think it's a curious coincidence?' Penny asked. 'That Archie Mitchell just happened to be on the bridge the night Harriet Barnes fell and a week or so later, he was found dead. And on that night you were the one who found him.'

Sarah's lips parted as if to reply, but no words came. She looked down at the bar and gave it a wipe with the cloth in her hand.

Penny lowered her voice. 'Sarah, we're not trying to cause trouble. But if there's something you know – anything at all – which could help us find out who killed Archie... That's all we want.'

Sarah didn't respond. But she didn't walk away either.

'And you knew Archie Mitchell, didn't you?' Penny continued. 'He was a regular here, wasn't he?'

Emma noticed Sarah's eyes flick briefly to a table in the far corner of the room.

'Yes, I knew him,' Sarah replied with a shrug. 'But there's nothing suspicious about it, if that's what you're thinking. Everyone knows everyone around here. Archie worked on the bridge and Johnny lives close by. Sometimes with me... sometimes elsewhere. But don't ask me where. Harriet Barnes was local too.'

'Did you know her?' Emma asked, watching Sarah carefully.

The barmaid shook her head quickly, as though the question made her uncomfortable. 'No. Never met her. What happened was awful, but Johnny says it was an accident. He doesn't like talking about it, and I know better than to ask him about it.'

'Sir Laurence Mulholland,' said Penny. 'Have you heard of him?'

'Who?' The barmaid's brow furrowed. 'Who's he?'

'He owns a construction company.'

Sarah shook her head. 'Never heard of him. Never known anyone with a title.'

She looked away, her gaze falling on the table in the far corner again. It gave Emma an idea. 'Did Archie have a regular seat here?' she asked.

'The bridge workers tend to sit over there.' Sarah pointed to the far corner she'd glanced at a few times. 'They'll be in later.'

They'd learned so little about Archie Mitchell that Emma felt the need to look at the place he'd sat so often. She turned to Penny. 'Shall we go and sit there for a moment?'

'Good idea. And let's have a sherry each while we're there.'

'Sherry?' said Sarah.

'Yes, please,' said Penny. 'In two small glasses.'

The sharp-eyed, wiry man watched Emma and Penny as they made their way to the table in the corner of the room. The tavern was quiet, but the few men who were in there seemed curious about the presence of the two women. Emma did her best to avoid their gaze.

Two sides of the table were flanked by benches built into the wood-panelled walls. Several rickety stools stood around the rest of the table and everything felt sticky from dried beer spills.

Emma sat on one of the benches. 'I can see why the labourers like this table,' she said. 'There's a good view of the rest of the tavern. They can keep an eye on who's in here and when they're coming and going.'

'Perhaps Archie Mitchell was keeping an eye out for someone,' said Penny, sitting beside Emma. 'Johnny Cooper maybe? If he'd walked in then Archie would have noticed from here. Who else could Archie have been looking out for? Seamus Byrne perhaps. Or even Sir Laurence Mulholland. Although I can't imagine this is the sort of establishment he would set foot in.'

'No,' said Emma. 'And I think Sarah Lyford spoke honestly when she said she'd never heard of him.'

'I think so too. We've finally found someone who's not heard of Sir Laurence!' Penny took a sip of her sherry. 'There are a lot of pieces to the puzzle, aren't there? And it's a struggle to see how they fit together.'

'And maybe some don't,' said Emma. 'Perhaps Inspector Simpson was right about Sir Laurence, and our discovery of his calling card in Mitchell's room was a red herring. I'd still like to prove him wrong, but I don't know how.'

The two women finished off their drinks and stood up to leave. As Emma moved, she felt her skirt catch on something behind her legs. She bent down to free it and found it was caught on a wooden panel which was coming loose beneath the bench. She tugged at her woollen skirt and the panel moved with it.

'Oh dear,' she muttered, feeling light-headed as she bent down.

'Do you need any help?' asked Penny.

'I'm fine, I'm just trying to free my skirt without it ripping.' She gripped the fabric and pulled it free. Then she crouched down to inspect the loose panel. She tried to push it back but it had clearly warped over time and no longer slotted neatly where it belonged.

'I wouldn't worry about repairing it,' said Penny. 'It's hardly our concern.'

'You're right.' Emma was about to stand up when something caught her eye – a flash of white beyond the loose panel.

'It looks like there's something in there,' she said.

She prized the panel open again and slipped her fingers behind it. She'd expected paper, perhaps a folded note, but the texture was soft. A piece of cotton wrapped into a small bundle.

'I think I've found something.' She eased the bundle out. It was a grubby cotton handkerchief, neatly folded and secured with a tiny knot.

Emma examined the find in her palm. 'There's something inside,' she said.

'Keep it hidden as you open it,' Penny lowered her voice, glancing around. 'We don't want anyone else in here seeing.'

Emma sat on the bench again and kept her hands beneath the table as she untied the knot in the handkerchief. The fabric fell open to reveal an oval of gold.

'A locket!' whispered Penny.

It was oval with a scalloped edge and engraved with a delicate design of fern leaves, flowers and berries.

She pressed her thumbnail into the clasp. With a satisfying click, the locket opened.

The photograph inside the locket was small and oval. A young man gazed out from behind the glass. He was dark-haired and dark-eyed with a serious expression. His hair was neatly parted and combed back, revealing a high brow and finely cut features. He wore a stiff, high collar and a dark jacket.

'Who's that?' said Penny.

'There's an inscription.' Emma read it out. '"Something to remember me by",' she said. 'And an initial. G.'

'Someone must be missing this locket,' said Penny. 'It's clearly been hidden behind the wood panel for safekeeping.'

Emma turned the locket over again in her hand, but there were no further clues. She examined the handkerchief. Two initials had been embroidered in blue thread in the corner.

'"A.M.",' she said.

Penny gasped. 'Archie Mitchell?'

Detective Inspector Simpson shook his head. 'I don't believe it,' he said. 'The young woman who gave us a critical alibi has now admitted she lied. Why? What possible reason could she have?'

'She was afraid of Seamus Byrne,' said Penny firmly. She and Emma stood with the inspector in the reception area of Scotland Yard. 'And for that reason, Inspector, you mustn't punish her.'

'Mustn't punish her?' he echoed, incredulous. 'She misled the police! She provided false testimony that skewed an entire investigation!'

'She did, yes. But she had her reasons,' said Penny. 'And I think you'll agree this isn't the first time someone has lied out of fear or misguided loyalty. You've seen it before. Family members, lovers, people who are intimidated... Sometimes they lie to protect someone they care for. Or sometimes they're simply frightened. Rosie Clark was both.'

Simpson frowned. 'Lying to the police is a serious offence, Mrs Blakely.'

'I know that,' Penny replied. 'But sometimes fear is the stronger force. I assured Miss Clark she wouldn't be punished for telling the truth now.'

'You assured her?' His voice sharpened. 'You gave your word on behalf of Scotland Yard, did you?'

An uncomfortable pause followed. Penny took in an audible breath, as if trying to keep herself calm. 'You asked us to help with this case,' she said. 'And I believe that through a few carefully chosen conversations, we've gathered information your officers didn't. That's not a criticism, it's simply a matter of approach. We're women speaking to other women, and that can result in quite a different outcome.'

Simpson folded his arms, still frowning. 'That's why I asked you and Mrs Langley to help us.'

'Indeed. So I ask you, Inspector, to consider Miss Clark's position. She's now told the truth. And her confession means you can question Seamus Byrne without the false alibi protecting him.'

He gave a sniff. 'We'll need to interview Miss Clark again to confirm her revised statement. And to understand what changed her mind. They're no longer close, I take it?'

'No,' said Emma. 'And her loyalty to him has now gone.'

The inspector gave a nod. 'That's good to hear.'

'But Miss Clark insists Seamus Byrne is not a murderer,' Penny added. 'She's admitted to the false alibi but she's still certain he's not guilty.'

He shook his head again. 'There's nothing quite so annoying as an unreliable witness. I shall be having a firm word with Miss Clark about this.'

'Is there any need to do that?' asked Emma anxiously. 'She already regrets providing the alibi for Mr Byrne.'

'A firm word, Mrs Langley. Not a punishment. Although there is a punishment for obstructing a police investigation like this, she's fortunate I'm showing her some mercy and have chosen not to apply the punishment in this instance. But if Byrne is the murderer then that means he's escaped justice for several months because of a young woman's despicable lies.' He blew out a sigh. 'This sort of thing makes me angry.'

'You'll be kind to her, won't you?' said Penny. 'She's been through a difficult time.'

The inspector gave a laugh. 'That's what she'll have you believe, Mrs Blakely. These people are all the same: they know how to tug at the heartstrings of gentle lady folk such as you and Mrs Langley.'

TWENTY-EIGHT

'I wish you'd tell me when you're going to turn up.' Sarah Lyford folded her arms and stared at Johnny as he finished off his food. 'It's difficult for my mother when you arrive out of nowhere. If we'd known, we could've made a larger meal.'

'Out of what?' He surveyed the basic room with a grimace.

Sarah felt her jaw tense. 'Ma can make anything go a long way.' Her mother and the children were in the neighbouring room. She continued, 'And if you tell us when you're coming then we can make sure there's enough food for the children too.'

'The children,' he repeated. He sat back in the chair and wiped his mouth on the back of his hand. 'Their father should be providing for them.'

'There's no chance of that and you know it. We live on my wages from the tavern.' She shifted from one foot to the next, nervous about what she had to ask him next. After a pause, she raised the subject, keeping her voice soft and low. 'You mentioned you would be able to give us something...'

Johnny scowled, his expression darkening. 'I can't at the moment, I'm waiting to get paid.'

'By who?'

He glanced at the curtained window, as if wary of someone

overhearing. Then he turned back to her. 'You know I can't say,' he said. 'It's the nature of my business.'

Sarah took in a breath and pushed her lips together, she didn't want to risk saying anything which would anger him.

'I'll give you something, I promise. I'll make sure you and your mother and those children... not that I have any responsibility for them... will be provided for.' He got to his feet. 'I'll make sure you're all provided for. Just you wait. You won't need to live in this place anymore.' He stepped over to her and lifted his face to hers. He smelled of drink. 'I protect you, don't I? You and your family don't get any trouble because of me. Just remember what I do for you. I sorted out your landlord when he claimed you owed him rent. Remember?'

Sarah winced. She couldn't forget. The landlord had nursed a black eye for a long time after the encounter and he hadn't demanded money from her since. She tried to pay him on time whenever she could but if she was late with the rent he didn't ask her for it anymore.

'I remember, Johnny.' She forced a smile which seemed to please him and he kissed her. She didn't enjoy it anymore when he showed affection, but she had to keep him by her side. It felt safer that way.

'There now,' he said. 'Just trust I'll do the right thing.' He stepped over to where his overcoat hung on a hook.

Sarah thought again of the two lady detectives who had called on her again that day. Were they going to keep bothering her until their questions were answered? The truth was, Sarah had questions too.

'Archie Mitchell...' she ventured. 'Did he see what happened that night?'

Johnny spun round, as if he'd been stung. 'Who?'

'You know who. I just said his name. Did he see what happened on the night Harriet died?'

He shrugged. 'I don't know. You'll have to ask him. Oh, wait a moment... you can't. Because he's dead.' He gave an ugly cackle.

Sarah felt her stomach turn. She opened her mouth to say more, but Johnny hadn't finished. 'And let's not forget how much time the police spent interviewing you about the whole affair.' His eyes bored into her. 'First on the scene, weren't you? There was just enough time to shoot him in the leg and throw the gun into the river, wasn't there?'

Sarah felt the indignation rise within her. 'That's not true and you know it!'

'No, I don't. Only you know what happened to Archie because you were there.'

'The murderer got away.'

'That's what you've always said. But did you see them running away? No. Now... I don't know what happened between you and Archie. Perhaps there was a lovers' argument—'

'I didn't know him in that way!'

'No? Well the only other person who can confirm it is a dead man. All very convenient if you ask me. Why have you brought him up again, anyway? Have those detective women called on you again.'

Sarah nodded, her mouth dry.

'Mrs Blakely and Mrs Langley, isn't it?'

She nodded again, surprised he'd remembered their names.

'Interesting.' Johnny put on his cap and turned away, heading towards the door. Just before he left, he turned to her, his voice low. 'You keep your secrets and I'll keep mine. Is that understood?'

TWENTY-NINE

Emma took the locket to a jeweller's shop once she'd finished her piano lessons the following day.

The shop was on Berwick Street, just south of Oxford Street, and was tucked between a tobacconist and a glove-maker. It had a smart black frontage with a gold sign and a bell jangled as she stepped inside. The sharp tang of metal polish hung in the air.

Emma approached the counter, where a man in a grey waistcoat was rearranging a tray of signet rings.

'I've just bought this locket,' she said, placing it carefully on the velvet mat. 'I'd like to know a little more about it. Can you tell me anything?'

The jeweller peered down at it. 'Where did you buy it?'

'From a friend.'

'And how do you know it's not stolen?'

'Because I trust my friend,' she replied.

He gave a short grunt and picked up the locket. Then he pushed an eyeglass in one eye and brought the piece close to his face.

'How much did you pay for it?' he asked.

'Five shillings,' she said, rather uncertainly.

He grunted again. 'Five shillings? Your friend got the better end of the deal. I wouldn't have paid more than three.'

'So it's not particularly valuable?'

'Not especially. It's nine-carat gold, and by the look of it, no more than a year old.'

'How can you tell that?'

'The hallmark tells me everything I need to know.' He turned the locket towards her and pointed with the nail of his little finger. 'See here? These three letters – BHJ – stand for BH Joseph and Company, a manufacturer in Birmingham.'

'Birmingham? So it wasn't made in London?'

'No, but that's not unusual. Much of the gold jewellery sold here is made in Birmingham. It's an important place for jewellery manufacture. Now see this? The number 375. That tells you it's nine-carat gold. The crown symbol after the number confirms that it's gold, and there's a sideways anchor here. See it? That's the assay mark for Birmingham. And this letter "O" at the end – that tells me it was hallmarked in 1888.'

Emma couldn't resist a smile. 'Goodness. All that information from just some small markings.'

'That's the beauty of hallmarks,' said the jeweller. 'I only wish all jewellery was marked with them. It's not mandatory, you know. But in this case, they've told us plenty. A modest little piece but well made. Do you mind if I open it?'

'Not at all.'

He clicked the clasp and peered inside. 'A young man,' he observed. 'Do you know who he is?'

'No.'

'And an inscription, "Something to remember me by". The initial is "G".' He glanced up again, one eyebrow raised. 'Is that your friend's name?'

'No,' said Emma. 'I don't know who the initial belongs to.'

The jeweller frowned. 'Then how did your friend come by it?'

'I believe it was a gift. And she didn't particularly want to keep it.'

'Ah,' he said. 'Well, this is clearly a sentimental keepsake. A token of affection, no doubt.' He closed the locket again and moved it delicately between his fingers. 'See the design on the front? Ferns and forget-me-nots. That tells you everything. A message of remembrance, perhaps even of lost love.'

He handed it back to Emma. 'It was probably exchanged during a courtship. Maybe one that didn't end well and that could explain why it's changed hands. Although I can't imagine why you'd want a locket with someone else's message and initial. For five shillings, you could have done better with something new.'

Emma suppressed a smile. 'Would a locket like this have been bought directly from BH Joseph?'

'Unlikely. BH Joseph manufacture in Birmingham, but they don't sell directly to the public. They supply jewellers across the country. Any modest shop could've stocked it.'

'So it could have been bought anywhere?'

'That's right. London, Manchester, Birmingham... you name it. There's no way to trace the exact shop.'

'Thank you,' said Emma. 'You've been extremely helpful.' She glanced down again at the locket in her palm. How were she and Penny going to find out who'd bought this locket? And who had they gifted it to? Somehow Archie was caught up in it and they needed to understand how.

THIRTY

Once the children were asleep for their afternoon nap, Penny sat at her typewriter to finish off her column – Musings of a Lady Detective.

She'd written about the Lizzie Dixie case which had been the first she'd worked on with James. The case which had changed everything.

It had been a puzzle from the start. Miss Dixie had been a well-known actress and much mourned when she'd been feared drowned in the sinking of the pleasure boat SS *Princess Alice* in 1878. Five years later, however, she'd been found dead in Highgate Cemetery. Somehow, she'd survived the sinking and carried on living in secret. As a friend of Lizzie's, Penny had been called on to help. By a youthful detective inspector from Scotland Yard.

She smiled as her mind drifted back to the cold, foggy afternoon when James had been waiting for her outside the British Museum. At the time, she'd been dismissive of him. She had no reason to trust a man from Scotland Yard. The institution had cost her her job as a reporter. Her editor had caved to pressure from the commissioner after Penny had criticised the Yard for prosecuting the wrong man. She'd written the truth and lost everything.

So when James asked to speak with her that day, she'd nearly walked away. But something about him... his gentle manner, the way he listened rather than talked... She'd felt persuaded to join him for a drink in the nearby Museum Tavern. He'd slowly earned her attention and then her trust.

How strange life could be. She'd never planned for marriage and a family. Her younger self had imagined a different path. Independence and a life-long career in a busy newsroom.

She had chosen work, thinking it meant forgoing family. She hadn't known it was possible to have both. It was a battle, but somehow – through resilience, compromise and the help of a capable housekeeper – she'd found a way to balance both.

Not perfectly. And there were days of exhaustion and guilt. Days when she longed for silence and others when she missed the chaos.

But here she was. The children asleep, the house still and the typewriter waiting for her to finish her account of how she'd solved the Lizzie Dixie case. She hoped readers would enjoy it.

Penny began typing the final paragraph. It was satisfying to look back on a case when the perpetrator had been caught and justice had been served.

The course of investigating, however, was often frustrating. At the present time it was difficult to know whether she and Emma were making any progress with finding Archie Mitchell's killer. Sometimes a small clue could pass unnoticed until a later revelation unveiled its significance. Sometimes witnesses bent the truth for their own gain. The ability to identify what was important and spot a liar was crucial. But few detectives got it right all the time. Penny felt proud of what she'd managed so far in her career, but she knew there was a possibility that one day she'd be presented with a case she was unable to solve.

It was quite likely, in fact.

Would Archie's murder become that impossible case? There were moments when she thought it likely. It could be dispiriting, but all she could do was continue what she was doing. It was important not to get disheartened.

She had just resumed her work on the final paragraph when a cry broke the silence.

Florence had woken up.

THIRTY-ONE

Sir Laurence enjoyed the way silence fell as he entered the room. The rustle of papers ceased, chairs were scraped back hastily, and every man around the table rose to his feet.

He chose a seat at the long, polished boardroom table and his secretary, Mr Gilbert, placed a heavy stack of files down with a thud.

The council officials remained standing until Sir Laurence took his seat. Only then did they sit down, each one wary under his gaze.

He steepled his fingers, leaned back in his chair, and let his eyes drift slowly along the line of gentlemen facing him.

'Well then,' he said at last, his voice low and commanding. 'Where do we stand with Bishop Street?'

Mr Mitford, a jowly man with a harried air and thinning grey hair, fumbled to respond. He shuffled the papers in front of him, pushed his spectacles higher up his nose and cleared his throat.

'Ah... yes, Bishop Street,' he said, blinking rapidly. 'The inspection is scheduled for next week, Sir Laurence.'

Sir Laurence frowned. 'Next week?' he repeated. 'It's been almost a month since we first discussed it. Why the delay?'

Mitford's fingers twitched nervously on the table.

'There's been a shortage of inspectors, I'm afraid. A bout of illness. We struggled to find someone available.'

No one else at the table spoke. They were quite content to let Mitford face the storm alone.

Sir Laurence narrowed his eyes at the man. 'Don't I get priority?'

'Of course,' Mitford stammered. 'Wherever possible, we... do prioritise your requests. But with the current situation...'

'Why not inspect it yourself, Mitford?' Sir Laurence interrupted.

Mitford gave a weak laugh. 'I'm not qualified, Sir Laurence. The law requires a certified inspector.'

'We're not paying him for his expertise. We're paying him for his authority. All we need is someone with a council badge to declare the property unfit for habitation. It's hardly complicated.'

Mitford managed a strained smile. 'Yes, of course. I agree in principle. But if we don't follow procedure, it may raise questions. And there's a risk of unwanted attention...'

'Then have the answers ready,' said Sir Laurence. 'The kind that satisfy. I'm not waiting another week.' He adjusted his collar. 'And quite frankly, I'm already losing interest in Bishop Street. That would be a pity, wouldn't it? For all of us.'

A silence followed and Sir Laurence enjoyed the effect his words had on the room. It was clear each man was worried he would put an end to their arrangement.

Another councillor cleared his throat and leaned forward with a sycophantic smile. 'I'm sure that won't be necessary, Sir Laurence. I'll speak to the inspector today. We'll rearrange his appointments and have him there by Thursday, if not sooner.'

Sir Laurence inclined his head slightly, acknowledging the effort. 'Good. That's what I like to hear.' He raised a finger. 'And when the report is completed and the recommendation proves satisfactory, you will receive my payment.'

Nods and polite murmurs were made around the table.

Sir Laurence got to his feet and his men did the same.

'Come along, Gilbert, we're late for our next appointment.'

The secretary nodded and picked up the important looking stack of files which hadn't been required for the meeting.

Sir Laurence strode out of the door, as if in a hurry. There was no appointment for him to go to next, but he liked to invent one now and again to create the impression he was in demand.

THIRTY-TWO

Clara Clifton arrived at the smart three-storey building that occupied a corner of Spring Gardens, just off Trafalgar Square. As she approached the shiny door, she noticed the brass plaque beside it was new. The old one had read 'Metropolitan Board of Works'; it had now been replaced with 'London County Council'.

She often visited the Metropolitan Board of Works to consult the archivist on her research into London's disused burial grounds. Mr Priestley, the archivist, had always been obliging and helpful. Clara could only hope that the same courtesy would continue under the council's new management.

She pushed open the heavy door and stepped into an austere marble entranceway where her footsteps echoed. A gentleman sat behind a polished reception desk, his expression impassive as she approached.

'I'm here to see Mr Priestley,' she said.

The man frowned. He was unfamiliar, presumably a new employee.

'Mr Priestley was the archivist,' Clara explained. 'I'm a regular visitor.'

'He was the archivist for the Metropolitan Board of Works?' the man asked.

'Yes, that's right. I'm assuming he's still the archivist here.'

The man shook his head and consulted a ledger on the desk. 'The archivist now is Mr Roberts.'

Clara's face fell. She had hoped Mr Priestley might have been retained. Perhaps he had chosen to retire.

'Very well,' she said. 'Could I see Mr Roberts, please?'

'Sign the visitors' book,' said the man, pointing to a large volume resting nearby. 'You know where you're going, do you?' he asked.

'Yes,' she replied. 'I assume the archives haven't been moved.'

He didn't answer. She crossed the hall to the stone staircase and descended to the basement. Gas lamps hissed faintly along the corridor, guiding her to a set of double doors at the far end.

The room beyond was a large basement chamber, cool and dim, its ceiling supported by thick brick pillars which disappeared into shadow. Rows of shelving stretched away in every direction, heavy with ledgers, files, and parcels of papers bound with faded ribbon. The air carried the dry, papery scent of dust and age.

A man aged about thirty now occupied the desk where Mr Priestley had once sat. She assumed he was Mr Roberts. He was reading a newspaper which he put down and folded up in a hurry.

'A visitor,' he said, his eyes widening with surprise. 'Did you mean to come down here?'

'Yes, I did,' said Clara. 'My name is Mrs Clifton. I work for the Metropolitan Public Gardens Committee, and I'd like to look at some of your records, please.'

'Oh.' He got to his feet. 'The Metropolitan Public Gardens Committee?'

'That's right. We're researching and documenting all of London's disused graveyards. Where possible, we work on turning them into public gardens.'

'Interesting,' said Mr Roberts. 'What sort of records do you want to see?'

'All sorts,' said Clara. 'I was a regular visitor when Mr Priestley was in charge of the archives.'

'Mr Priestley no longer works here.'

'I can see that,' she replied. She edged towards the shelves that lined the room. Mr Priestley had always allowed her to browse freely, but the new archivist seemed less accommodating.

He raised a hand to stop her. 'Perhaps you can tell me exactly what you wish to look at, and I'll find it for you.'

'Lots of things,' she said. 'It would be far easier for both of us if you simply let me look around. That's what Mr Priestley used to do.'

He folded his arms. 'That was then. The Metropolitan Board of Works did things rather differently. This is the London County Council now, and we can't simply let anyone walk in and start rummaging through our records.'

'Very well.' Clara took out her notebook from her bag and opened it at a page filled with her notes. She showed it to him. 'Here is a list of all the documents I'd like to examine.'

He glanced down the page. 'All of these? I can only permit you to view two or three.'

'But that's impossible,' said Clara. 'I need to see all of them. It's essential for my work.'

'It also creates a great deal of work for me, finding them,' he said.

'Then let me look myself,' said Clara. 'I know where everything is.'

The young archivist rolled his eyes. 'I shall have to accompany you.'

'Very well.' Clara strode towards the shelving units, Mr Roberts trailing behind. 'I'm interested in slum clearance,' she said. 'There's been a great deal of it in recent years.'

'Yes, indeed there has.'

'I believe this is the relevant section here,' said Clara, pausing before a shelf thick with files and ledgers. 'I know there's been some work in Hackney... Ah, here we are.' She pulled out a thick bundle of papers. And Clerkenwell too...' She found another bunch of papers tied together.

She turned to Mr Roberts who stood nearby, offering little assistance. 'Would you mind holding these for me?' she asked, handing him the Clerkenwell papers.

'Of course.'

Clara continued with her search, finding all the documents she needed. A short while later, Mr Roberts accompanied her to a row of desks lined up against a wall. Grey daylight filtered through a pavement light above their heads.

The archivist placed down the heavy pile of documents then stood back. 'It's going to take you a long time to look through all of these.'

'Yes,' said Clara wearily. 'But it has to be done. I want to find out which construction companies have been involved in the slum clearance projects.'

She sat down at the desk, took out her notebook and lifted the first stack of papers from the pile nearest her.

Mr Roberts pulled at his ear, clearly unsure what to do next. Eventually he cleared his throat. 'I've got some spare time at the moment. Perhaps I could help you, Mrs Clifton?'

THIRTY-THREE

A short train ride from London Bridge railway station brought Emma and Penny to Greenwich the following evening. The pair had decided to call on Archie Mitchell's uncle, Robert, to confirm whether or not the locket had been wrapped in one of Archie's handkerchiefs.

On the way, Emma told Penny about her visit to the jeweller's shop. 'The jeweller gave me lots of information,' she said. 'But nothing which could lead us to the person who owned the locket.'

'So it's impossible to trace where it was bought?' asked Penny.

'Yes, it could have been purchased in just about any jeweller's. It's not particularly unique or valuable.'

'If we're lucky, we might discover Archie mentioned the locket to his uncle,' said Penny. 'But the locket was well-hidden, so whoever put it there probably wished to keep it secret.'

Robert Mitchell's home was in a row of terraced houses on a neat, well-lit street near Greenwich railway station. In his parlour, Emma and Penny watched as he turned the locket over in his hands.

'I don't recognise it,' he said, frowning. He pressed the tiny clasp and opened it carefully. His brow furrowed as he peered at the inscription inside. 'No... I've never seen this before. Who does the initial G refer to?'

'We don't know,' said Penny. 'But we assume it's the person in the photograph.'

'And you say Archie was in possession of this?' He handed the locket back to Emma.

'We think so. We found it hidden behind a loose wooden panel in the corner of the pub where he used to sit. And it was wrapped in this.' She unfolded the handkerchief and held it up. 'The initials A.M. are stitched into the corner.'

Mr Mitchell leaned closer, squinting at the embroidery. 'Yes... I can see that. I suppose it's possible it belongs to someone else with the same initials, but when you say you found it where he used to sit...' He bit his lip as he thought for a moment. 'Let's have a look in his trunk. I'm quite sure his handkerchiefs are in there. We can see if this one matches them.'

He rose from his chair and led them to a small box room at the top of the stairs. A single bed stood beneath the window, and at its foot rested a battered trunk with scuffed corners.

Mr Mitchell knelt beside it and slowly unbuckled the straps.

'I've only looked through this a few times,' he said quietly. 'But it never gets any easier. Archie didn't own much and it's difficult to see a man's life reduced to a single trunk of belongings.'

He pushed open the lid to reveal a pair of boots, a few neatly folded shirts and some worn work trousers. Silence followed and Emma felt a lump in her throat as she surveyed the small number of humble belongings.

'And to think Archie never had a chance to find a wife,' said his uncle. 'No children. No family of his own...' His voice cracked and he ran a hand over his face. The only sound was the distant tick of a clock downstairs.

At last, he cleared his throat. 'Anyway,' he said, forcing a thin smile. 'Let's have a look for his handkerchiefs, shall we? If they match the one you've got then we'll have to start wondering what he was doing with that locket.'

He lifted a shirt, carefully mended at the collar, and put it to one side. Beneath it was a threadbare jacket with frayed cuffs. Next to the jacket, a battered tin cup lay on its side, the rim faintly stained with tea. He lifted each item slowly, respectfully, as though disturbing them might unsettle something.

Then he pulled out a bundle of handkerchiefs folded neatly together. The stub of a clay pipe fell out of them, its bowl blackened from use.

Emma picked up the pipe and placed it back in the trunk. She felt an odd shiver as she handled something so personal to a man who was now dead.

Mr Mitchell unfolded one of the handkerchiefs and Emma noticed its corner embroidered in the familiar blue thread.

'A.M.,' said Penny.

Emma took out the handkerchief which had contained the locket and found the corner with the embroidered initials.

'The stitching is identical,' said Penny. She turned to Robert Mitchell. 'Do you have any doubt this handkerchief belonged to your nephew?'

He shook his head. 'No. No doubt whatsoever.' He scratched his chin. 'Someone must have given this to him. A young man? That seems quite unthinkable to me.'

'Why hide it?' asked Penny.

Mr Mitchell shrugged.

'Perhaps it wasn't a gift,' said Emma. 'Perhaps he found it somewhere or perhaps...' She paused for a moment, choosing her words carefully in case she offended Mr Mitchell. 'Perhaps he happened across it somewhere?'

'Perhaps,' he agreed. 'I don't think he could have stolen it though. Archie wouldn't have done that. Perhaps someone else did and asked him to look after it for them. He was a firm believer in right and wrong.'

'Perhaps he simply found the locket?' said Emma. 'And he didn't know what to do with it so he put it in a safe place while he thought about it.'

'In the tavern?' said Penny. 'That doesn't strike me as a safe place. After all, you found it there, Emma.'

'Only because my skirt caught on the loose panel. If that hadn't happened, then we wouldn't have found it.'

Mr Mitchell rubbed his chin thoughtfully. 'Hiding it in that way is an odd thing to do,' he said. 'Do you know if the locket is valuable?'

'No, not really,' said Emma. 'The jeweller I showed it to said it was worth about three shillings.'

'I see. Well, it seems this locket is a mystery.' He turned back to the open trunk again, his expression sombre.

'Have you ever come across this man?' Penny handed him the calling card which belonged to Sir Laurence Mulholland.

He squinted at it and shook his head. 'No. Who is he?'

'He owns a construction company,' said Emma. 'Mulholland and Son.'

'I've not heard of them. Did Archie know this man?'

'We don't know. We found this calling card in the room which Archie rented,' said Penny. 'But it's possible it was dropped there by someone else.'

'Yes, perhaps it was. I think Archie would have mentioned it to me if he knew someone that grand. He didn't know anyone like that.' He paused for a moment then gave a wistful smile. 'A mysterious locket and a calling card from someone important. Perhaps Archie was a bit of a magpie, picking up shiny things and tucking them away.' He handed the card back to Emma. 'Maybe he found this and meant to show it to someone as a joke. He could have pretended he'd met Sir Laurence Mulholland and was moving in sophisticated circles.' He gave a fond laugh. 'He liked to play the fool sometimes.'

'Would you like to put this handkerchief with the rest of Archie's belongings?' Emma asked him.

He gave a weak smile. 'Thank you. That's a nice thought. I don't suppose you need it anymore, do you? Keep hold of the locket though. We don't know for certain it belonged to Archie. Perhaps you'll be able to find out who the mysterious G is.'

'I hope so,' said Penny. But she had no idea how they were going to find him.

THIRTY-FOUR

'Thank goodness you're back,' James said when Penny arrived home. 'I always worry when you're out late.' He stood in the hallway, newspaper in his hand. 'Is everything all right?'

'Everything's fine,' said Penny, leaning in and giving him a kiss. 'There's nothing to worry about. Emma and I travelled by cab back from Greenwich.'

She took off her coat and hung it on the cloak stand.

'Well, it doesn't stop me worrying,' said James as they went into the front room.

'We called on Robert Mitchell just as I said we would,' said Penny, sinking into an easy chair by the fire. It always felt comfortable to be home. 'He's a pleasant gentleman, you don't need to worry about him.'

'Good,' said James, returning to his armchair. 'You don't think he murdered his nephew then?'

The thought hadn't occurred to Penny. 'No. Why do you say that?'

'Everyone's a suspect at the moment, aren't they?'

'Yes...' Penny gave this some thought. 'But not Robert Mitchell, though. I don't see why he would attack his nephew.'

James nodded. 'I think you're a good judge of character, Penny. If you think he's innocent then—'

'You're right though, James. Perhaps he should be considered a suspect? Just because he seems pleasant doesn't mean he's not a murderer.' She paused and wearily ran a hand over her face. 'There's always so much to consider, isn't there?'

'Yes, there is. But I feel sure you and Emma will make progress soon, though.'

'I'm not so sure about that,' she replied. 'I don't feel we're making much progress. How have the children been?'

'I haven't heard anything from them all evening. They've both been sound asleep since you left.'

'You checked on them?'

'Three times. Just to make sure Thomas hadn't got out of his bed and was quietly playing with his toy train.'

Penny laughed. 'That was a surprise the other evening. I've no idea how long he was awake for. Quite a long time I think because he was very tired the next day.' She gave a yawn. 'I think I'll make a cup of cocoa before I go to bed. Would you like one?'

'I'll make it,' said James, getting to his feet. 'You can have a rest after your busy evening.'

While he was making the drink, Penny fetched the column she'd written for Musings of a Lady Detective.

'Here,' she said when he returned to the room. 'I've written about the Lizzie Dixie case. I thought you might like to read it.'

James smiled. 'The first case we worked on together? I'd love to read it.' He swapped the cup of cocoa for the manuscript and they both sat down. 'The autumn of eighty-three, wasn't it?'

Penny nodded. 'Five and a half years ago. It feels like a long time and yet... somehow not long ago at all.'

'Who'd have thought then that we'd end up where we are now? Married with two children. I'd never have guessed it. You absolutely terrified me.'

Penny laughed. 'Terrified you? Really?'

'You were brisk and unsmiling, striding out of the British

Museum like a woman with no time to waste. I'd been warned about you, of course.'

Penny frowned. 'Warned?'

James nodded. 'They told me you'd been dismissed from your job on the newspaper at the commissioner's request and that you wouldn't be pleased to speak to someone from the Yard. So there I was, standing outside in the fog, heart thudding like a schoolboy about to recite a poem. And when you finally appeared... I almost lost my nerve.'

Penny rested her hand on his arm. 'I'm happy you didn't.'

A quiet moment passed between them.

'Sometimes when we're busy with the children or bickering about something, it's easy to forget what came before,' said Penny.

James reached for her hand. 'But it's still there. All of it. And it's rather nice to remember, now and then.'

She smiled and felt her eyes misting. 'Yes. It is.'

A knock at the door interrupted them.

James started and let go of Penny's hand. 'Who's that at this hour?' He got to his feet.

'Maybe it's Emma,' said Penny, also getting up. 'But she would only call round in an emergency. Oh goodness... I hope nothing awful has happened.'

As she spoke James marched towards the hallway. 'I'll go and see who it is.'

Penny followed.

James opened the door and Penny noticed a moment's hesitation as he saw the person on the doorstep. 'Who are you?' he said, his hands on his hips. 'What do you want?'

Penny joined him and felt a prickle of anxiety run through her as her eyes fell on the visitor.

THIRTY-FIVE

The visitor on the doorstep was a tall, broad man with a strong jaw, sharp green eyes and a cap pulled over a shock of straw-like hair. He wore a well-tailored expensive overcoat over a shabby tweed jacket and matching trousers. His heavy boots were flecked with dirt and his hands were shoved into his overcoat pockets. His choice to keep them there and not remove his cap showed insolence. Penny immediately disliked him. Even more so when he gave a smile which didn't reach his eyes.

'Good evening, Inspector Blakely,' he said. 'I'm here to speak with your wife.'

James stepped forward, ensuring he formed a barrier between the visitor and Penny. 'Oh no you don't,' he said sharply. 'You haven't even told me who you are.'

'Johnny Cooper's the name,' he said with a grin. 'And I understand Mrs Blakely has been speaking to a good friend of mine.'

'Who's your friend?' Penny asked.

'Sarah Lyford.' He addressed her directly now and she didn't like his gaze. He looked her up and down, clearly a deliberate glance designed to make her uncomfortable.

James noticed it too. 'It's too late in the evening to be calling on us like this. You need to push off.' He grabbed the edge of the door, readying himself to close it.

'I'll be more than happy to do as you ask, Inspector, once I've understood why your wife keeps talking to my friend.'

'We're trying to find out more about Archie Mitchell,' said Penny. 'Did you know him?'

He shook his head. 'No. Who is he?'

'He was murdered last December but I suspect you know that already. He spoke at the inquest into Harriet Barnes's death. She was with you on that night, wasn't she?'

'She was and it's an evening I'd rather forget.' His expression remained impassive.

'Archie Mitchell saw what happened,' said Penny.

He took a hand from his pocket and rubbed his nose. 'I remember who he was now. He's dead, you say?'

'You know he is,' replied Penny.

'I don't know what makes you say that. I remember him at the inquest but I had nothing to do with him before or after it. If he's dead then I'm very sorry to hear it. Especially murder. That's a terrible tragedy.'

His voice lacked sincerity and it angered Penny. 'Why are you here?' she asked.

'To speak with you, Mrs Blakely. Am I allowed in?'

Penny's thoughts immediately went to her sleeping children upstairs. 'No,' she replied.

James moved to close the door. 'My wife has nothing more to say to you this evening, Mr Cooper,' he said. 'I bid you goodnight.'

Johnny Cooper pushed a foot over the threshold and barred the door's progress. 'I'm not finished,' he said.

Penny's heart thudded. Johnny was taller and broader than James. If he chose to use his strength, there could be trouble.

'Mrs Blakely, keep out of it.'

'Watch how you speak to my wife!' said James.

'It's all right, James,' said Penny. 'Mr Cooper is clearly a straight-talking man and I shall hear him out.' She turned to

Johnny, aware the man's temper was probably as volatile as a powder keg. 'Keep out of what, exactly?'

'Whatever you're doing. This lady detective business. It's upsetting Sarah and when she's upset, I get upset too.'

'I'm sorry to hear we've upset her, that was certainly never our intention. Do please pass on my apologies.'

'I will.' He gave a nod, briefly disarmed by Penny's apology. 'However, you and your friend, Mrs Langley, need to stay away. Keep out of The Tiger Tavern and stay away from her home. She doesn't like it, you know. It was upsetting enough for her that she was the one who found Archie Mitchell that night...'

'I thought you didn't know he was murdered?'

Johnny bit his lower lip for a moment, clearly annoyed she'd caught him out. Then he bared his teeth in a humourless grin and Penny calmed her breath, keen not to show any fear. She felt like she was dealing with a calm but aggressive dog.

'I don't think I need to say anything more, Mrs Blakely. You understand my meaning, don't you?' He turned to James and doffed his cap in mock deference. 'Thank you for allowing me to speak with your wife, Inspector Blakely.'

He turned on his heel and walked off into the night.

James swiftly shut the door and pulled the bolt across. 'Well, he's an unpleasant chap, there's no mistake about that.' He sighed and leaned against the door. 'I'll have a word with the chaps at the Yard tomorrow and see what we can bring him in for. He can't get away with behaving like that towards a detective inspector and his wife. How did he find out where we live?'

'I don't know,' said Penny. 'It's worrying. He could call on Emma next. I'll send her a telegram and ask her not to answer the door to anyone tonight.'

THIRTY-SIX

After breakfast the following morning, Clara opened her notebook once more. Her head still ached from the hours spent the previous night poring over documents. She had worked late with Mr Roberts, the London County Council archivist, sifting through piles of papers until her eyes had grown weary and the smell of old paper clung to her clothes.

Now, seated at her dining table with the remains of breakfast still about her, she reviewed the notes she had compiled from the mountain of paperwork. A soft morning light from the window fell across the pages. As she read her tidy handwriting, she felt quiet satisfaction.

She was confident she'd drawn the right conclusion. Mulholland and Son had been involved in a series of suspiciously similar projects in Hackney, Clerkenwell, Southwark and Camden Town. In each case, the pattern was the same: buildings were condemned by the local vestry and purchased soon after by Mulholland and Son for a curiously low price. They were then swiftly demolished and replaced with new buildings where rooms were let out at much higher rents.

The speed of the work was astonishing. Within months, entire streets had been cleared and rebuilt. It was unusual in an industry where paperwork and bureaucracy could grind progress to a crawl. Something – or someone – was smoothing the way.

Among the papers, Clara had examined the original contracts between Mulholland and Son and the Metropolitan Board of Works. She had seen Sir Laurence's signature many times, written in his bold, assertive hand. But another name appeared beside his on several key documents: a Mr Oscar Garland.

THIRTY-SEVEN

Penny turned up with Thomas and Florence on Emma's doorstep. She'd sent a cryptic telegram the night before asking Emma not to answer the door. Fortunately no one had called and she hadn't needed to worry Mrs Solomon about it. But she was keen to find out why Penny had sent the message.

Emma waited patiently while her landlady greeted Penny.

'Oh, what lovely children!' said Mrs Solomon as she helped them into the house.

'I'm so sorry for the surprise visit,' said Penny.

'No, don't be sorry at all! I love seeing your children, Mrs Blakely. I don't think I'll ever have grandchildren of my own so I'll dote on yours instead.' She took Florence into her arms and made funny faces. Then she turned to Thomas. 'Do you like biscuits?'

'Yes!'

'Come with me then and we'll go and find some.'

'Is everything all right?' Emma asked Penny once Mrs Solomon had taken the children into the dining room.

'Not really.' Penny sighed, taking off her hat and gloves. 'Johnny Cooper called on us yesterday evening.'

Emma gasped. 'Cooper?'

'That's why I asked you not to answer the door. I was worried he would come here too.'

'Fortunately he didn't.' Emma felt relieved about it. 'What did he want?'

'He wants us to keep away from Sarah Lyford. I don't know why but he's obviously unhappy we've been asking her questions.'

'How did he know where to find you?'

'I don't know. The Post Office Directory, perhaps? Miss Lyford must have told him about us and he looked us up.'

Emma felt a twinge of anxiety. 'So he could call here too.'

'Possibly. And if he does, don't challenge him too much. Just be prepared to go along with what he says. I think he could be a violent man.'

'Oh no.' Dread began to coil in her stomach. 'Why is he so bothered about us speaking to Miss Lyford?'

'Because he has something to hide. A secret to protect. And she must do too.'

'If you think he's a violent man then he could have murdered Archie Mitchell, couldn't he?'

'Yes, he could.' Penny turned to her. 'But don't worry—'

'Don't worry?' Emma gave a laugh. 'Of course I'm going to worry!'

'If he comes here, just say what you need to say to appease him. We can deal with him, but we just need to do it carefully.'

'Very well.' Emma took in a shaky breath. 'Hopefully I won't encounter him.'

Emma couldn't shake the feeling that danger was drawing closer. Johnny Cooper knew their names now and their addresses. She took in a breath, trying to steady herself against what was coming.

THIRTY-EIGHT

Clara Clifton stifled a yawn as she listened to the bookkeeper of the Metropolitan Public Gardens Committee that evening. He was giving an update on the charity's accounts.

The other members appeared to be giving him their full attention, but she struggled to summon any interest in the figures. Still, she had to remain patient. Her time to speak would come soon enough.

To keep herself awake, she tried to read the small inscription beneath the oil portrait of a local dignitary hanging opposite her. If she squinted, she could just about make out the name. Sir John someone. Or was it Sir Joseph? He looked a rather glum fellow, his dark clothing blending into the murky background. His pale face, tinged red at the cheeks, stood out starkly. The painter had paid particular attention to the eyes, giving them a stern, imperious expression, the sort that suggested everyone must do exactly as he said.

'Now we come to an item on the agenda which, I believe, was tabled at the very last minute,' announced the chairman. He turned to the committee secretary, Mr Wheeler, seated at his left. 'Who put this on the agenda?'

'Mrs Clifton,' said the secretary, nodding in Clara's direction.

Clara cleared her throat and smiled. 'That's right. I'm sorry I only just managed to get in touch with Mr Wheeler in time. It's regarding the St Pancras project.'

'Ah,' said the chairman. 'We discussed that in great detail at last month's meeting.'

'Yes, we did,' said Clara. 'But we haven't done much about it yet, have we? From what I've learned about Sir Laurence, he gets on with things very quickly indeed. If we waste any more time, the disused burial ground will be built over.'

'Waste time?' spluttered a spectacled man with grey whiskers. His name was Mr Sturgeon. 'Are you accusing us of wasting time, Mrs Clifton? I don't think anyone at this table wastes his time!'

'Perhaps I chose the wrong words,' said Clara. 'What I mean is we need to act more swiftly. I've carried out some research into Sir Laurence's other projects and he seems to get buildings demolished and rebuilt in no time. When he's involved, everything happens suspiciously quickly.'

'Suspiciously?' asked the chairman. 'Are you suggesting some dishonesty, Mrs Clifton?'

'I suspect it.' Clara opened her notebook in front of her. 'I looked at Sir Laurence's projects in Hackney, Clerkenwell, Southwark and Camden Town—'

'How?' asked Mr Sturgeon.

'I worked with the archivist at the new London County Council. He helped me look through the records for the Metropolitan Board of Works.'

'That must have taken a great deal of time.'

'It did. And I believe it was necessary. We're trying to challenge Sir Laurence on his plans for St Pancras and I believe we need to know what sort of man we're dealing with.'

'And what are your conclusions, Mrs Clifton?' asked the chairman. 'Dishonesty?'

'Yes. There was a name which appeared on many of the documents and I couldn't understand why his name was so prevalent.

When you consider the different locations the projects are in, you would expect to see a wider variety of names. But instead, the same name keeps coming up.'

'Whose name?' asked the chairman.

'Mr Oscar Garland. I think he helped Sir Laurence make his land purchases quickly and easily. In exchange, I suspect Sir Laurence greased his palm—'

'Absolutely not!' said Mr Sturgeon, slapping his palm on the table. 'Mr Garland is a fine gentleman who has just retired from the Metropolitan Board of Works after many years of dedicated service. I will not hear his name besmirched!'

News of Mr Garland's retirement interested Clara. Perhaps he had retired on the proceeds of Sir Laurence's bribes? Although she felt tempted to suggest it, she decided it would enrage Mr Sturgeon even more.

'Bribery is a serious accusation,' said the chairman. 'And it appears to be based on pure speculation I'm afraid, Mrs Clifton. Now we don't have the time to discuss this in greater detail at this meeting. However, I'll remind you that we drafted a letter to Sir Laurence after last month's meeting—'

'Have we received a reply?' Clara cut in.

'No, not yet. Although I'm sure we will.'

'I don't have confidence that we will,' said Clara. 'After all, I suspect he's bribing officials.'

The chairman turned to the secretary. 'Can you omit the comments regarding bribery from the minutes please, Wheeler.'

'Omit them?' said Clara.

'Yes, Mrs Clifton. Nothing can be proven at the moment.' He turned to the secretary again. 'Don't include that either, Wheeler.'

Clara sighed. Why was the chairman so reluctant to publicly criticise Sir Laurence? She wondered if he was scared of him. 'Perhaps Sir Laurence will reply to our letter once he's built over the graveyard,' she said. 'And what will we do then?'

'I think you're worrying yourself unnecessarily, Mrs Clifton,' said the grey-whiskered man. 'It's possible Sir Laurence will move quickly, but we still have time. The buildings he means to demolish are still standing, after all. It will take weeks to pull them down completely.'

'Why don't we write him a second letter and invite him to a meeting with us next week?'

'A meeting of the full committee?' asked the chairman.

'Yes,' said Clara. 'We can arrange that, can't we?'

'But the committee only meets once a month, Mrs Clifton. You know that.'

'Yes, and if we wait until next month it will be too late.'

The chairman raised a hand. 'No, Mrs Clifton. There's no need to be hasty. I understand your concern, but we don't need to panic.'

'I'm not panicking,' said Clara, trying her hardest to hide her irritation. 'I'd just like us to move a little faster. We need to protect that burial ground.'

'Yes, we know that,' said Mr Curtis. 'That's why we're all here. Now then...' He glanced at the clock on the wall, 'we're running short of time this evening. I propose we give Sir Laurence another two weeks to respond. If he hasn't replied by then, we'll discuss our next step.'

Clara gritted her teeth. A great deal could happen in two weeks.

'All those in favour?' asked the chairman. 'Show of hands, please.'

Every hand around the table was raised, except Clara's. She kept her arms folded firmly in front of her.

'Very good,' said Mr Curtis, making a note on his copy of the agenda. Then he looked up at her. 'Don't worry, Mrs Clifton. He won't get past us. We'll make sure of it.'

Clara forced a faint smile, but she had little confidence in his reassurance.

When the meeting finally adjourned, Clara gathered her papers with brisk efficiency. The men lingered, chatting amiably as though nothing of consequence had been discussed. She offered her usual good evenings and stepped out into the cool night. The air outside felt sharp and bracing after the stuffy committee room. Two weeks, they'd said. She wasn't prepared to wait that long. If Sir Laurence Mulholland thought he could build over the graves in St Pancras without resistance, he was very much mistaken.

THIRTY-NINE

'Johnny Cooper won't be bothering us for a while,' said James to Penny during dinner that evening. 'I had a word with Detective Inspector Bradshaw in H Division and he's had him brought in.'

'Well, that's a relief, I suppose,' said Penny. 'What was the reason for arresting him?'

'Suspicion of robbery. H Division are well acquainted with Cooper, their friendship goes back a long way. Ideally he would be charged and sentenced for a spell in jail but that depends on the evidence against him. A jury would want something to convict him on.'

Although it felt reassuring to hear Johnny Cooper had been arrested, Penny worried his detention would only be short. 'Won't it make him angry?' she said.

'Probably,' said James, cutting into a piece of beef fillet. 'But he should know better than to call at the home of a detective inspector and make threatening remarks to his wife. In fact, that's a crime in itself and I've asked Bradshaw if he can find some charges he can bring against Cooper for appearing on our doorstep yesterday evening.'

'But if Cooper is free again soon, he'll be even more resentful of us,' said Penny. 'He might call round again and who knows what he would do?'

'He'd be a foolish man indeed if he chose to call on us again. In fact, I shall visit him at Commercial Street station again and remind him of that.'

'Really?' Penny put down her knife and fork and gave a shiver. She worried about James, even more so after he had been attacked during the investigation into the murder of Lord Harpole. 'I think you need to be careful, James. You don't want to make him angry...'

'It's my job to make these men angry, Penny. Police officers can't spend their time tiptoeing around these men hoping not to upset them. They're ruffians. Scoundrels. They have no scruples at all.' He stuck his fork into a potato and held it aloft. 'It's important they realise they can't mess about with the police. Especially Scotland Yard.'

'Very well.' Penny picked up her cutlery again. 'As long as you're careful, James. I worry about you.'

He leaned forward towards her. 'And I worry about you too, Penny. Even more than you worry about me. I'm a chap, I can deal with men like Johnny Cooper. But you're a lady. You stand no chance against a chap like him.'

'I can when it comes to wits,' said Penny. 'Cooper may be large and strong but I doubt he's particularly clever. If I can find evidence he murdered Harriet Barnes and Archie Mitchell then he won't be able to bother another person ever again.'

James gave a nod. 'That would be impressive.'

'If he murdered them, then I believe Emma and I can prove it,' she said. 'But we need to speak to someone who was there the night Harriet died. I made some notes from the inquest reports...' She pushed a piece of beef onto her fork as she thought. 'And there's probably the name of someone I can speak to in my notes somewhere...' She put down her fork and went to fetch her notebook.

FORTY

The letter sat on the hallway table while Jane Fielding made breakfast for her lodgers then carried out the morning chores. She scolded the coal delivery boy for spilling the coals and she placed her weekly order at the grocer's shop.

She made herself a cup of tea at ten o'clock and chose this time to pick up the envelope and take it into the parlour. Now it lay on the parlour table in front of her while she sipped her tea and prepared herself to open the envelope.

She knew who the letter was from. The envelope was made of good quality cardstock and she recognised the slanting handwriting on it. He'd called at the house three times in the past fortnight but she hadn't answered the door. She had nothing to say to him, but there was clearly something he wanted from her.

Now he'd resorted to writing her a letter. It was tempting to throw it onto the fire without reading it, but she was too inquisitive to do that.

After she'd topped up her cup from the teapot, she picked up the envelope and slit it open with the letter opener. Her heart thudded heavily in her chest. What was the letter going to say?

She pulled out the letter which had been folded in half. As she expected, the thick paper was headed with a coat of arms.

Dear Mrs Fielding

I have called on you at home several times recently but have had little success in speaking with you.

There's little need to explain what I wish to discuss with you; I think you know only too well what the matter is regarding. If you would agree to a meeting with me then I feel sure we can have the issue resolved without any more bother.

Although I have many reasons to be aggrieved, I'd like to remind you that I'm a reasonable gentleman who desires nothing more than to ensure this small dispute between us reaches a satisfactory conclusion.

I urge you to please call on me at your earliest convenience.

With kindest regards,

Sir Laurence Mulholland

Jane ripped the letter in half and tossed it to one side. Its polite tone didn't fool her; she knew what Sir Laurence was really like.

She didn't want to reply and she didn't want to call on him. But a worry nagged at the back of her mind – what would he do if she continued to ignore him? What was he capable of?

FORTY-ONE

Penny called on Emma. 'Do you remember we made some notes from the newspaper reports on the inquest?' she asked.

Emma nodded.

'Well, I happened to write down the name of the constable who was the first police officer to help when Miss Barnes fell into the river. His name is Constable Dickinson and he's with the City of London Police. Do you have some time now to find him?'

After inquiring with the desk sergeant at Old Jewry police station, Emma and Penny discovered Constable Dickinson was based at the police station on Cloak Lane. They made their way there and spoke with another desk sergeant who confirmed the constable was out on his beat.

'Which streets does his beat include?' Penny asked.

'Upper Thames Street, King William Street, Cannon Street...' The sergeant paused and narrowed his eyes. 'I'd like you ladies to understand that Constable Dickinson can't be bothered while he's patrolling his beat.'

'We won't bother him,' said Penny.

'He can't be distracted from his work.'

'Absolutely not,' added Penny. 'We understand.'

They went out again onto the busy streets of the City. Smartly dressed gentlemen bustled officiously in and out of banks and offices. Carts and delivery vans tethered to bored-looking horses called at the many warehouses and businesses.

'Cannon Street is the nearest to us, I think,' said Penny, glancing around. Emma couldn't be so sure; she didn't know the City of London particularly well. Her last visit here had been to the bank she and her husband had banked with on Lombard Street.

'Yes, it's just over there,' said Penny, pointing. 'I think that's Cannon Street railway station.'

Emma had made a note of the constable's beat in her notebook. She and Penny tried to follow the route as best they could. As they turned into King William Street, Emma caught sight of a constable across the road – distinctive in his domed helmet and blue jacket with brass buttons.

'Over there!' she said.

'Well done!' said Penny. She looked over her shoulder and dashed through a gap in the traffic. Emma followed and a cabman shouted at them for not looking properly.

'Constable Dickinson?' said Penny breathlessly as they reached him. He was a young man with a fair moustache and a slightly crooked nose.

'Yes, what is it?' He rested his hand on the wooden truncheon at his belt, as if preparing for action.

'Can we speak to you about the death of Harriet Barnes after she fell from London Bridge last December?'

'Erm... if you must. There's no emergency then?'

'No,' said Penny. 'No emergency. We'll walk with you.'

'I see... Well, that's not really strictly allowed. I'm on my beat, you see.'

'This really won't take long, Constable.'

'Very well. Just a minute or two then. Let's walk on.' He gestured in the direction they should move.

As they walked, Penny explained she and Emma were assisting Scotland Yard with investigating the murder of Archie Mitchell.

The constable raised an interested eyebrow but continued to glance around him as he continued his steady walk.

'We want to find out more about Johnny Cooper,' Penny added. 'Archie Mitchell was on London Bridge at the same time as Johnny Cooper and Harriet Barnes. We know you were the first constable on the scene that night and gave evidence at the inquest into her death.'

'That's right.' He stopped to cross the road at the junction at the top of King William Street. When they crossed, he greeted the policeman who was directing the traffic with a friendly nod.

'So perhaps you can tell us what you saw that night?' Penny asked once they continued along Cannon Street, retracing the steps she and Emma had just taken.

'I was on night patrol when Miss Barnes fell from the bridge,' said Constable Dickinson. 'I was just at the end of Lower Thames Street when I heard a man calling for help. I realised he was probably near the river and I immediately assumed someone had fallen in. I ran around the corner and came across Johnny Cooper. He shouted to me that a lady was in the river. I ran on to the river and down the steps. But I could see very little, even when I lit my lantern. Mr Cooper told me she'd fallen off the bridge and the river was so wide and dark at that point... and so cold too. I already feared the worst.'

They passed a public house where a drunk man was being pushed out onto the street by a grumpy landlord. The drunkard staggered in the path of the constable before straightening himself and giving him a salute.

The constable stopped. 'Do you need to be taken somewhere to sober up?' he asked.

'No, Constable. I'm quite all right. I'm going home now for a lie down.'

'Where's your home?'

'That way.' The drunk man swayed and pointed. Then changed his mind and pointed in the other direction.

'Well, make your way there now and mind how you go. If you make a nuisance of yourself I shall take you to the cells.'

The drunkard saluted him again and stumbled away.

'I shall probably be picking him up on my next circuit,' muttered Constable Dickinson. He continued on his way.

'So you saw no sign of Harriet Barnes?' Emma asked him.

'Sadly not. A few people went out in boats to try to reach her. And the river police arrived too. But she'd been pulled under and her body wasn't found until the following day. Down near Hammersmith as I recall.'

'How dreadful,' Emma said.

He gave a weary nod. 'The river can be treacherous around the bridge piers and the water is bitterly cold at that time of year. Once someone goes in, it's hard to bring them out alive. We didn't give up hope and the river police did all they could. But I've seen it before, and I know I'll see it again. It's a dangerous place to be, especially if you're not careful. Standing on the wall of a bridge... well, let's just say it's not wise. Then again, Miss Barnes was under the influence of drink.'

'Did you encounter Archie Mitchell that night?' Penny asked.

'Yes. Once I'd realised there was nothing I could do from the side of the river, I climbed the steps again to find him standing on the edge of the bridge. I asked him what he was doing there and he told me he wanted to help because he'd heard Miss Barnes fall. Then Mr Cooper appeared and he was angry and upset. He told me I should be doing something to help and I replied that I could see the lights of the river police boat and they were doing all they could to pull his friend from the river. I went down to the riverside on the other side of the bridge in the hope Miss Barnes had been able to swim to safety but sadly there was no sign of her on the mud flats there. So I returned to Mr Mitchell and Mr Cooper and took statements from them both.'

'And what did Mr Mitchell say?' asked Penny.

'He told me he was walking southwards along London Bridge when he heard a woman singing.'

'Just heard. He didn't see her?'

'No.'

'But why not?' Emma asked. 'We passed over London Bridge recently at night and could see it's lit with gas lamps.'

'Yes, but they're widely spaced. A lot of the bridge remains in darkness at night. Anyway... Mr Mitchell told me he'd heard singing, then a cry, then a splash. A man cried out for help shortly afterwards and I believe that was Mr Cooper.'

'Did Archie Mitchell seem upset when he told you this?' Penny asked.

'Yes, he was very shaken.'

Emma gave this some thought. 'So Archie Mitchell was walking southwards and Johnny Cooper and Harriet Barnes were walking northwards.'

'That's right,' confirmed the constable.

'And when you went down to the riverside for the second time, Johnny Cooper and Archie Mitchell spoke to each other?'

'I don't know. I couldn't say.'

'But they were standing together when you returned to them?' asked Penny.

'Yes.'

'Then you took statements from the pair of them?'

'That's right.'

'And Archie Mitchell was quite clear he saw nothing of what happened? He just heard it.'

'Indeed.'

Penny cleared her throat before her next question. 'Constable, do you think it's possible Johnny Cooper could have pushed Harriet Barnes off the bridge?'

He frowned for a moment. 'Pushed her while she was balancing on the wall?'

'Yes.'

'Why would he do that?'

'I don't know,' said Penny. 'But I do know he's an extremely unpleasant man.'

'Oh yes. He's a criminal all right. But they're not all murderers, you know. Harriet Barnes was the worse for drink that night and she paid with her life. That's all there is to it. Now please excuse me, ladies, but I must get on with my beat without further distraction.'

'Of course.'

Emma and Penny stopped and watched the constable stroll on away from them.

'Johnny Cooper and Archie Mitchell were alone together before Constable Dickinson took their statements,' said Emma quietly.

'Yes they were,' replied Penny. 'And that means Johnny Cooper had time to influence Archie's account of the events that night.

FORTY-TWO

At lunchtime, Emma and Penny met with Clara Clifton at the ladies' dining room in Café Monaco.

'Have you got anywhere with Sir Laurence Mulholland?' she asked them.

'No,' said Emma. 'His name keeps coming up but we haven't been able to find the connection between him and Archie Mitchell. He denies he ever knew him but we're not sure we believe him.'

'We've discovered Rosie Clark worked for him,' said Penny. 'But she claims she never met Archie Mitchell.'

'Or so she says,' replied Emma.

Penny smiled. 'True. You can't always believe what people tell you, can you? I thought Rosie seemed honest enough, but...' She gave a shrug. 'You can never be sure.'

'Well, I have a theory,' said Clara.

'You do?' Penny's eyes brightened with interest. 'Well, let's hear it because Emma and I are in danger of chasing our tails at the moment. It's difficult to find a definite lead.'

The waiter arrived to take their order and Emma grew impatient as he took his time writing it down. She wanted to hear what Clara had to say.

Once he'd left again, Clara lowered her voice and Emma and Penny leaned in to hear.

'There's little doubt Sir Laurence is up to no good,' said Clara. 'I've done some research into his projects.'

Emma and Penny listened intently as Clara explained she suspected Sir Laurence had bribed a gentleman called Oscar Garland at the Metropolitan Board of Works.

'And this is what's happened in St Pancras where the disused burial ground is in danger of being built on?' asked Penny.

'Yes. I think Sir Laurence ensured the buildings in the area were all condemned so he could buy the leasehold cheaply.' She lowered her voice further. 'Perhaps Archie Mitchell discovered Sir Laurence was bribing officials?'

'It's certainly possible!' said Penny. 'But how did Archie find out? And does that mean he confronted Sir Laurence with what he knew? The two men were from such different walks of life that it's hard to imagine.'

'Perhaps Archie worked as a labourer for Sir Laurence?' suggested Emma.

'For his company? Yes! Now that's something we could find out.' Penny scratched her chin as she thought. 'Although Robert Mitchell hadn't heard of him, had he? If Archie had worked for Sir Laurence, I think his uncle would have known about it.'

'Perhaps you'd like to come and visit the St Pancras site?' Clara suggested. 'Then you can get an idea of what Sir Laurence is up to.'

Once they'd finished their lunch, the three ladies travelled by omnibus to Euston railway station. From there, they made a short walk to the down-at-heel area between Euston and St Pancras stations.

Thin sunlight filtered through a veil of drifting smoke from the chimneys above. The air smelled of damp timber, coal smoke and the sour tang of the nearby railway. The cobbles were uneven and speckled with puddles from the morning's shower. Wheels rattled over them and children darted between the carts.

Clara led them along Chalton Street to a row of buildings with their lower storeys obscured behind tall wooden hoardings. Bill posters had been pasted onto them advertising seaside excursions, patent medicines and shows at nearby theatres.

'I'm relieved the buildings are still here,' said Clara. 'The last time I visited one of the workmen told me demolition was sched-uled to begin within the fortnight. It gives me hope we might still stop it. Once the buildings are knocked down, the workers will waste no time building over the burial ground behind.'

Emma glanced up at the buildings; they seemed fairly modern to her, little more than fifty years old. Apart from a few broken windows, they looked to be in reasonable condition.

'I don't understand why this site has been condemned,' she said.

'Sir Laurence's money,' said Penny. 'That's why.'

'But shouldn't someone be doing something about it? Why's he allowed to proceed unchallenged?'

'It's not right,' agreed Penny. 'And it's exactly the sort of matter I would have investigated as a journalist.'

Emma was suddenly struck by an idea. 'Perhaps Harry Wright could investigate? I think he'd be good at it.'

'I agree,' said Penny. 'I think you should suggest it to him. He'd certainly listen to you.'

Emma felt warmth creep into her face. 'I don't think he'd listen to me any more than anyone else.' But she knew her voice lacked conviction.

Penny grinned, then her expression turned quickly to alarm as she noticed what Clara was doing.

Emma heard the wrench of splintering wood and turned to see Clara pulling open one of the hoardings. 'Goodness!' she said. 'Are you allowed to do that?'

'No,' replied Clara, peering into the gap she'd created. 'But there's no one around to stop me at the moment, is there?' She'd managed to pull part of the hoarding out of its timber support. The gap was wide enough to fit through.

'Behind here is the shop where I borrowed the key from the nice shopkeeper to access the burial ground,' said Clara. 'Now it's closed up and he's gone. It's sad, isn't it? Let me show you the burial ground.'

Emma exchanged a bemused glance with Penny. 'Isn't it trespassing?' she said.

'I don't know,' said Clara, squeezing herself through the gap. 'But whatever we're doing, it's not as bad as Sir Laurence's activities. Come on... Just mind these nails which are poking out. You wouldn't want one of them in your eye.'

Penny headed for the gap in the hoarding and Emma followed. As she turned sideways to edge herself into the gap, she noticed a stooped elderly gentleman watching from the other side of the road. She quickly glanced away, hoping he wouldn't alert anyone to what they were doing. The sharp end of a nail almost caught her on the chin but she managed to get past and did her best to pull the hoarding back into position behind her.

Penny and Clara had walked on past the dark-windowed shop and stopped by an alleyway on the other side of it. Emma joined them.

'There,' said Clara, pointing down the dark alleyway. 'That's the old burial ground. You can just see the gate.'

The alleyway had a damp, acrid smell and Emma pinched her nose, not wishing to investigate any further. But Clara and Penny stepped into the gloom of the alleyway.

'It's believed the burial ground was a seventeenth-century plague pit,' said Clara, her voice echoing within the passageway. 'In those days it was obviously on the periphery of the city but these days it feels like it's in the centre.'

Reluctantly, Emma followed her two friends. She had little interest in the burial ground but she didn't like waiting about on her own.

'It looks very creepy,' said Penny, peering through the bars of the gate. 'You went in there on your own, Clara?'

'Of course. I'm quite used to it now. These places don't bother me. The dead can't do any harm.'

Penny stepped aside so Emma could look through the gate. She gripped the rusty bars with her gloved hands and leaned in. Tall buildings surrounded the graveyard giving it a grey, gloomy air. It looked like a damp place, permanently in shadow. Weeds climbed and twisted around the sunken headstones and tombs. A chill ran through her as she thought of all the burials in there. 'I don't believe in ghosts,' she said. 'But this place looks haunted to me.'

Clara laughed. 'All it needs is some maintenance. Someone to look after it. I think it's a very peaceful place.'

Her words were interrupted by a deafening crack.

FORTY-THREE

Emma felt her knees buckle and she immediately dropped to the ground.

The noise reverberated around the little graveyard followed by the flapping sound of birds taking flight.

Silence fell as all three women crouched huddled together. Emma's heart pounded in her chest and she felt a cold sweat break out on her forehead.

'What on earth...' said Penny, her voice hushed and breathless. 'What was that?'

'I don't know,' whispered Clara. 'A gunshot?'

'Stay still,' said Penny. 'We mustn't move.'

Emma felt every muscle in her body trembling. She wanted to run but didn't feel able to. What was safer? Remaining still or moving? She screwed her eyes shut for a moment and took in a breath. The danger would pass. Perhaps it had already?

Opening her eyes again, her breath was shaky and shallow as she glanced around her. Penny and Clara hadn't moved. Their faces were pale and their eyes wide.

'I think the shot came from in there,' whispered Clara, pointing to the graveyard. 'Maybe from a window—'

The top of the nearest tombstone shattered, sending shards of stone scattering against the bars of the gate. Emma felt a cry leave her throat but it was lost in the deafening echo of a second gunshot.

Clara scrambled away from the gate on her hands and knees. Penny remained huddled where she was, her head buried in her arms.

A sickening dread lurched in Emma's stomach. Had Penny been hit?

She lunged over to her, her movements feeling clumsy and careless.

'Penny!'

Luckily her friend lifted her head. But she had never seen her looking so stricken before.

'We should go,' said Emma, glancing in the direction in which Clara had just vanished.

'But what if they...'

'Clara's got away. We should too.'

Penny nodded and the pair of them crawled on the damp, gritty ground. Sharp little stones pushed through Emma's gloves and skirts. She felt giddy now. The ground seemed to lurch a little as an odd sensation of floating came over her. Was this really happening?

Then she heard footsteps behind.

'Hurry!' said Penny leaping up. A moment later, she was hauling Emma to her feet. She gripped on to her friend's hand as they ran back through the alleyway, their feet flying across the ground.

As they rounded the corner, the gap in the hoarding came into view. They pushed through it, no longer caring about the long sharp nails which protruded from it. Emma heard a small rip as one tugged at her coat, but she ran on and out onto the uneven cobbles of the street. She joined her friends, and the three of them ran as fast as they could.

FORTY-FOUR

Emma's body trembled as the three women hurried down the street towards Euston Road. Her mouth felt dry.

Had they just cheated death?

'I think we should report this to a constable,' said Penny. 'That shot may not have been aimed at us, it could have been someone else. Someone who could be lying in the graveyard at this moment horribly injured.'

'But how would they have got in there?' Emma asked. 'The gate was locked.'

'Perhaps they had a key. Who knows?'

'If we report it then we could get into trouble for going behind the hoardings,' said Clara.

'We'll just tell the police we were looking for our missing cat,' said Penny.

Clara turned to her, puzzled. 'A cat?'

'It's an excuse I've used frequently when I've been discovered in places I shouldn't be,' said Penny. 'It's always worked.'

Clara smiled. 'Then I shall try it myself!'

'Who do you think fired the gun?' Emma asked. 'Someone who works for Sir Laurence?'

'It's possible,' said Penny. 'If it was a security guard then that suggests Sir Laurence could be very worried about people discovering what he's really up to.'

'I can't tell you how delighted I am, Laurence,' said his wife, Eugenia, at dinner that evening. 'Our first grandchild! Gregory says the baby is expected in September.'

She passed him the letter which had arrived in the afternoon post. Sir Laurence put down his knife and took it from her. As he read Gregory's words, he felt a smile on his face. 'Wonderful news,' he said. 'He married a fine young lady and now she's going to give him a child. It's just as I had hoped.'

'Me too. It's a shame they're so far away up there in Scotland.'

'Then you must go and visit them again.' He handed her back the letter and picked up his cutlery. 'The train is very comfortable these days.'

'Yes, you're right. I can catch the early morning service and be in Edinburgh before dinner time. I would love to see them both. I miss Gregory.'

'So do I.' He took a sip of wine. 'All our business has to be conducted by mail.'

'It would be so much easier if he was in London.'

'Not at the moment it wouldn't. It's much better that he's up there and out of the way. And he's doing marvellously. He'll prove himself to us yet.'

Eugenia sighed, sitting back in her chair. 'Oh, I do hope so. And to think how worried we were about him. I still do worry of course but marriage to Lydia has changed him for the better. Just as you said it would, Laurence.'

He picked up his serviette and dabbed at his lips. 'That's because I chose the right family for him to marry into. If the choice had been Gregory's then... Well, we know what happened.' He didn't wish to talk about it.

'Yes...' Eugenia gave her glass of wine a wistful gaze. 'You do wonder how it's all turned out, don't you?'

He frowned. 'Turned out for who?'

'Well... the girl.'

His stomach clenched with anger. He scrunched up his serviette and placed it on the table. 'As far as I'm concerned, she doesn't exist. Forget about it, Eugenia. It's a waste of our breath even discussing it.'

'But—'

'I said forget about it!' His jaw felt tight as he snapped at her. The maid who was waiting to clear their plates startled.

Eugenia pushed her lips together and stared ahead of her at the wall. 'Very well.'

The mood in the room had changed. He knew his wife would be silent for the next few hours or so. Why had she felt the need to ruin what had been a perfectly good dinner?

He got to his feet and addressed the maid. 'I shan't be wanting dessert. If anyone needs me, I'll be in my study.'

As he marched across the hallway, he caught sight of a visitor who'd just arrived. A slight, sharp-faced man with a thin black moustache. 'Pugh?' he said. 'What are you doing here?'

Mr Pugh had just handed his hat and coat to the footman. He gave a little bow. 'I'm sorry to call on you unannounced at this hour, sir. But I've made some progress.'

Sir Laurence felt some weight lift from his shoulders. 'Is that so? Come and join me then.'

He continued on his way to his study, listening to Pugh's footsteps hurrying behind him. Once inside the room, he stepped over to his whisky decanter and poured out two drinks.

'Well then, Pugh. What's happened?'

'I decided to use a different tactic.' He ran a thumb and forefinger over his moustache. 'I employed a chap who knows how to make people talk.'

Sir Laurence couldn't resist a smile. 'That sounds like my sort of chap.'

'Yes... It's not how I usually do things. But I came to realise that merely asking polite questions doesn't necessarily get one anywhere.'

'Absolutely. I can't say I've ever resorted to politeness myself. There's no need for it. I've always considered it a trait of the lower classes.'

Pugh gave a grin. 'Absolutely. Anyway, this chap found a friend of Archie Mitchell's and... under duress I should say... the fellow confessed he and Mitchell had discussed hiding places for something valuable. He didn't know what valuable item Mitchell was talking about but they discussed a hiding place in a public house. He wasn't sure if Mitchell went ahead with his plan in the end but Mitchell swore him to secrecy. That's why he hasn't spoken of it until now.'

'In a public house? Where?'

'The Tiger Tavern on Tower Hill.'

'No! Where in the public house?'

'Oh.' Pugh gave a polite laugh. 'Hidden behind a loose panel apparently.'

'And did this fellow see what Mitchell hid there?'

'No. But I'd wager it was the locket.'

Sir Laurence drained his glass. 'Right. We'll go there now.'

'Absolutely.' Pugh finished his drink too.

'Do you know where the loose panel is in the tavern?'

'Yes, it's all been described to me.'

'Excellent. We'll leave now.'

Buoyed by the whisky and the news, Sir Laurence left his study with a spring in his step.

He hadn't felt this happy for months.

FORTY-SIX

'You could have been killed!' James's eyes were wide, his jaw slack with disbelief. 'Why did you even go there?'

Penny knew he was frightened for her. She had expected this reaction when she told him that someone had fired shots at them. But his implication that she had been reckless to visit the disused graveyard made her bristle.

'We weren't expecting to be shot at,' she said, keeping her voice steady. 'No one could have predicted that.'

He ran a hand across his brow, exhaling sharply. 'No, I suppose not. I'm sorry, I'm not blaming you for what happened. But it's horrifying to think that my wife, the mother of my two children, could have lost her life this afternoon!'

'Well, that's something Sir Laurence Mulholland will have to answer for,' said Penny. 'I feel sure he's behind it.'

'If he is, then I'll have a word with him myself. Did you see who fired the shots?'

Penny shook her head. 'No. They may not even have been aiming at us, there could have been another person in the graveyard. I don't want to assume they were trying to kill us. That would be...' She hesitated. 'A terrible thing to believe. That someone would stoop to shooting three harmless women.'

'It sounds very much as if someone was firing at you,' said James. 'Please promise me, Penny, that you won't ever go back there.'

'I won't. I shall stay well away.'

'So who did you report it to?'

'We found a constable on Euston Road. He took down everything we told him and said E Division would send men to investigate. With any luck, they've already arrested someone.'

'I'll find out,' said James. 'I'll speak to one of the inspectors at E Division myself. This is absolutely terrifying.'

'We weren't supposed to be there,' Penny admitted. 'We were trespassing. But even so, whoever it was shouldn't be discharging a gun in that area. Children could wander into that graveyard out of curiosity. The thought of one of them being harmed...' She broke off, her voice faltering.

James nodded gravely. 'It troubles me too. I know how determined you are to uncover the truth, Penny. But you're a mother now, and...' He rubbed his brow again. 'Sometimes I find it hard to reconcile the woman who chases after murderers with the woman who is a mother to our two children. I don't want one role to destroy the other.'

Penny felt a lump rise in her throat. Until that moment she hadn't allowed herself to think about what might have happened. The thought was unbearable. The noise of the gunshots still echoed faintly in her mind, and the realisation that her children could have lost their mother pressed on her chest like a weight.

They fell into silence. Penny could feel her hands trembling. 'I think I'll just look in on the children,' she said. 'I know they're asleep but I just want to see them.'

The house was quiet as she climbed the stairs. In the nursery, the glow of the fire had dwindled to embers, casting a soft orange light across the room. Thomas was curled up in his little bed, one arm flung across his blanket. Florence slept soundly in her cot, her curls spread across the pillow.

Penny stood for a long moment watching them. Their faces

were peaceful and untroubled. She reached down and brushed a strand of hair from Florence's forehead, her fingers lingering there.

A shiver ran through her as she thought of how close she had come to never seeing this scene again.

Downstairs, she could hear the faint creak of James moving about. Pacing, perhaps. Still uneasy. He had always worried and she couldn't blame him.

She sank into the rocking chair by the fire, the old wood creaking beneath her. For a moment, she let the rhythm of it calm her.

How could she give up the work that defined her? The pursuit of truth, of justice, had always felt necessary. Yet tonight, with the echo of the gunshots in her mind, she worried that her determination might cost her everything.

FORTY-SEVEN

Sarah Lyford knew someone unexpected had walked into the tavern when she heard a hush fall and faces turn towards the doorway. Moments later, a tall, distinguished gentleman approached the bar. He wore a long dark overcoat and carried a top hat in his hand. His dark hair was neatly parted and greying at the temples. A gold pin secured his silk cravat and a gold watch chain hung on his waistcoat. He had handsome features but his prominent brow shadowed his dark eyes and gave him a slightly intimidating appearance.

Sarah chose not to feel intimidated. If she could handle Johnny Cooper, she could handle anyone. She continued to pull the handle of the pump as she filled a tankard with beer.

'Can I help you, sir?' She kept her tone nonchalant. The men at the bar were quiet as they listened to what the visitor had to say.

'I believe Archie Mitchell frequented this establishment,' said the gentleman. 'I'd like to know where he sat.'

Sarah's heart sank at the sound of Archie's name. He was dead and gone. Why did people keep talking about him?

'Over there,' she said, pointing to the corner of the room. She couldn't see the table from where she stood, there were too many customers in the way.

'Perhaps you could show me?' asked the visitor.

'Very well, sir. I'll just finish this order.'

She glanced around, hoping the landlord would appear and deal with the upper-class gentleman. Frustratingly, there was no sign of him.

Once she'd served the drinks, she wiped her hands on her apron, stepped out from behind the bar and made her way across the room to the table Archie Mitchell had sat at.

The labourers sitting there now quietly got to their feet, their usual boisterous conversation had stopped.

The posh gentleman turned and nodded at someone and Sarah realised now that he was accompanied by a slight man with a thin black moustache. He walked over to the seat and began examining the wood panelling beneath it.

Sarah suddenly recalled a memory she had forgotten about. The two lady detectives – Mrs Langley and Mrs Blakely – had sat in this very spot four or five days previously. And she had seen one of them stoop down... just as the man with the black moustache was doing now.

'Anything there, Pugh?' asked the visitor. There was a note of impatience in his voice.

'I've found a loose panel,' came a reply. 'But I can't see anything else.'

The upper-class gentleman turned to the labourers. 'Did any of you chaps see Archie Mitchell hide anything here?'

They all shook their heads and stepped away a little, keen not to be involved.

The gentleman gave his companion a sharp tap on the shoulder. 'Out of the way, Pugh.' As his companion stood up, the gentleman handed him his top hat. 'Here. Hold this.'

In a swift, sharp movement, the gentleman moved the table out of the way. The tankards on it wobbled and spilled some of their beer.

Then he took a step back before launching one of his long legs at the panelling beneath Archie Mitchell's seat. The heel of his well-polished shoe splintered the wood.

Sarah let out a gasp at the sudden aggression. 'Wait!' she said. 'You can't do that!'

But the visitor ignored her, launching another kick at the panels. Fragments flew out and scattered across the floor. One of the labourers gave a nervous laugh. Others moved away.

A third kick demolished most of the panelling beneath the seat, creating a large hole. Sarah felt herself trembling. Who was this man? Why was no one standing up to him?

He snatched his top hat back from his companion. 'Now have another look, Pugh.'

The man did as he was told, crouching down onto the floor and putting his hand into the gaping hole which had been made.

He got to his feet. 'Nothing, sir.'

'Nothing? Are you sure about that?'

'Quite sure, sir.'

The visitor pursed his lips. His face was pale now and Sarah noticed his gloved hand ball into a fist.

She knew the signs of anger.

Moving away, she headed for the bar and the door behind it. She'd tried to stop him kicking the seat but no one else had. A room full of men and not a single one had done anything about the visitor's wanton vandalism. It was remarkable how a man of his position could get away with such reckless behaviour; he looked like a gentleman but didn't behave like one. If he'd been a labourer or sailor, there would have been no shortage of men ready to stop him.

The visitors left shortly after that. The atmosphere was muted for a while as everyone speculated about who he had been. Before long, everything began to return to normal.

And somehow Sarah was going to have to explain to the landlord what had happened.

The visitors had been looking for something which Archie Mitchell had hidden in the panelling beneath the seat. It clearly wasn't there anymore. But whatever it was, Sarah had a good idea who now had it.

FORTY-EIGHT

'Mrs Langley,' said Harry Wright the following morning. He got to his feet and straightened his jacket. 'This is a pleasant surprise. What can I er... do for you?'

Emma couldn't resist smiling at his awkwardness. In truth, she felt awkward too. She'd knocked at the door of the *Morning Express* newsroom expecting Harry's colleagues to be there too. But instead it was just the pair of them.

'I have a story for you,' she said. 'If you're interested.'

'Interested? I'm extremely interested!'

'But I haven't told you what the story is yet.'

'Oh right.' His face flushed. 'Of course... Well, I'm sure you're only here because it's a good story, one which you clearly already know I would want to look into.'

'Yes,' said Emma. 'That's right.'

She could feel a little perspiration on her forehead, partly from embarrassment and partly from the excitement of being alone in a room with Harry Wright. It didn't feel appropriate for the pair of them to be together like this, but she reminded herself they were in an office – a professional place. She felt sure a chaperone would only be required in a social situation.

She sat in Frederick Potter's chair. 'Have you heard of Sir Laurence Mulholland?' she asked.

He thought for a moment. 'Mulholland and Son? The construction company?'

'Yes. That's the one.' She then explained to Harry what she'd learned about Sir Laurence's business activities and the possibility he'd bribed Oscar Garland. He perched on his desk and listened intently, making notes as she spoke.

'And then someone fired shots yesterday while we were at the site in St Pancras,' she added.

Harry's mouth dropped open. 'Someone shot at you?'

'Well, we can't be sure they fired directly at us. Perhaps it was just a warning shot. Or perhaps they were aiming at someone else.'

'That's terrifying! Did you see who it was?'

Emma shook her head. 'We think it could have been someone who's been paid to guard the empty buildings.'

Harry made some more notes then asked, 'Did you report it?'

'Yes. We found a constable close by and told him what we'd heard. We had to tell him a small lie. We said we went behind the hoardings because we'd heard a cat mewing there and we thought it was trapped and needed rescuing.'

Harry smiled. 'That's a good excuse.'

'But we had to report the gunshot because we were worried someone may have been injured. The constable called on some colleagues and they searched the buildings and the old burial ground. They found no sign of anyone.'

Harry frowned. 'Not even the chap who fired the shot?'

'No. Nothing.'

'That's odd. You'd have thought that a guard would have stayed on the site and explained to the police why he fired his gun.'

'Yes. It strikes me as very strange. The fact no one was there at all suggests they ran away.'

'And they ran away because they've got something to hide,' said Harry. 'Thank you for this, Mrs Langley. I'm going to start looking into

Sir Laurence Mulholland right away. Buildings which are mysteriously condemned, old graveyards at risk, rumours of bribery... There's certainly a lot to look into here.' He closed his notebook and fixed her gaze. 'Thank you,' he said. 'This is the sort of story every journalist would like to investigate. I'm grateful to you for considering me.'

'Well...' Emma felt her face flush. 'You're the only news reporter I know. But I also know you're a very good reporter and that you'll do a good job.'

He gave a bashful smile. 'Well, I'll try.'

A pause followed as Emma struggled to know what to say next. Harry seemed to feel the same. He glanced over to the window and ran a hand over his chin as if preparing some words.

Emma took in a breath and tried to relax her shoulders. She could feel a tension between them, charged by unspoken feelings.

Finally, Harry spoke. 'I wonder if...'

The door flung open and stocky, curly-haired Frederick Potter strode in. 'Good morning!' he trilled. 'And good morning to you, Mrs Langley!'

They both greeted him as he hung his bowler hat on the hatstand. Emma got to her feet, knowing this was her signal to leave.

The disappointment on Harry's face was evident. She felt the same.

'Good luck with the story, Harry,' she said. 'I'm looking forward to hearing how you get on.'

'Absolutely!' He was on his feet now, too. 'I shall keep you posted, Mrs Langley.'

FORTY-NINE

'You've impressed me, Mrs Blakely,' said Inspector Simpson that evening.

'Have I?' said Penny. She and James sat with the inspector in their sitting room. The officer sipped his tea; the cup and saucer looked small and dainty in his large, chubby hands.

'Absolutely. Discovering that Seamus Byrne provided us with a false alibi for the evening of Archie Mitchell's death was the breakthrough the Yard needed.'

'Have you spoken to Mr Byrne?' Penny asked.

'Absolutely. And I wish you'd been there to see the look on the fellow's face when I told him he no longer had an alibi!' He and James both laughed.

'I can imagine he was rather disappointed,' said Penny. 'Has he told you what he was doing that evening?'

'Well yes, a chap like that knows how to tell a good tale, doesn't he? He related a cock and bull story about exploring the riverside wharves.'

'To break in and steal something?' asked Penny.

'His confession didn't admit it but I think we all know why a chap of his class would be doing such a thing. He says he was on his own and therefore has no alibi for that evening.'

'Which is why he asked Miss Clark to lie for him,' said Penny. 'He knew he'd be considered a suspect in Archie Mitchell's murder and he couldn't properly account for his whereabouts that evening.'

'Yes, I had a firm word with Miss Clark about lying to the police, she won't be doing that again.'

'Not too firm, I hope? She realised the error of her ways.'

'It was as firm as it needed to be. There was no chance of the young lady appealing to my sympathies as she did to yours.'

Penny hoped Rosie Clark didn't regret speaking frankly to her and Emma. 'So what do you think Seamus Byrne was really doing on the night of Archie Mitchell's murder?' she asked. 'Do you believe his story about exploring the wharves?'

'There could be some truth in it. Perhaps he was trying to break into a warehouse earlier that evening. But I think it's quite likely he murdered Archie Mitchell and – for that reason – he's being kept in custody for the time being.'

Although Penny could understand why Seamus Byrne was a suspect in Archie's murder, there was little doubt he was one of many. 'Do you have any other evidence?' she asked.

She noticed the inspector's brow lower a little when she asked this, as if he resented the question. 'Archie Mitchell seriously injured him and prevented him from working,' he said gruffly. 'If that's not a strong motive, then I don't know what is.'

'I agree it's a strong motive,' said Penny. 'But there are other people to consider too. Johnny Cooper, for example. It's possible Archie Mitchell witnessed him push Harriet Barnes off London Bridge—'

'The inquest ruled it as an accident,' interrupted the inspector.

Penny gritted her teeth and exchanged an exasperated glance with James. 'And there's Sarah Lyford,' she said. 'Until recently, she was your main suspect.'

'She had the opportunity but the motive is elusive,' he responded. 'I had hoped you would be able to help us uncover that, Mrs Blakely.'

She chose to ignore the pointed remark. 'And Sir Laurence Mulholland,' she said. 'I don't think we can consider him a suspect yet, but we found his calling card in Archie Mitchell's room.'

'And I told you at the time that it had to be a red herring, Mrs Blakely. Have you established a connection yet between Sir Laurence and Archie Mitchell?'

'No,' Penny admitted.

'Well, there you go. I think you can put that gentleman out of your mind.' He took another sip of tea.

'I think Sir Laurence fired some shots at me and my friends yesterday,' said Penny.

The inspector spluttered some tea back into his cup. Muttering an apology, he pulled his handkerchief from his pocket and dabbed at his mouth.

'I'm sorry, Mrs Blakely. But did you just say Sir Laurence fired a gun at you?'

'Yes. Well, I suspect it was one of the men who works for him. Someone guarding the site at St Pancras where Sir Laurence is planning his next building project.' She explained what had happened while Inspector Simpson finished his tea.

'Goodness,' he said, putting his cup and saucer down. 'What a terrifying thing to have happened. The three of you could have been seriously injured—'

'Or worse,' added James.

'Indeed. Or worse. Who's looking into this?'

'E Division,' said James. 'I spoke to Inspector Campbell there and they haven't been able to find who fired the shot.'

'I think they need to speak to Sir Laurence,' said Penny. 'He'll know who it was.'

Inspector Simpson scratched his head. 'Perhaps he will,' he said. 'I'm sorry to hear you experienced something so frightening, Mrs Blakely. Hopefully E Division will find out exactly what happened. In the meantime, there is nothing to connect Sir Laurence and Archie Mitchell. These are two separate inquiries from what I can see.'

Penny wasn't sure she agreed. She forced a smile to relieve the tension in her jaw.

James turned to the inspector. 'You mentioned when you arrived here this evening, Simpson, that you have a favour to ask.'

'Oh yes. That.' He gave Penny a sidelong glance, suggesting his feelings weren't as warm towards her as they'd been a few minutes previously. 'Yes... I was wondering if you and your colleague, Mrs Langley, would like to speak with Seamus Byrne? You clearly have a talent for getting information out of people.'

'Yes,' said Penny, smiling genuinely now. 'I can't promise we'll succeed. But if there's a chance we might help uncover the truth, we'll certainly try.'

FIFTY

Jane Fielding was delighted to find fresh asparagus at the market the following morning. She added it to her shopping basket along with potatoes, rhubarb and watercress. After a visit to the butcher's, she made her way home.

Turning into Shand Street, she saw two men running away towards the long tunnel beneath the railway lines at the end of the street. Although it struck her as unusual, she thought little of it as she approached her house.

When she noticed her door standing open, she felt her heart drop to her feet. Her breath quickened as she glanced around her.

The street was quiet and the men had gone.

Cautiously, she approached her door. 'Who's in there?' she called out. 'Come and show yourself!'

She was met with silence.

Whoever had left the door open had presumably gone.

Her pulse sounded in her ears as she slowly stepped into her home. The doors leading from the hallway had been left open. Door frames had been left broken and splintered where the doors had been locked.

The money.

She gave a cry and dropped her shopping basket as she ran through to the parlour.

It was as she'd feared.

Cupboards and drawers had been pulled out and emptied. The rug had been pulled aside and the loose floorboard prised open. It had been ripped up with such force that it was bent.

And the money which had been hidden beneath the floorboard had gone.

All twelve bags.

Jane sank to her knees with a wail and wept.

FIFTY-ONE

Emma recognised Seamus Byrne as soon as they stepped into the interview room at Leman Street police station.

He was the sharp-eyed, scruffy-haired wiry man she'd seen sitting alone at the table in The Tiger Tavern. If they'd known who he was, they could have spoken to him sooner. However, she felt more comfortable speaking to him in the relative safety of the police station.

'Not these two,' he said, sitting back in his chair. He had a thick Irish accent and his tone was contemptuous. 'I've seen these two in the Tiger asking questions.'

'Is that so?' said Inspector Simpson.

'Yes,' said Emma. 'And I recall seeing you there, Mr Byrne.'

He grinned, revealing wide gaps between his teeth. 'So you're the sort who never forgets a pretty face?'

'That's enough,' snapped Inspector Simpson. 'You behave yourself with these ladies or I'll box your ears.'

Seamus folded his arms.

The inspector gave Emma and Penny a weary glance. 'I'll let you speak with him. Perhaps you'll get further than I have.' He turned to the constable by the door. 'Constable Greaves, stay put and make sure Byrne behaves himself, won't you?'

With a nod, he left them.

Emma and Penny took their seats opposite Seamus. He stared at them like a man forced to suffer a dull sermon.

'I didn't kill Archie Mitchell,' he said flatly. 'There. I've said my bit.'

'Then who do you think did?' Penny asked.

He gave a dismissive snort. 'It was probably the barmaid at The Tiger Tavern. Sarah. She's the one who found him, so I say she did it.'

'And why would she do that?' Emma asked.

He shrugged, eyes shifting. 'How should I know? She must have had her reasons. But she's the most obvious one, isn't she? And if it wasn't her, then I've no idea.'

'How well did you know Archie Mitchell?' asked Penny.

He rolled his eyes. 'I worked with him. On the bridge with about half a dozen other men.'

'Were you friends?'

He shook his head. 'He wasn't exactly the lively sort. Too quiet for me. Too boring.'

'So he was just a colleague?'

'If you want to call it that, yes.'

'We heard you blamed him for an accident,' said Penny. 'An accident which injured your hand.'

He stared at her for a moment, then slowly uncrossed his arms. He extended his right hand across the table. Emma winced as she saw the palm thick with pink scar tissue, the skin twisted and taut. His fingers curled inwards, resistant and stiff.

'He messed up my hand, all right. I can't work at the moment and I'm not sure I ever will again.'

An uncomfortable pause settled in the room.

'How did it happen?' Penny asked.

'A red-hot rivet. He'd just pulled it out of the furnace and he dropped it. I was reaching behind me for my hammer at the time and I accidentally picked up the rivet.'

'Ouch,' said Penny. 'That must have been painful.'

'I can't tell you,' said Seamus. 'I passed out. I've not worked a day since. When Archie was shot, everyone seemed to think I was the one who did it. But I'll ask you what I've asked the coppers many times. Could I possibly pull the trigger of a gun with this hand?' He held up his scarred palm for them to see.

'Maybe you used your other hand,' said Penny.

'My left hand?' He smiled. 'I can tell you now I've got more chance of firing accurately with my injured hand than my left hand. Or maybe I did shoot him with my left hand which is why he was shot in the leg rather than the chest.' He gave a bitter laugh. 'To be quite honest with you, I find this idea I murdered him complete nonsense. I was angry with him. Angrier than I can tell you. But I'm no murderer.'

'So why did you ask Rosie Clark to lie for you?' Penny asked.

'Because it was obvious everyone was going to suspect me. I know I wasn't there that night he was shot so I wanted to make that clear for everybody. By getting Rosie to say I was with her just made it easier for everyone. How is she by the way? Were the police angry with her because she lied?'

'She's all right,' said Penny. 'And Detective Inspector Simpson understands why she lied about the alibi. She wanted to protect you.'

He nodded. 'I feel bad for making her lie now, it wasn't fair on her. I just didn't want the police to waste their time with me because I know I'm innocent of murder.' He sighed. 'I thought they would get on with finding the real killer. But it turns out they're no good at that and they've got you two ladies doing it instead.' He gave an amused smile.

'You told us you think Sarah Lyford, the barmaid at The Tiger Tavern, murdered Archie Mitchell,' said Emma. 'If she had done it, she'd have needed the revolver with her. Are you suggesting she kept it hidden behind the bar?'

He shrugged. 'I've heard of worse. Maybe Johnny Cooper put her up to it.'

Penny raised an eyebrow. 'Johnny Cooper? What do you know about him?'

Seamus scratched the side of his nose. 'Same as anyone. He's trouble. The kind of man you don't cross unless you want to end up with broken ribs. People say things about him... dark things.'

'Did Archie Mitchell ever mention Johnny Cooper to you?' Emma asked.

Seamus shook his head. 'No. But I know he was on the bridge when Johnny's girl fell in the river. Archie wasn't the same after that. Kept to himself more.'

'Do you know what he saw that night?'

'No. We weren't friends.'

'But you noticed he changed afterwards?'

'Yes, I think so.'

'Do you think Johnny Cooper's capable of murder?'

Seamus rubbed his face. 'I'm not going to say anything more about Johnny. I know what he's like and I'm not getting into trouble with him.'

'So you're saying you didn't kill Archie Mitchell,' said Penny. 'What were you doing that night?'

He leaned forward, his voice dropping a little. 'I wasn't doing anything wrong, just... things that don't look good. And I don't fancy being locked up for something else just because I told the truth.'

'Are you admitting to something criminal?' asked Emma.

He leaned back again with a slight smile of mischief. 'It depends on what you call criminal. I was just... taking a look at some of the warehouses along the river.'

'With the intention of stealing something?'

He spread his hands, mock-innocent. 'Do I look like a thief to you?'

They didn't answer.

Seamus grinned and folded his arms again. 'Anyway, I've said enough.'

'Detective Inspector Simpson will be back shortly,' said Penny.

'And if you won't tell us exactly what you did on the night of Archie's murder, he'll continue to assume you were involved in it. It's in your best interest to admit you were up to no good. Otherwise, it looks like you've got something much worse to hide.'

He shook his head again. 'That's all you're getting out of me.'

'Very well,' said Penny. 'One more question and you only need answer yes or no. Does that sound simple enough?'

'All right.'

'Have you ever heard of Sir Laurence Mulholland?'

He gave a groan and rubbed his hand over his face. 'That family...'

'So you have?'

'Yes, but I've never met him. Rosie used to work in his household. Until... Well, you know what happened. That's a secret she kept from me and I wasn't too happy when I found out about it either.'

'How did you find out?'

'I called on her one day and saw the baby. I asked her if he was her son and she admitted it. She couldn't bring herself to deny it, I know how much she adores him.'

'Do you know if Archie knew Sir Laurence?'

'Archie? Why would he know him?'

'So he didn't?'

'No. I can't see why Archie would have anything to do with him. Rosie on the other hand... Well, I suppose you could call Sir Laurence the grandfather.'

'Grandfather of who?' Emma asked.

'Her baby, of course.' He gave a bemused smile. 'She didn't tell you then?'

'Tell us what?'

'Who the baby's father is. It's Gregory Mulholland. Sir Laurence's son. They had a love affair when she was working as a maid. Quite a scandal, wouldn't you say?'

'Yes,' said Penny. 'That is quite scandalous. She told us the baby's father was dead.'

Seamus gave a hollow laugh. 'That sounds like Rosie! Too ashamed to tell anyone the truth. Especially as young Gregory got sent up to Scotland to marry the daughter of a lord or someone or other. Poor Rosie...' He looked down at the table now and when he spoke, Penny could hear the emotion in his voice. 'I think she really loved him. If only she'd cared for me the way she cared for him... perhaps things would have been different. Baby or no baby.'

'What did you make of Seamus?' Penny asked Emma once they'd left Leman Street police station. It was a grey day and the wind whisked along the road tugging at clothing and awnings. The opposite side of the street was dominated by the grand red-brick offices of the Co-operative Wholesale Society.

'He seemed to speak honestly enough,' Emma replied as they headed northwards. 'But you can never be too sure, can you? Archie Mitchell appears to have caused an accident which left Seamus too injured to work and he must be extremely resentful about that. I don't know what the future holds for him and I doubt he knows either.'

'People murder out of anger,' said Penny. 'But in Seamus's case, what would murdering Archie Mitchell achieve? He's unable to work whether Archie was dead or not.'

'I suppose it feels like revenge,' said Emma. 'And revenge can make some people feel a bit better.'

'I suppose so.' Penny sighed. 'I don't think our conversation with Seamus has helped us that much. It's neither convinced me he's the murderer nor persuaded me he isn't. I don't think Detective Inspector Simpson is going to be very impressed when we call back. However...' She stopped and pulled her notebook out of her bag. 'I think Johnny Cooper remains a very strong suspect and I had an idea the other day about finding out what happened exactly on the night of Harriet Barnes's death.'

'Is Johnny Cooper still in custody?' Penny asked James when he returned home that evening.

'Yes, I think so.' He kissed her and baby Florence who she was holding in her arms. 'Why do you ask?' He stepped over to Thomas and ruffled the young boy's hair.

'I think he needs to be questioned again about Harriet Barnes's death.'

Penny told her husband about the conversation she and Emma had had with Constable Dickinson. 'Johnny Cooper had the opportunity to influence Archie's statement about what happened on the bridge that night. I struggle to believe Archie only heard what happened and didn't see anything.'

James made himself comfortable in his armchair. 'So you think Archie Mitchell saw Cooper push Miss Barnes off the bridge. But Cooper then threatened him and made him change his story so it appeared to have been an accident.'

'Yes,' said Penny. 'It's what I've thought for a while. Johnny Cooper needs to be asked about it.'

James wiped a hand across his brow. 'But it's just as possible that Archie Mitchell told the truth,' he said. 'Cooper may not have influenced his statement at all.'

'So why did Archie Mitchell's mood change shortly before his death?' Penny asked. 'I think he was being threatened. And why did Johnny Cooper turn up here making vague threats? He pretended he was protecting Sarah Lyford but I think he was actually trying to protect himself.'

James sighed. 'I can see it's a possibility, Penny. I really do. But it's just a theory. And asking for Cooper to be interviewed about it when an inquest has already established what happened on the bridge that night—'

'Possibly based on an inaccurate witness statement.'

'Possibly yes... and also possibly no. But we don't actually know either way.' Thomas clambered up onto James's lap and showed him a toy soldier.

'Just question Cooper and see what he says,' said Penny.

'That's not quite as easy as it sounds. The accident happened within the jurisdiction of the City of London police. They're the force who investigated Harriet Barnes's accident and they'll need to be the ones who interview Johnny Cooper again.'

'Do you think they'd agree to it?'

'Probably not, Penny. There's no evidence Cooper or Mitchell lied.'

Penny sighed. 'But all the signs are there! How do we find evidence?'

'I don't think you can. Not in this instance. Too much time has passed. The inquest has been held, ruled Miss Barnes's death as an accident and Archie Mitchell is no longer around to tell anyone whether he lied or not.'

Penny gritted her teeth. 'So Cooper could get away with murdering both Harriet and Archie!'

'Perhaps it's impossible to determine the truth about Harriet Barnes's death now. But for Archie Mitchell, who knows? There's more evidence to be found.'

Penny nodded. 'The murder weapon for example; what happened to that?'

'Exactly,' said James. 'There's a lot of work to do yet, Penny. But I know one thing, you and Emma are quite capable of solving this.'

FIFTY-THREE

Harry Wright made his way up Chalton Street to where the buildings were surrounded by large wooden hoardings. It was a dispiriting place. The shops had dusty window displays and faded signs. A cartwheel lay broken by the kerb and a scrawny dog was eating something which had been discarded on the pavement.

Children played nearby. One of them chased a hoop which struck the hoardings with a hollow thud before rolling away.

Everything about the place felt worn and weary. A half-forgotten street which Sir Laurence Mulholland was scavenging for profit.

Thankfully, Emma Langley and her friends had noticed what Sir Laurence was doing. Harry smiled as he recalled Emma calling on him the previous day to tell him about Sir Laurence's suspicious activities.

You're a very good reporter. That's what she had said. And she'd told him he would do a good job with the story.

He could feel himself growing bashful again as he recalled her flattering words. Did they mean she liked him as a person too? Or did they only refer to the fact she thought he was a good reporter? Harry couldn't decide. He was sure Emma felt as he did. But was she as fond of him as he was of her? He had no way of telling. All he could do was hope that she was.

He paused by the wooden hoardings and looked around him. He needed someone to talk to about Sir Laurence's plans for the buildings which were shortly going to be demolished.

Further up the street, he noticed a grocer's shop sign. He made his way towards it, hoping he could find someone useful to talk to.

The grocer's shop was a cramped, untidy little place where every inch of space was filled. Firewood was stacked in piles on the floor before the counter. Behind the counter, shelves bowed under the weight of jars whose labels had long since peeled away. Faded advertisements for Bride's Custard and Bovril hung on the wall.

'Just three weeks ago there were people living there,' said the grocer when Harry asked her about the empty buildings. She was a short lady with thick forearms and a frizz of grey hair. 'Families,' she continued. 'Lots of children. A man came along one day and condemned the lot of it.'

'Do you know who he was?'

'No. Couldn't tell you. He must've been from the vestry or the works. Something like that. He just came in and condemned it all and everyone had to move out. The shops too. Their businesses just gone. Just like that. I'm lucky I'm still here but it's probably only a matter of time. They'll be coming for me next.' She glanced over at the window as if looking out for them.

'What condition were the shops and homes in?' Harry asked.

'They weren't perfect, but they weren't beyond saving. They just needed a landlord who was willing to look after them properly.' She paused and looked at his notebook. 'Are you going to put all this in your newspaper?'

'Yes.'

'Good. It needs to go in the newspaper. People need to know what's happened.'

'So where did everyone go?' Harry asked.

'They went where they could. Most people tried to stay around here but there are only so many rooms, aren't there? Some have gone north, some have gone east. And some have been living on the street. Old Mr Lodge was one of them. He said he didn't want to take a room which a family could have so he slept in my doorway. I would've taken him in but I've got my mother living upstairs and she wouldn't have taken kindly to it. Anyway, the police moved Mr Lodge on.' She shook her head in dismay. 'He had nice rooms over the road. Only small but he had what he needed. Now he's in the workhouse for the rest of his days I should think.'

'Do you know of anyone I can speak to who lost their home when the buildings were condemned?'

She folded her arms. 'Lots of people. You could try number sixty-four, above the boot repairer. Lily Jones lives there with her children. She's got a lot to say about it all.'

'Thank you.'

'Here, have some biscuits.' She picked up a tin from a pile stacked on the counter.

'Erm... I don't need any right now...'

'Free of charge,' she said, holding the tin out to him. 'Go on. A little gift for writing about this in your newspaper.'

'Very well.' Harry smiled as she pressed them into his hands. 'That's very kind of you.'

Lily Jones was a young, gaunt-faced lady with an incessant cough. Harry felt worried for her, especially when she told him she had five children.

He spoke to her in a cramped little room above the boot repairer's shop. Damp laundry hung in front of a small range and the wallpaper was peeling from the wall.

Two of the children sat with their mother on the family's bed. Harry guessed the others were out with the other children he'd seen playing in the street.

'This room isn't big enough for us,' said Lily. 'But it was the only place nearby.'

'What happened when you were asked to leave your home?'

'A man just turned up and told us. He hammered on the door as if he was angry with us. He said I should have read the sign he put up on the wall in the hallway. I told him I can't read. But that didn't matter to him. He told us we had to leave there and then. I tried arguing but there was nothing we could do about it. The same was happening to everyone else. So we had to pack our things and leave and here we are.'

'Do you know who the man was?'

Lily coughed for a moment, then shrugged. 'Someone to do with the landlord, I think. From what I hear a gentleman has bought the buildings and he's going to knock them all down. He wanted us out of there.'

Harry felt a tug of concern for her. She wasn't well. How was she going to look after her five children for the years to come?

He picked up the tin of biscuits and handed them to her. 'Have these,' he said.

'Are you sure?' Her eyes widened.

'Of course. I'm sure your children will appreciate them. And if you're lucky, they might even let you have one or two as well.'

She smiled again. 'Thank you.' Then she turned to the children. 'Thank the gentleman for his gift.'

Both muttered shy gratitude.

A coughing fit overcame Lily again.

'I'll do what I can to make sure people understand what's happened here,' he said. 'It's not right that you lost your home so suddenly and have to live here in one room.'

'Oh, we get by,' said Lily, recovering herself from her cough. 'There are people worse off than us.'

Harry knew she was right. And he also sensed she didn't want him feeling sorry for her. He thanked her for her time and as he made his way out, he took three shillings from his pocket and rested them on a little table by the door.

FIFTY-FOUR

'I've decided I quite like "Für Elise" now,' said Mrs Solomon as she sat at the piano that evening. 'And I'm finding that ten minutes of practice a day makes all the difference.'

'That's wonderful,' replied Emma, pleased her landlady had finally heeded her advice.

'Let me play it for you now,' said her landlady, stretching out her fingers in readiness.

Before Emma could reply, Mrs Solomon launched into a halting rendition of the first twenty bars of "Für Elise". She didn't seem to notice when she played a wrong note, instead she carried on with a confident smile on her face.

'What do you think?' she asked once she'd finished.

'It's coming on very well,' said Emma, groaning inwardly. 'Although you're occasionally playing a D instead of a C.'

'When?' Mrs Solomon scowled, a little offended.

'Here,' said Emma circling the note on the sheet of music with her pencil. 'And here... here... and here.' There were a few others too but she decided not to mention those.

Her landlady peered at the sheet of music as if there was something wrong with it. 'That's a D, is it?'

'A C,' said Emma.

'C?'

Emma took in a breath, trying to remain patient. She realised now why she preferred teaching children. They rarely questioned her when she tried to point out a mistake.

She was grateful when the doorbell interrupted them.

'Just as I'm getting the hang of it,' muttered Mrs Solomon, getting up to answer the door.

Emma hadn't expected her to return with Sarah Lyford from The Tiger Tavern.

'Goodness.' Emma got up from her chair. 'Miss Lyford. What brings you here?'

The barmaid stood awkwardly in the parlour, gripping her shawl. 'I'm sorry for calling on you unexpectedly, Mrs Langley, but there's something I think you should know.'

'I'll make some tea,' said Mrs Solomon, eyes wide with interest.

Emma gestured for Sarah to sit. 'How did you find me here?' she asked.

'I looked you up in the directory. I hope you don't mind.'

'No that's fine,' said Emma, feeling a little disconcerted. 'So what do you want to tell me?'

'A gentleman came into the tavern two nights ago,' said Sarah. 'I didn't know who he was at the time but I later found out his name. Some of the customers told me.'

'Who was he?'

'Sir Laurence Mulholland.'

'Sir Laurence?' Emma felt her eyebrows raise. 'What was he doing there?'

'He came in looking for something which Archie Mitchell had hidden in the tavern.'

The locket. Emma hadn't given it much thought recently.

'What was he looking for?' she asked, pretending she didn't know.

Sarah shrugged. 'I don't know. But he went over to the seat where Archie used to sit and then he kicked it in!'

'Kicked it?'

'Yes! With all his strength. Everyone just stood by and watched him. I tried saying something but he ignored me and no one helped me out. The landlord wasn't there at the time but he wasn't happy when he got back and saw all the damage.'

'Why did he kick the seat?' Emma asked, keeping her expression as innocent as possible.

'He thought Archie had hidden something there. Apparently there was a loose panel. Well, there were a lot of loose panels by the time he'd finished with it! And he didn't find anything.'

'How did he know Archie had hidden something there?'

Sarah shrugged. 'I don't know.'

A pause followed as Emma gave this some thought. Why was Sir Laurence so interested in the locket? Had Archie stolen it from him?

Sarah adjusted her shawl. 'I couldn't help noticing, Mrs Langley, that when you and Mrs Blakely last visited you sat where Archie used to sit.' She was looking at Emma pointedly. 'And shortly before you left, I couldn't help noticing you were bent down looking at the panels under the seat.'

Emma took in a quiet breath. Should she tell Sarah what she'd found? 'That's right,' she said calmly. 'My skirt caught on the loose panel there. A panel which was presumably loosened because Archie Mitchell had pulled it in order to hide something there.'

Sarah watched her, keeping her gaze steady. 'Did you find what he put there?'

Thoughts raced through Emma's mind. If she told Sarah she'd found a locket then word could get back to Sir Laurence. She didn't like the idea of him turning up on her doorstep demanding she return it.

'No,' she said, returning Sarah's firm gaze. 'I didn't see anything there. I didn't know Archie had hidden anything. Did you?'

'No,' said Sarah. But Emma couldn't decide if she was telling the truth or not.

Sarah got to her feet. 'Well, I thought I should tell you what happened just in case you did find something. It looks like Sir

Laurence wants it and he seems like the sort of man who won't stop at anything until he gets it.'

'I see,' said Emma, trying to ignore the heavy pound of her heart. 'Well, let's hope he finds it before he damages anything else. And if he's a decent gentleman, he'll pay for the repairs to Archie's seat.'

'I won't hold my breath,' replied Sarah as she headed for the door.

As soon as Sarah had left, Emma dashed upstairs to her room. She pulled out the drawer of her nightstand and pulled out the locket. Then she sat on her bed and cradled the locket in the palm of her hand.

How had Archie Mitchell come by it? Was it a gift or had he stolen it?

Emma reasoned that if it had been a gift, he would either have worn it or kept it safe in his lodgings. The fact he'd hidden it in a public house suggested he'd come into possession of it by other means.

Why did Sir Laurence want it so desperately?

She put her thumbnail into the locket clasp and the locket opened with a click. Inside was the photograph and the inscription.

SOMETHING TO REMEMBER ME BY. G.

Suddenly the answer struck her. How had they missed it?

Sir Laurence's son was Gregory. And Gregory was the father of Rosie Clark's son, Edward.

FIFTY-FIVE

'Rosie doesn't want anything to do with you,' said Mrs Clark, standing in the doorway of her Stepney home the following morning. 'Not after you got her into trouble with the police.'

'I'm sorry Detective Inspector Simpson had a strong word with her,' said Penny. 'I told him not to. It could have been worse; she could have been prosecuted.'

'Well, what you did was bad enough. Why couldn't you just leave it as it was? She's not the first to lie about an alibi and she won't be the last.'

'It's important the police know the truth,' said Penny. 'And because Rosie was honest in the end, Seamus Byrne remains a credible suspect.'

Mrs Clark leaned against the door post and folded her arms. 'Is that so? I can't say I was ever fond of him.'

'Please may we speak with Rosie?' pleaded Emma, impatient to find out what her reaction to the locket would be. 'We have something we believe belongs to her.'

Mrs Clark looked her up and down. 'I can pass it on.'

'I'd rather do it myself,' said Emma. 'I need to give her an explanation.'

Mrs Clark blew out a sigh. Then she turned over her shoulder and shouted. 'Rosie! These gentlewomen have got something for you! They won't give it to me. Apparently it needs an explanation!'

A few moments later, Rosie appeared behind her mother's shoulder, cradling her son. She gave Emma and Penny a long hostile glance.

'I told them what happened with you and the police,' said her mother. 'Apparently it could have been worse, they say. But it wouldn't have happened at all if they hadn't stirred all this up, would it?'

'No,' said Rosie. Then she turned to Emma and Penny. 'What have you got?'

Emma opened her bag and reached inside it for the locket.

'Tell you what,' said Mrs Clark. 'Come inside. I don't want the neighbours staring and talking.'

In the small, simply furnished room, Emma gave the locket to Rosie.

The young woman took it in her hand as she held her baby in the other arm. A long pause followed. Then Emma noticed her shoulders give a little shudder and a tear ran down her cheek.

'Oh Rosie, love,' said her mother, putting an arm around her. 'You've got it back.'

Rosie nodded and wiped away her tears with the back of her hand.

Her mother guided her to the battered armchair.

'Thank you,' she said quietly to Emma and Penny once she'd helped her daughter sit down.

Rosie opened the locket and stared for a while at the photograph and inscription. Emma felt a lump in her throat. The locket clearly still meant a lot to her.

Rosie clicked it shut and looked up. 'Where was it?' she asked, her voice breaking.

'We believe Archie Mitchell hid it,' said Penny.

'Archie Mitchell? What was he doing with it?'

'We don't know. We were hoping you might be able to tell us.'

Rosie shook her head. 'I never met him. I don't know how he got this. He hid it?'

'Yes, behind a wooden panel in The Tiger Tavern,' said Penny. 'When did you last see it?'

'It went missing from my room one day when I was working for the Mulholland family. It must have been... about a year ago now. I never thought I'd see it again.' Her voice cracked and another tear ran down her cheek.

'Someone in the house took it from your room?' Emma asked.

Rosie nodded.

'Could Archie Mitchell have stolen it?'

'I told you, I never saw him there. He didn't know anyone in the house. Perhaps someone took it and gave it to him for safekeeping. I never understood why someone took it.'

'We know the name the initial G stands for,' said Penny.

Rosie gave her a coy look, then glanced away.

'We can understand why you told us Edward's father was dead,' said Emma. 'You had to keep your love affair secret.'

Rosie nodded but said nothing.

'And you presumably had to keep the locket secret,' said Penny. 'You didn't want to risk anyone finding it.'

'No,' said Rosie. 'I didn't. I kept it hidden in my pillow. But somehow someone found it there. I was so upset when I found it had gone. Gregory was upset too...'

It was the first time she'd mentioned him by name.

Mrs Clark shook her head. 'It doesn't do to remember him. He's best forgotten about. All this causes nothing but heartache. He's in Scotland now, married to the daughter of a peer, I heard. The Mulhollands wanted to make sure they sent him far away.'

'But I still want to remember him!' said Rosie, tearful. 'And now I have this locket to show Edward when he's older. A photograph of his father.' She smiled through her tears and Emma felt an ache in her chest. A doomed love affair seemed to her to be the greatest tragedy of all. Two people forcibly separated because their love for each transcended the strict boundaries of class.

The rules of society meant baby Edward would grow up without knowing his father. Rosie was likely to remain in poverty for the rest of her life, rejected by suitors who didn't want to take on the responsibility of an illegitimate child.

It all seemed overwhelmingly unfair.

'Well, I suppose it's nice you've got the locket back, Rosie,' said her mother. 'But I don't think it's a good idea you having it here in the house.' She gave Emma and Penny a disapproving sidelong glance.

'But I want to keep it here!' Rosie protested. 'It's the most important thing I've ever owned!'

'It's been stolen once already. Someone might come here and try to take it again.'

Rosie shook her head and clasped it to her bosom. 'They won't. And besides, no one knows it's here, do they?' She looked at Emma and Penny for confirmation.

'No, they don't,' said Penny.

Mrs Clark sighed. 'Very well. But put it in a safe place and don't go dwelling on that young man again. You need all your strength for being a good mother to little Edward.'

'We need to solve the mystery of how Archie Mitchell got hold of that locket,' said Penny. 'If anything comes to mind, then you'll let us know, won't you?'

Rosie nodded. 'I will. Thank you for returning it to me. How did you know it was mine?'

Penny gave a short sigh. Emma caught her eye. They both knew the next part of their explanation might be difficult for Rosie to hear.

'We know the locket means a lot to Sir Laurence Mulholland,' said Emma. 'He's looking for it. And he's so keen to find it that he caused some damage in The Tiger Tavern recently in his attempt to retrieve it from behind the wood panelling.'

Mrs Clark gave a groan and put her head in her hands. 'Oh, the Lord save us.'

'When we heard he wanted the locket, we realised who the G on the inscription referred to,' said Penny. 'His son, Gregory.'

Rosie had paled a little. 'Does Sir Laurence know I have the locket?'

'No,' said Penny. 'And we won't tell anyone we've returned it to you.'

'He wants that locket so he can destroy it,' said Mrs Clark. 'It's evidence of his son's love affair with a humble maid and their illegitimate child. It's not obvious what the G stands for, but it contains his photograph. In the wrong hands, that locket could bring disgrace onto the Mulholland family.'

'But it's safe now,' said Rosie. 'It's where it belongs.'

'I hope it's safe now,' said her mother. 'Sir Laurence isn't the sort of man any of us want to cross.'

FIFTY-SIX

'We're going to have to call on him again, aren't we?' said Penny as she and Emma left Rosie Clark's home.

'Sir Laurence?' said Emma. 'Yes. But I wish we could find out how he and Archie knew each other. The locket and the calling card connect them. But how?'

'We could ask Jane Fielding, Archie's landlady. Perhaps Sir Laurence called at the house to see Archie?'

On Shand Street in Bermondsey, it took Mrs Fielding a while to open the door. When she did, she seemed much smaller and paler than Emma remembered.

'Oh, it's you,' she said. 'What do you want?'

'We'd like to ask you about Sir Laurence Mulholland,' said Penny.

A long pause followed. An expression of contempt flickered on Mrs Fielding's face, followed by a harder expression which thinned her lips. Resentment perhaps. Possibly anger.

'You'd better come in.' The landlady turned and they followed her to the parlour. Emma closed the door behind them. As they walked along the hallway, Emma noticed a couple of the door-frames had small pieces of timber nailed to them – rudimentary repairs perhaps. She hadn't recalled seeing them before.

In the parlour, Mrs Fielding sat down at the table and propped her chin on her hand. Her shoulders slumped and there was something resigned about her manner. Defeated, even.

Emma felt a little sorry for her. It seemed something bad had happened. 'I noticed some repairs to the doors,' she said. 'Did someone damage them?'

'No.' Her reply was so curt that it seemed suspicious.

'Really? But I don't recall seeing the repairs the last time we were here.'

Mrs Fielding's eyes grew wide and bulging. 'I don't want to talk about it!' she snapped.

Emma recoiled, surprised by the outburst. The twisted expression on the landlady's face was unsettling. 'I'm sorry for mentioning it,' said Emma, feeling the need to calm the situation.

Eventually Mrs Fielding's expression returned to normal and Penny took in a breath before asking her question. 'Do you know Sir Laurence Mulholland?'

'Oh yes.' The landlady glanced down at the lace tablecloth. 'My late husband, Stephen, used to work for him.'

'Your late husband?'

'Yes. He was his coachman.'

'How long ago was that?' asked Penny.

'He did it for many years until he died last year.'

'So you know Sir Laurence well?'

'No.' She scowled. 'Not well at all.'

'Did Archie Mitchell know him?'

Mrs Fielding lifted her chin from her hand and stared at them for a moment. 'Archie Mitchell? Why would he know Sir Laurence?'

'We think Sir Laurence could have called on him here.'

She wrinkled her nose, as if the suggestion was preposterous. 'Sir Laurence call on Archie Mitchell? He'd have had no reason to. They didn't know each other. Not to my knowledge, anyway.'

'Has Sir Laurence ever called here?' Emma asked.

'No.' She recoiled a little, shaking her head. 'Why would he? I've not seen him since my husband died.' She took out a handkerchief and dabbed her nose with it.

'Did Archie Mitchell ever mention a locket to you?' asked Penny.

'A locket?' She wiped her nose again. 'No. What locket?'

'We think Archie Mitchell might have stolen it.'

'He stole it? Well I didn't think he was the sort of chap who'd do something like that. How disappointing.'

'We can't be sure how he came by it,' said Penny. 'So you never saw it or heard about it?'

The landlady shook her head. 'No. What's this got to do with Sir Laurence?'

'We think the locket had a connection to the Mulholland family.'

'So the Mulholland family has it now?'

'The rightful owner has it now,' said Emma.

'I see. Well if Archie Mitchell stole it then that's a big shame. Do you think that's why he was murdered?'

'No, we don't think so,' said Penny. 'But we're still trying to learn more about him. And if we can understand if he and Sir Laurence knew each other, then that could help us.'

Jane Fielding gave a sad sniff. 'I don't know Sir Laurence well, but I can tell you one thing about him.'

'What's that?'

'He's a very unpleasant man. And dangerous too. He's not the sort of man you want to fall out with.'

FIFTY-SEVEN

Harry Wright stood on a quiet Kensington street lined with plane trees. He'd stopped by a large three-storey house of cream-coloured stucco. Steps rose from the pavement to a portico supported by fluted columns. Tall sash windows looked out over the street, each framed by heavy mouldings. The basement area below the railings was half-hidden in shadow where a coal chute and scullery door broke the symmetry of the grand frontage above.

Harry walked up the steps to the shiny black door and sounded the brass knocker which was shaped like a lion's head. A maid answered.

'Is Mr Oscar Garland at home?' he asked.

'No, I'm afraid he isn't. Do you have a calling card?'

Before Harry could answer, he heard a carriage behind him. He turned to see it coming to a halt. It was pulled by two shiny black horses and the coachman wore a smart uniform. The maid dashed past Harry and ran down the steps to open the carriage door.

A silver-whiskered man in a top hat and black overcoat climbed out of the carriage. He headed for the steps, tapping a gold-topped cane on the pavement as he went.

'Mr Garland?' asked Harry.

'Yes. What of it?'

'My name is Harry Wright and I'm a reporter for the *Morning Express.*'

'What do you want?'

'I believe you've retired recently from the Metropolitan Board of Works.'

Oscar Garland climbed the steps until he stood level with Harry. 'I'm neither confirming nor denying it until you tell me what you want.'

'Did you work with Sir Laurence Mulholland on his building projects?'

'That's what you want to know, is it? Well yes, I did. What does it matter to you and the *Morning Express?*'

'Can you explain why Sir Laurence's projects were always approved so quickly?'

'Quickly?' Mr Garland frowned. 'I've no idea what you mean. Now please excuse me, I have a busy day of appointments.' He stepped past Harry and into his house.

'Why does your signature appear on so many of the project documents?' Harry asked him. 'Did Sir Laurence receive special treatment from you?'

Mr Garland spun on his heel. 'Clear off! You're making a nuisance of yourself!'

'So you don't deny it then? Why did you give Sir Laurence special treatment? Did he pay for it?'

'I said clear off!'

The shove from Mr Garland sent Harry half-tumbling down the steps. He managed to right himself before completely losing his balance, but he felt a painful twist in his knee and he dropped his notebook.

The maid gasped and made a move to help Harry.

'Leave him be and get inside!' barked Mr Garland. 'Men like him are vermin!'

As Harry stooped down to pick up his notebook, the shiny black door was slammed in his face.

FIFTY-EIGHT

The cell block at Commercial Street police station had an acrid odour which hit the back of Sarah Lyford's throat.

The custody sergeant hammered on Johnny's door. 'You've got a visitor, Mr Cooper!' He unlocked the door, slid the bolts and pulled it open. 'No funny business, now.' He put one arm across the doorway as a barrier and his other hand went to his truncheon in his belt. 'You've got two minutes.'

Johnny was sitting on a bed which was bolted to the tiled floor. He met Sarah's gaze but didn't get to his feet. He looked tired and had a rough stubble on his chin. 'Oh it's you,' he muttered. 'I thought you'd come sooner.'

'I wanted to but it's been busy. I've had to work.'

Johnny shook his head as if he thought this was a poor excuse.

'How long are they keeping you here for?' she asked.

'I don't know. They won't tell me.'

'Why did they arrest you?'

'For harassing a detective inspector from Scotland Yard and his wife,' replied the sergeant.

Sarah felt her shoulders sink with disappointment. 'Johnny... You visited Mrs Blakely? Why did you do that?'

He jumped to his feet, his mouth twisted. Sarah noticed the sergeant flinch.

'To protect you, that's why I did it! And now I've been locked up for it and you're not even grateful?'

'Yes, I'm grateful, Johnny,' said Sarah, keen to appease him. 'Very grateful. Thank you. But look where it's got you. And you've been here three days now.'

'Four days,' he spat.

'Perhaps I can have a word with Mrs Blakely,' said Sarah. 'Perhaps I can get you out of here.'

He paced the small space. 'You can if you want. But she can't do anything. It's her husband who's the problem.' He stopped and put his hands on his hips. 'And I didn't harass them! It was just a little word asking them politely to leave you alone. They'll find any excuse to put me in here. It shouldn't be allowed.' He began to pace his cell again.

'Sir Laurence Mulholland came in to the Tiger looking for something Archie Mitchell hid,' Sarah said. 'Do you know what it was?'

'No.' His mouth twisted again. 'Why would I know what it was? All I'm interested in is getting out of this place. And if I hear Archie Mitchell's name once more...'

'Right then. Time's up,' said the sergeant taking a step back to close the door.

'Time's up?' said Johnny. 'That wasn't two minutes. It was barely one!'

'Goodbye for now, Mr Cooper.'

Sarah stepped away as the sergeant shut the door with a resounding slam.

FIFTY-NINE

'So the Metropolitan Public Gardens Committee—'

Sir Laurence Mulholland thumped his desk. 'I've heard quite enough about them!'

'Yes, I realise that, sir,' said Mr Marshall the estate manager. 'However—'

'However what?'

Marshall cleared his throat. 'If you could allow me to finish, sir. The Committee does have the law on its side when it comes to the old burial ground. The Disused Burial Grounds Act of 1884 states that—'

'Yes, I know what it states, Marshall. We've been over this. If demolition had started when it was supposed to have done, then the Metropolitan Garden people – or whoever they are – wouldn't have had any time to object. This burial ground... it was hidden away. No one knew it was there!'

'On the contrary, sir.' Marshall leafed through some papers in front of him. 'The committee employs a lady, Mrs Clara Clifton, to survey London's disused burial grounds.'

'What?' Sir Laurence could scarcely believe what he was hearing. 'A lady wanders about looking at them?'

'Yes, sir. And she documents what she finds in great detail.'

Sir Laurence gave a laugh.

'She actually surveyed this particular burial ground last year,' added Marshall. 'She noted that it was in a poor state of repair—'

'Which is why it's best to bury it in the foundations of a building.'

'Which has recently been outlawed, sir. And the Metropolitan Public Gardens Committee wish to transform the burial ground into a public garden—'

'Transform?' Sir Laurence gave a derisive snort. 'The only way to transform such a place is to bury it beneath concrete. And besides, who can possibly enjoy a public garden with the knowledge of all those souls interred beneath it? If we build over these places then no one is any the wiser. Now get onto this, Marshall, we need those buildings knocked down before our work is obstructed. If the garden people get any more time, people will start listening to them and we don't want that happening.'

'We think some of them tried to access the burial ground a few days ago, sir.'

Sir Laurence let out a loud sigh. 'Why doesn't that surprise me? These people have nothing better to do with their time. What happened?'

'The guard on site fired a warning shot and that solved the problem.'

'Good. Hopefully it scared the wits out of them.'

'It did, sir. Although they reported the incident to the police.'

'Even though they were trespassing at the time? They have a remarkably twisted interpretation of the law. They're not of sound mind. What did the police have to say?'

'The guard avoided them, sir.'

'As he should. We're not answerable to anyone.'

A knock sounded at the door.

'Come in!'

'But sir,' protested Marshall. 'I haven't finished yet...'

'Yes, you have. Get those buildings knocked down.'

His secretary stepped into the room. 'Mr Pugh is here, sir.'

'Excellent. Show him in.'

Marshall left, casting a bitter glance at Mr Pugh as he passed him.

Sir Laurence got to his feet and made the private investigator a drink.

'Well?' he said as he handed it to him. 'Have you found it?'

Pugh's sharp features remained dour. 'I'm afraid not, sir.'

'So nobody knows who took the locket from the tavern?'

'No.'

'And it wasn't the landlady?'

'No.'

'So who's left?'

Pugh took a sip of his drink. 'The girl.'

Sir Laurence took in a breath. 'You think she's found it?'

'I can't think of anything else, sir.'

'How did she find it?'

Pugh shrugged. 'I'm doing my best to discover that.'

Sir Laurence sank into a chair by the fireplace and rested his head against the leopard skin arranged over the back of it. 'Clearly you're not doing your best, Pugh, because you haven't found it.'

'If the girl has it... then it's not a terrible problem for you, sir.'

'That depends on who else knows.'

Pugh ran a finger over his thin dark moustache as he thought. 'There is another way of managing this.'

Sir Laurence drained his drink. 'What other way?'

'Well... if something were to happen to the girl and the child for example.'

Sir Laurence paused for a moment. He hadn't expected Pugh to come up with an idea as dark as that. 'Are you suggesting what I think you are?'

'It could resolve the problem. And then your son could return to London and assist you with the business properly.'

'Indeed. It's always been my intention he'll return one day. He's going to run the company when age or infirmity catches up with me.'

'Well, he could return sooner rather than later.'

Sir Laurence gave a slow nod. 'My wife, Eugenia, would like that.' Both men fell silent for a moment, considering a plan which was very unpleasant but could spare the Mulholland family the risk of disgrace.

'If she has the locket… then all three problems could be dealt with at once.'

'Absolutely, sir.' There was something rather shocking about the way Pugh discussed the horrific plan with such a deadpan expression. Sir Laurence found it a little thrilling. He hadn't expected to find a private investigator with such loose morals.

'Right then,' he said. 'Find out if she has it, and then we can put our plan into action.'

'And if she hasn't?'

Sir Laurence thought for a moment. 'Well, if she hasn't… it does seem like a rather appealing solution anyway.'

'Very good, sir.'

Then Sir Laurence felt a small prick of conscience. 'But don't do anything until I say, Pugh. I need to be in charge of this.'

'Absolutely, sir.'

SIXTY

A fortnight after Edgar had tasked Penny with writing her new column, Musings of a Lady Detective, she arrived at the *Morning Express* offices with her manuscript in her hand.

Edgar sat at his untidy desk and sipped a cup of coffee as he read it.

She watched his expression for signs of approval or criticism and felt encouraged that he appeared to be engrossed by it.

'Wonderful,' he said once he'd finished. 'Our readers are going to enjoy it.'

Penny gave a smile of relief. 'Thank goodness. I was worried I'd gone into too much detail.'

'Detail is what our readers like! Many of them will remember the Lizzie Dixie case and they'll be fascinated to read about the work you undertook behind the scenes, as it were. And it serves as a reminder about some of the events which have happened in recent years. That *Princess Alice* tragedy...' He shook his head as he trailed off. 'I remember I was a young reporter at the time and getting the train down to Woolwich and...' He ran a hand down his face. 'Goodness... what a day. One of the worst events I ever reported on. Six hundred... seven hundred dead. They never knew the exact figure, did they? And Lizzie Dixie was presumed to be one of them. Quite extraordinary.'

After a moment's pause, he returned to Penny's article.

'I must say, Mrs Blakely, that I think you give Inspector James Blakely a lot of credit for solving this case. As I recall, you did most of the work. In fact, I was quite jealous of you working on the case because I wanted to have a go at it myself.'

Penny smiled at the memory. 'I suppose it's natural that I praise my husband; I couldn't have solved the case without him.'

'Ah, that's what you think. But I think perhaps you could have done. So I hope Inspector Blakely won't take offence if I edit out some of the praise which has been lauded upon him here.' Edgar took out his pen and made a few notes in the margin. 'After all, this is supposed to be the musings of a lady detective, not a Scotland Yard detective.'

'Very well,' said Penny. 'But I don't want anyone thinking I solved the case completely by myself. A few people helped me.'

'The story is much more compelling for our readers if they think you worked alone,' said Edgar. 'Your husband won't be offended by that, will he?'

'No. Probably not.'

'Good.' Edgar made some firmer strokes with his pen, now. Crossing out a few sentences. 'So then... what's next? The murder in St Giles Rookery? It makes sense to write your columns sequentially.'

'Yes, it does,' said Penny. 'I shall find my old notebook and write about that one next.'

SIXTY-ONE

Clara Clifton stood on Chalton Street and watched as the men on the scaffolding chipped away at the building. The roof tiles had gone, leaving the bare rafters exposed to the grey sky. Now they were hammering at the walls, loosening them brick by brick and sending the rubble tumbling to the ground. There were more men than she could count, all busy hammering and calling out to each other. One of them doffed his cap as he noticed her watching.

She estimated the building would be gone within a few days. And after that, work would start quickly on the new one.

And the old burial ground would be built over before anyone in authority could do anything about it.

The authorities were so slow to act that she wondered if they were doing it deliberately. Was Sir Laurence Mulholland really that influential?

With a bitter taste in her mouth, she turned and walked away. She felt powerless. How could one man manage to do whatever he wanted?

SIXTY-TWO

Penny joined Emma later that morning at Park Crescent – a semi-circle of grand houses at the north end of Portland Place. The homes were large and overlooked a pretty crescent-shaped garden which was surrounded by railings and closed to the public.

'I wonder what sort of mood Sir Laurence Mulholland will be in?' said Emma.

'I'm preparing myself for the worst type of mood,' said Penny. 'But it's possible he might surprise us, isn't it?'

They made their way down Portland Place, neither hurrying their step too much.

The footman answered the door again and the sombre housekeeper in the grey woollen dress wanted to know the purpose of their call.

'We want to ask him about a locket,' said Penny.

'Which locket?'

'I feel sure he'll know which one when you mention it to him.'

After disappearing to speak to Sir Laurence, the housekeeper returned quite quickly for them. Once again they were led to his large study furnished with mahogany wood and hunting trophies.

Emma felt a sense of trepidation as they stepped into the room. Sir Laurence stood at the window with his back to them. 'The lady detectives are back,' he said to the pane of glass. Then he turned and gave them a mocking smile.

Penny cleared her throat. 'We asked you about Archie Mitchell when we last visited. And you denied ever hearing of him.'

'That's correct.'

'But we've discovered something which connects him to your family.'

'And what's that?'

'A locket,' she said. 'We believe he stole it.'

The glint of recognition in his gaze was unmistakeable, but he controlled his reaction well. 'A locket?'

'I believe you know about it,' said Emma, trying to keep her voice calm and measured. 'You went looking for it in The Tiger Tavern on Tower Hill.'

Sir Laurence grinned before sinking into the chair behind his desk. 'I did what?'

'You visited The Tiger Tavern and the place where Archie Mitchell used to sit. You looked for the locket behind the loose wooden panels beneath his seat, but it wasn't there.'

He gave a laugh. 'I don't know who you've been speaking to, but you've clearly mistaken me for someone else.' He sat back in his chair, obviously amused. 'Why on earth would I do that?'

'Because the locket is important to you,' said Penny, her voice firm. 'Your son gave it to a young woman he had a love affair with. A young woman who worked in this household as a maid. While she was here, the locket was stolen from her room and it somehow found its way into the possession of Archie Mitchell.'

The silence which followed this statement stretched on for so long that Emma felt her toes squirm. Sir Laurence's eyes were dark and still. Unblinking.

When he eventually spoke, his voice was so quiet that it was barely above a whisper. 'Where did you hear this?' he asked, his eyes fixed on Penny.

'It's what we've been able to piece together over the last couple of weeks,' said Penny.

'And you call yourselves lady detectives?' He shook his head, as if bitterly disappointed. 'You're wasting my time, ladies. I should have learned from our last encounter that the pair of you are completely deluded—'

'So you deny the existence of the locket?' Penny interrupted.

'Oh no. I'm sure it exists. But it has nothing to do with my family.'

'And you deny the love affair your son Gregory—'

'You're not worthy of mentioning his name!' he hissed, slamming a fist onto his desk.

Penny fell silent, much to Emma's relief. She could sense the man had a quick temper and she didn't want to antagonise him any further.

'Now leave,' he said, pointing to the door. 'The pair of you. Get out of here. Now!'

SIXTY-THREE

Emma felt her eyes prickle with tears as she and Penny left Sir Laurence's home. Then she felt ashamed of them and tried to blink them away. She couldn't understand why she'd allowed him to bother her so much.

'Well, I thought that went better than I'd expected,' said Penny breezily. 'I thought he'd completely refuse to speak to us. At least he gave us a few minutes of his time, he revealed that he's ashamed of his son's affair with Rosie Clark. He also proved himself to be a liar which we suspected already.'

She took Emma's arm and gave it a comforting pat, clearly aware that Emma had been a little shaken by the encounter. 'He was horrible to us because we saw through his lies,' she added. 'Despite his denials, we've managed to establish the truth.'

They walked northwards to Park Crescent. 'But we're still no closer to understanding how he and Archie Mitchell knew each other,' said Emma. 'That's what puzzles me more than anything.'

Penny stopped for a moment, thoughtful. 'Perhaps we're looking for a connection which doesn't exist. The calling card and the locket link them, but perhaps the two men never met?'

'Perhaps they didn't,' agreed Emma. 'Maybe we're wasting our time trying to link them.'

'Detective Inspector Simpson suggested the calling card is a red herring,' said Penny. 'Perhaps the locket is too. We've managed to return it to its rightful owner and I don't think we can do much more.'

'But Sir Laurence wants that locket,' said Emma. 'Perhaps he'll try to take it from Rosie Clark?'

Penny sighed. 'It's certainly a worry. Rosie asked us if he knew she had it, didn't she? He's actually made a bit of a mistake.'

'What?'

'By refusing to acknowledge the locket's existence, he was unable to ask us if we knew where it was,' said Penny with a chuckle. 'He couldn't even ask how we knew about it, could he? I feel reassured at the moment that he has no idea where it is.'

SIXTY-FOUR

Rosie had just finished feeding Edward when a knock sounded at the door.

'I'll go,' said her mother, putting down her needle and thread.

Moments later, Rosie heard raised voices. She sighed, got to her feet, and joined her mother at the front door.

'I've told you, she's not interested!' said her mother to a scruffy-haired young man on the doorstep.

'Seamus,' said Rosie.

Her mother turned round. 'I've just told him you don't want to see him!'

'I don't.'

'So what are you doing here? Get back inside.'

'I came to see who it was.'

'And I want to have a word about what you said to the coppers!' said Seamus. He looked weary and Rosie felt a stab of guilt about telling the police the truth. She actually felt a little sorry for him.

'Did they arrest you?' she asked.

'Yes! I spent three days in the cells. For what? Nothing.'

'Well, you're out now.'

'I'm out on bail,' he said. 'I go in front of the magistrates tomorrow. I've been charged with conspiring to commit a burglary.'

Rosie gasped. 'When did you do that?'

Her mother gave a heavy sigh. 'Well, if the pair of you are going to start holding a conversation then I'm wasting my time standing here, aren't I?' She stepped away from the door and left them alone.

'I was looking around the warehouses on the night Archie Mitchell got shot,' said Seamus. 'That's what I had to tell them I was doing because you wouldn't give me an alibi anymore!'

'You left me, remember?'

'Yes. But that's because you didn't tell me about him!' He pointed at Edward in her arms.

She cuddled her baby closer. 'I had my reasons.'

'And I had my mine.' He pushed his hands into his pockets and stuck out his lower lip.

'Well, at least you've not been charged with murder,' said Rosie. 'You won't get much for planning a burglary, will you? Maybe just a fine.'

'And how do I pay that? I've got no money. I can't work, can I?' He pulled out his scarred hand to demonstrate what she already knew. Then his eyes went to her neck. 'What's that?'

She put a protective hand up to it. 'A locket. What do you think it is?'

'Where'd you get it from?'

'It was stolen from me a long time ago but I got it back again.'

'How?'

'Why'd you have to ask me so many questions, Seamus? It's none of your business.'

'Is it from him?'

She shifted from one foot to the other. 'Yes. But he gave it to me a long time ago. Before Edward was born.'

His shoulders slumped. 'And you still want to wear it.'

'I like it.'

'Because he gave it to you.'

'Yes,' she said, sadly. 'I don't have many nice things, you know.'

He glanced away, nodding. 'I know. I wish I could've bought you nice things like that.'

They both fell quiet for a moment.

Rosie still felt some fondness for Seamus. They had enjoyed some good times together until he'd found out about Edward. 'I'm sorry I went back on my word,' she said.

He shrugged. 'That's all right. I shouldn't have got you to lie for me.' He paused for a moment, then continued, 'I wish you'd told me about Edward from the start. I might've... Well, who knows.'

Rosie nodded, it seemed they both wished things had been different.

But it was too late now. 'I've got to go,' she said. 'The baby's getting cold out here on the doorstep. Good luck in the magistrates' court. I hope you don't get too much of a punishment.'

'Thanks.' He sighed and gave a small smile. 'It was nice to see you again. Take care of yourself, Rosie.'

She returned his smile before she closed the door. As men went, Seamus Byrne wasn't too bad.

SIXTY-FIVE

'I'm very sorry to disturb you at this hour, Mrs Blakely.' Detective Inspector Simpson gave Penny a polite but weary nod.

'What's this about?' asked James. 'We were just about to retire for the night.'

'I do apologise, Blakely,' said Simpson as he lowered himself into a chair in their sitting room. 'But I feel it's important to relay this message to you as swiftly as possible.'

Penny's heart gave a thump. Had there been a breakthrough in the case? A new clue? An arrest? However, the inspector's expression suggested he wasn't bringing good news.

'Has something happened?' asked James, clearly thinking the same.

'There's been an instruction,' said Simpson. 'From high up.'

James scowled. 'How high?'

'From the commissioner himself. He's decided that Mrs Blakely and Mrs Langley are no longer to be involved in the investigation into Archie Mitchell's murder.'

Penny felt her breath leave her. She stared at the hearthrug for a moment, gathering her thoughts. Then she turned to Simpson again. 'No longer involved?' she said. 'Why?'

'The commissioner didn't offer a reason. He simply asked me to convey his decision in person.'

'And you accepted that?' snapped James. 'Without asking him for an explanation?'

'I did ask,' said the inspector. 'But he made it clear no discussion was required. His decision has been made.'

James looked as though he might explode. 'It's outrageous! Penny and Mrs Langley have done far more to progress this case than the Yard has ever achieved. What kind of interference is this?'

Penny laid a calming hand on his arm. 'James,' she said softly. 'Let's not—'

'No, Penny, it isn't right!' He turned back to Simpson. 'Could you not have questioned the commissioner about his reasoning?'

'It's above my head,' he replied. 'I don't like it either, Blakely, but my hands are tied.'

A pause followed. 'I'm sorry again, Blakely,' said Simpson, his voice softer now. 'As a good friend of your father's, I find this news particularly difficult to deliver. Clearly the commissioner has decided on a new approach to the investigation.'

'It's all right, Simpson,' said James, a little calmer. 'It's above your head as you rightly point out. There's not a lot either of us can do about it.'

James saw the inspector to the door and Penny slumped in her chair, her head in her hands. Despite the lack of explanation, she knew the reason for the commissioner's decision.

She lifted her head again when James returned to the room.

'Can you believe it?' he said. 'What on earth is the commissioner thinking?'

'Oh, I can believe it all right,' she replied. 'It's no great coincidence that Emma and I called on Sir Laurence Mulholland today. Clearly the commissioner is a good friend of his.'

James groaned. 'You think Mulholland had a word with him?'

'I'm sure of it. He wants to stop us working on this case. And the obvious question now is why?'

SIXTY-SIX

Emma stared at Penny in disbelief, her breath catching as the words sank in. 'The commissioner of Scotland Yard has removed us from the investigation?' she repeated, barely able to believe it. Her chest clenched with rising fury. They sat together in a tea room just off Oxford Street.

'Yes,' said Penny. 'Just like that. No explanation, no courtesy. We've been shut out.'

'Because we spoke to Sir Laurence Mulholland.'

'That has to be the reason, doesn't it?'

'Do we know if he's friendly with the commissioner?'

'I wasn't aware of it, but I think it's clear he must be! Our swift removal suggests Sir Laurence has a lot of influence.'

'Which isn't surprising,' said Emma. 'Gentlemen like him often do. And if he's responsible for Archie Mitchell's death, then this is serious. A police commissioner under Sir Laurence's influence isn't going to press charges against him, is he?'

Penny rubbed her brow. 'And maybe that explains why the Yard haven't solved the case. Their efforts were obstructed.' She shook her head. 'I'm not sure what we can do now. We can't just stop...'

'No, we can't.' Emma lowered her voice. 'We can keep going – but quietly. We've come too far to stop now.'

Penny smiled. 'I'm happy you say that, Emma, because I feel exactly the same. If we can find some proper evidence, then the commissioner can't ignore it.' She stopped for a moment and sighed. 'But being shut out from the case makes our job much harder.'

'But not impossible,' said Emma. 'Every investigation hits a problem, doesn't it? And I've watched you keep going when things seem hopeless. You taught me that. Now it's my turn to remind you.'

Penny grinned. 'You're becoming rather good at this.'

'I'm learning from the best.'

'Perhaps,' Penny said. 'But I think you're learning from experience too. That sense you have when you know you're on the right track.'

'Let's keep going. We'll find out what Sir Laurence is hiding. And we'll make sure everyone knows the truth.'

'I'll drink to that.' Penny raised her cup of tea then took a sip. Emma did the same.

'So who do we speak to next?' asked Penny. 'Quietly, of course.'

'Harry Wright.'

'Harry?'

'He's been investigating Sir Laurence's business dealings. I want to find out what he's discovered.'

SIXTY-SEVEN

'You're free to go, Cooper,' said the custody sergeant.

Johnny Cooper rubbed his eyes, blinking in the bright light that now invaded his cell. 'Now?' he said. 'Couldn't you have waited until I woke up?'

'We need the cell.'

'And I was joking,' said Johnny, swiftly getting to his feet before the sergeant changed his mind. 'Am I being released on bail?'

'The charges have been dropped.'

He felt a skip of excitement. 'Dropped?'

'The inspector at the Yard has decided not to pursue the matter. But you're under orders to stay away from him and his wife.'

'Don't worry, I intend to,' said Johnny, impatiently waiting by the door. 'So can I go now?'

The sergeant stepped aside. 'You can go.'

Johnny smiled as he stepped out onto Commercial Street, relieved by the familiarity of the sights and sounds around him. Even the air somehow smelled good: chimney smoke, horse dung in the road and the malty smell of the Truman brewery.

He stopped at a tobacconist's then lit his clay pipe and enjoyed a slow saunter along the street. He was free again. For the time being.

With beer on his mind, he saw the sign of The Ten Bells public house up ahead. Crossing the road, he skipped across the rails of the horse tram and headed for the sanctuary of the tavern.

Inside, he was greeted with lively chatter and warm stuffy air. The contrast with the cold, antiseptic police cell couldn't have been greater.

'Johnny!' Molly, an old flame, draped an arm around his neck. 'Where've you been?'

'Here and there.' He gave a well-practised enigmatic smile and signalled to Mabel the barmaid that he'd like his usual pint.

An old friend called Tom slapped him on the back and offered to pay for his drink. Johnny thanked him graciously. It felt good to be doing what he enjoyed the most. Drinking in the company of good people.

After three pints of pale ale, Johnny rested against the bar in a contented haze.

'Another one, Johnny?' asked Mabel.

'Maybe.' He lit his pipe again. 'I'm just deciding if I need to go somewhere.'

He could call on Sarah and see if her mother had made a pot of stew. He had little desire to see Sarah; he didn't like the way she'd been looking at him recently – stern and disapproving as if she suspected he was up to no good. But what did she expect? She'd known from the start he was no angel.

It always went this way with women. It was fun to start with and then they turned serious and expected things from him.

Disapproved of him.

He caught Mabel's attention and ordered another pale ale.

'I'll pay for that,' said a man next to him.

Johnny turned round to thank him. Then he saw who it was.

Detective Inspector Blakely.

He gave a groan. 'You do realise everyone in here will know you're a copper?'

The inspector nodded. 'I'm used to it.'

'Well I don't like being seen talking to coppers.'

'That didn't stop you calling at my house.' He ordered a pint of stout from Mabel.

'I've been told to stay away from you,' said Johnny. 'So I'm going to have to leave.'

'And leave a pint of ale behind? I'd make the most of it and drink it if I were you. And don't you think you should be thanking me for dropping the charges so we can have this conversation?'

Johnny gave a snort. 'I don't thank coppers for anything. You lot make my life a misery.'

'Only because you make life a misery for innocent people.'

He sneered at this exaggeration. 'I do what I need to get by.'

Mabel placed the pint of ale in front of him and it looked too tempting to leave. Inspector Blakely picked up his pint of porter and sipped it.

'So what did you say to Archie Mitchell that night?' he asked.

Johnny blinked for a moment, surprised by the question. 'Archie Mitchell? He died months ago. I don't know why everyone's still talking about him.'

'They're talking about him because he was murdered and the killer hasn't been caught yet.'

'Well, it's not me.'

'I didn't say it was. But I do want to know what you said to Archie on the night Harriet fell into the river.'

It was a night Johnny would rather forget. 'I don't know. I don't even remember seeing him there.'

'He was on the bridge when Harriet fell, wasn't he?'

'So I heard. I didn't see him. It was dark.'

'You saw him after you'd raised the alarm. You spoke to Constable Dickinson who was the first policeman on the scene.'

Johnny nodded. 'I remember now. Next to useless, he was. Wouldn't even go in after her.'

'He would have perished if he had,' said James. 'Presumably you didn't go into the river yourself for the same reason?'

Johnny took a gulp of beer and chose to say nothing.

'Archie Mitchell joined you,' said James. 'He was distressed by what he'd seen. Constable Dickinson left the pair of you alone for a few minutes while he checked the riverside. What did you two talk about?'

'I'm blowed if I remember,' said Johnny. 'And I don't like talking about this.'

'I'm sure you don't. It was a tragic evening. When Constable Dickinson returned and took statements from the pair of you, did you tell the truth?'

'Of course I did! Why would I lie?'

'So your memory of the evening is quite clear then.'

'Yes.'

'So you weren't particularly drunk?'

'A bit, but not much.' He prickled with irritation. 'Why are you asking me this?'

'I've spoken to a barman at The Rose and Crown, the public house on the south bank of the river which you and Harriet visited shortly before her death. The landlord of that establishment told the inquest you were both intoxicated and bothering the other customers so he asked you to leave. That's not true, is it?'

Johnny's breath quickened. 'I don't know why you would bother speaking to them there.'

'The barman told me neither of you were particularly intoxicated that night and that he saw you call on the landlord the following day to discuss the incident.'

'So what if I did?'

'Did you tell the landlord what to say in his police statement?'

'Of course I didn't!' Johnny took another gulp of beer. He had to get out, he couldn't stand the way the inspector was questioning him.

'Did you tell Archie Mitchell what to say in his police statement?'

'No!' Johnny felt his fists clench.

Voices fell quiet around them. The inspector fixed him with his steely gaze. 'Did you threaten both men into lying for you? Covering for you because you pushed Harriet into the river that night?'

A flash of rage gripped him. Perhaps he'd tried to punch the inspector, he couldn't be sure. But when he came to his senses, he found Tom had pushed him up against the bar.

'Easy now, Johnny,' he said into his ear. 'Don't get carried away.'

'Where is he?' Johnny hissed through his teeth. He twisted his head around, trying to see where the inspector had got to.

'He's gone now. Calm down. Don't do something you'll regret. Not again, Johnny.'

SIXTY-EIGHT

'It's been a busy few days,' said Harry when Emma and Penny joined him in the newsroom of the *Morning Express* offices. 'I've visited council offices and building sites. I've spoken to vestry officials, construction workers and people who've been evicted from their homes and businesses. I think it's fair to say the tentacles of Mulholland and Son stretch far and wide across London. I've found evidence of a dozen building projects.' He lifted a pile of papers from his desk to demonstrate. 'And there's at least half a dozen more being planned.'

'Goodness,' said Penny. 'Sir Laurence is a busy man indeed. Have you found any evidence he's bribed officials?'

'Not yet,' said Harry. 'But I'm convinced it's happening. I paid a visit to Oscar Garland and asked him about it. He pushed me down his front steps. I think that is enough evidence in itself.'

Emma gasped. 'He pushed you down the steps? Were you hurt?'

'I twisted my knee and that hurt a little. But I'm fine.' He smiled, clearly appreciating her concern.

'What a horrible man,' said Penny. 'He clearly has something to hide.'

'I agree,' said Harry. 'And I feel sure I can find some evidence he received money from Sir Laurence. In fact, his aggression towards me has simply made me more determined to find it.'

Penny grinned. 'I like your spirit, Harry. You're a true journalist.'

'To be honest, I don't feel I can rest until I see it through,' he said. 'I want to see justice done.' He turned to Emma. 'Thank you for passing this story on to me, Mrs Langley. It's been fascinating work.'

His eyes held hers for a moment and she couldn't resist a smile. 'That's quite all right,' she replied. 'Thank you for working so hard on it, everything you've done here is invaluable.'

'We need evidence of Sir Laurence's wrongdoing,' said Penny.

'I agree,' said Harry, pulling his gaze away from Emma. 'And I think *Morning Express* readers are going to be deeply saddened when they hear stories from the people Sir Laurence has evicted.' He picked up his notebook and turned a few pages. 'Here's what one lady who lived at the St Pancras site said. She was holding a baby and had two young twins. "It was our home for five years and we'd always paid the rent on time, then some men turned up and told us we had to leave. Just like that. No warning, no explanation. They said the building had been condemned and we had to get out."'

'Goodness,' said Penny. 'With no warning?'

Harry continued, '"The men said a notice had been posted by the front door but I can't read. They said the place was too dangerous to live in, but we were still living there with no problems. There was damp in the walls and the windows rattled. The roof leaked if the rain came in sideways, but we managed. We fixed what we could and the landlord could have seen to the rest. All it needed was a bit of maintenance. We had neighbours we trusted. It felt safe. Especially for the little ones."'

'So where did they go once they were evicted?' Emma asked.

'This lady said she and her family had to sleep on the street for the first night.'

'On the street?' said Penny.

'She managed to find somewhere to stay the following night and when I spoke to her she'd lived in three different places. She was still looking for a proper home. Here's what her friend said, "I don't like feeling helpless and I've always done what I could to keep us going. My husband died three years ago. I scrub steps. I take in sewing when I can. I don't drink. I keep the children out of trouble. But none of it matters. You do everything right, and still someone can show up one morning and take your home from you."'

Emma shook her head. 'Sir Laurence needs to hear this.'

'And he will!' said Harry. 'I've discussed this with Mr Fish the editor and he's agreed we're going to run a series of articles about Sir Laurence's activities.'

Penny grinned. 'Excellent! The police will do what they can to stop us but journalists will always manage to print the truth.'

Harry frowned. 'The police have stopped you?'

Emma explained the commissioner had decided he no longer wanted her and Penny to help with the case.

'Well, that's a foolish decision!' said Harry, his expression bitter.

'We suspect Sir Laurence is behind it,' said Penny. 'We called on him yesterday and I don't think he liked us asking him questions. We think he's had a word with the commissioner.'

'Sir Laurence has clearly got a hold over him,' said Harry. 'But he doesn't have a hold over this newspaper. Mr Fish and I plan to publish the first article about his activities in a couple of days. Tomorrow I'm meeting with some officials from St Pancras vestry and the new London County Council. I've invited Mrs Clara Clifton to join me because she knows a lot about the St Pancras site. Perhaps you would both like to attend too?' He smiled. 'The more the merrier.'

'We'd love to,' said Emma.

SIXTY-NINE

Rosie Clark knew something was wrong the moment she turned into Prince's Square. Her step slowed as tightness coiled in her chest. The front door to their building was ajar, creaking gently as the wind nudged it back and forth.

That wasn't right.

She adjusted the baby in her arms and quickened her pace, her boots scuffing on the cobbles. An odd hush had fallen on the square.

She stepped over the threshold and into the rooms she and her mother shared. The rooms looked like they'd been struck by a whirlwind. Rosie dropped her shopping basket in the doorway and stared. Everything lay scattered across the floor, the pictures from the mantelpiece were smashed in their frames. Drawers had been wrenched out and their contents tossed about.

And her mother was there, white-faced and clutching the edge of the chair as she spoke with a constable. Her eyes were rimmed with red.

'Ma?' Rosie's voice broke as she said it.

Her mother turned sharply. 'Rosie! Oh, thank heavens you're here.'

'What's happened?'

'We've been burgled,' she said. 'I'd only gone out to see Betty for a few minutes. Twenty at the most. I locked the door – I swear I did – but when I came back, it was like this.'

Rosie's hand went to the locket around her neck. At least that was safe. 'What did they take?'

'Money. The shillings I'd set aside for the rent... they've gone.' She sighed. 'I'm going to have to pawn my ring to pay for it now...'

She trailed off and the constable made some notes. 'Anything else missing?' he asked.

'No,' said Rosie's mother. 'We don't have much, as you can see.' She bent down and reached for one of the drawers strewn across the floor. 'I should tidy,' she said. 'I can't bear to look at this.'

'Best to leave things as they are for now,' said the constable. 'Just until we've finished checking everything here.'

But she'd already lifted the drawer and was trying to slide it back into place. It caught on something inside the cabinet. 'Oh, what's that now?' she muttered.

She tugged the drawer free and reached cautiously into the cabinet. Her brow furrowed. Then her hand emerged slowly, palm open.

A small, black revolver rested there.

Rosie gasped.

'Give that here!' said the constable, holding out his hand.

Her mother's hand trembled as she held it up. 'I swear... I've never seen this in my life, Constable. It's not ours. It was hidden in the cabinet.'

The policeman put his notebook away and took the revolver from her, handling it like a venomous snake. 'It's loaded,' he said, inspecting the chamber. 'And you say you've never seen this before, Mrs Clark?'

'No! Never.'

'Miss Clark?' he said, turning to Rosie.

'I've never seen it before,' she replied. 'I don't know how it got there.'

The constable narrowed his eyes. 'Who else lives here?'

'No one,' said Rosie's mother. 'Just me, Rosie, and baby Edward.'

'Who's visited recently?'

'We don't have visitors as a rule... but two women – Mrs Blakely and Mrs Langley – called round recently. Twice in fact.'

'They wouldn't have had a gun with them,' said Rosie. 'And they didn't go anywhere near the chest of drawers.'

'Anyone else?' asked the constable.

'Seamus Byrne,' said Rosie's mother. 'He called here yesterday.'

'He didn't come inside,' said Rosie. 'He stayed on the doorstep. We don't get many visitors, just as my ma has said. I think the burglar must have left it there.'

'Thieves don't tend to leave loaded revolvers behind,' said the constable. 'Especially not where someone else might find and use them. No. This wasn't left by accident.' He emptied the bullets from the revolver's chamber and put them in his pocket. Then he wrapped his handkerchief around the gun and put it in another pocket.

'Are you sure Seamus didn't give you anything to look after, Rosie?' said her mother.

'Quite sure!'

'Because he's the most likely owner of this.'

'He's not!' protested Rosie, feeling the need to defend him.

Her mother turned to the constable. 'Seamus Byrne has been arrested in the past as a suspect in the murder of Archie Mitchell.'

The constable's eyebrows rose halfway up his forehead. 'Is that so?'

He took out his notebook and made more notes. 'This could be very serious indeed; I shall summon my superiors. The pair of you are to stay right where you are.'

Rosie's mother shook her head as the constable left the house to get help. 'Somehow Seamus hid that gun in our house,' she said.

'It's not his, Ma!' cried Rosie. 'He would never murder anyone. He's not perfect, but he's not a murderer!'

'Well, I used to think he wasn't capable of it. But there's too much coincidence now. He asked you to lie for him to provide an alibi and now this. He knows this house well and he knew we were out. He was probably watching the house and waiting for his opportunity.'

'No!' Rosie felt tears prickling her eyes. 'I don't believe he would do it!'

They remained in sullen silence until the constable returned with Detective Inspector Simpson and another officer with small piggy eyes.

Simpson was holding the revolver in his hand. 'I've little doubt this was the weapon used in the murder of Archie Mitchell,' said Detective Inspector Simpson. He turned to his companion. 'What do you think, Harmsworth?'

'I think it's extremely likely,' he said. 'We know one shot was fired at Mitchell and from the casing left at the scene we suspected a small revolver had been used. Very much like this one. These Bull Dog revolvers hold five cartridges and this one had four left in its chamber. That suggests that someone loaded up the chamber and fired only one shot.'

Edward began to grow restless in Rosie's arms, as if the tension in the room was bothering him.

'Seamus Byrne must have hidden it here,' said Rosie's mother.

'He didn't!' added Rosie quickly.

Simpson frowned a little and examined the gun again. 'I believe you hid this weapon for Seamus Byrne,' he said. 'And you kept company with him until recently, didn't you, Miss Clark? Why are you still protecting him?'

Rosie closed her eyes for a moment, trying to remain calm. 'I'm not protecting him, not anymore. I don't believe he's a murderer. He never gave this gun to me to hide...' She trailed off as she felt everyone's gaze on her. Taking in a breath, she continued, 'I know I lied to begin with. But I'm telling the truth now. If Seamus had given me that gun, I'd admit to it now. And if I thought he murdered Archie then I'd admit to that too. But he never did those things. Someone else put the gun there to get me and Seamus into trouble.'

'Is it possible Seamus Byrne gained access to your home and hid the revolver there without your knowledge?'

'No.' Edward gave a little cry and Rosie rocked her arms to soothe him.

'When was the last time he visited?'

Rosie swallowed. 'Yesterday.'

'Yesterday?' Simpson raised an eyebrow.

'He called on me because he was angry I withdrew his alibi. That's all there was to it.'

'And during the visit, could he have concealed a revolver in the chest of drawers?'

'No. He never stepped into the house.'

'That's right, he didn't,' said her mother. 'I was there. But I think he came back here today when we were out and left it here. Then he messed everything up to make it look like a robbery.'

A pause followed. Then Inspector Harmsworth spoke. 'Do you see the difficulty we're in, Miss Clark? This revolver was hidden in your home and someone had a reason to do that. If it wasn't you, and it wasn't your mother... then who? A burglar who stole your money and left behind a murder weapon? It doesn't make sense. It can only have been Mr Byrne.'

Rosie's heart thudded in her chest. The walls felt like they were closing in on her. Was she ever going to be believed? Even her own mother doubted her. All because she'd lied one time... everyone now assumed she would do it again.

'Unless,' said Inspector Simpson, 'someone wanted this gun to be found.'

'Wanted it to be found?' said Mrs Clark. 'You've been saying it was hidden.'

'Hidden but not too hidden. And if you say the intruder put it there...'

'They must have done!' said Rosie, relieved they were finally considering her theory.

The two police inspectors exchanged a glance. Edward made a louder cry this time and Rosie wished the officers would leave so she could nurse him.

An understanding appeared to pass between the two men before Simpson addressed Rosie and her mother again. 'There's a possibility Archie Mitchell's murderer placed this weapon in your home to make it seem that you carried out his murder,' said Inspector Simpson. 'And I'm not ruling out Seamus Byrne from that. In fact I remain even more suspicious of him than before.'

He tucked the gun away in his pocket. 'I'm going to take my leave of you ladies now.'

Rosie could feel herself trembling as she let out a long sigh. Seamus was innocent, she felt sure of it.

But what if she was mistaken?

SEVENTY

'James has discovered that Johnny Cooper lied about Harriet Barnes's death,' Penny told Emma the following morning. They were walking along Pancras Road to St Pancras Vestry Hall for the meeting with the council officials.

Emma stopped and gasped. 'James has proof that Johnny lied?'

Penny nodded and told her that James had spoken to a barman from the Rose and Crown public house who'd seen Johnny and Harriet shortly before her death.

'His version of events doesn't fit with what the landlord told the police and the inquest,' Penny added. 'And Johnny called at the public house the morning after Harriet's death to speak with the landlord. James suspects that's when he encouraged the landlord to tell a story which fitted his.'

'So if Johnny told the landlord what to say, it's likely he told Archie what to say too?' said Emma.

'Exactly. It's possible we've been right about Johnny all along. He pushed Harriet off the bridge and threatened the witnesses.'

'So poor Archie witnessed it and was left feeling frightened afterwards,' said Emma, shaking her head. 'How awful. No wonder he was upset shortly before his death.'

'James is going to ask the City of London police to speak to

Johnny again,' said Penny. 'And I really hope they can make some progress.'

'Me too.' Emma smiled. 'This sounds hopeful. It feels frustrating that we're not supposed to be working on this case, but thankfully we have people like James and Harry who can do some of the work instead.'

They met Clara Clifton and Harry Wright outside the Vestry Hall then made their way to the boardroom. Portraits of local dignitaries lined the walls and tall, narrow windows looked out over the busy road outside.

A long, polished table stretched through the centre of the room and a line of officials sat on one side of it. Each had an air of self-importance. Some peered over spectacles while others had mutton-chop whiskers or neatly oiled hair. All wore dark suits with high starched collars.

Emma felt pleased she and Penny had agreed to accompany Harry and Clara. Without them, the pair would have been extremely outnumbered.

Once everyone was seated, Harry began to speak. 'Thank you, gentlemen, for agreeing to meet with us. We've come with a few questions regarding the plans for the buildings and graveyard in Chalton Street. Mrs Clara Clifton here is from the Metropolitan Public Gardens Committee which has raised concerns about the burial ground being built on. Mrs Langley and Mrs Blakely are lady detectives who have assisted me with looking into the activities of Mulholland and Son.'

A thick-set man with a florid complexion arched an eyebrow. 'Lady detectives?' he said with faint amusement. One of the other gentlemen smirked.

Emma felt Penny stiffen beside her. 'That's correct,' said Penny. 'There's little doubt we'd be taken more seriously if we were gentlemen. But I can assure you our work is no less rigorous.'

Harry continued, 'From what I've gathered, the properties on

Chalton Street weren't in dire condition. I've spoken to many people who lived and worked there. And yet the buildings were quickly condemned and sold off and the tenants evicted. That speed is unusual. Unprecedented, even.'

'They were in poor condition,' said the florid-faced man, folding his arms across his chest. 'Our buildings inspector was called in after receiving several complaints.'

'From who?' asked Harry. 'The former tenants I've spoken to admitted the properties needed attention, repairs to windows and that sort of thing. But they were all problems which were easily fixed.'

'That's what the tenants think,' the man blustered. 'But our inspector took a different view. And I remind you that under the Artisans' Dwellings Act, the authorities may clear properties deemed unfit for habitation. Everything is done legally and within our remit.'

'And the speed of the sale?' said Harry. 'I can't help wondering whether Mulholland and Son was given special consideration.'

'There was no favouritism,' the man said sharply. 'Sir Laurence made a perfectly valid commercial offer. He's taking on a financial risk in order to invest in the parish.'

Clara cleared her throat and spoke, 'Including building over a burial ground.'

The man gave her a withering glance. 'That matter is still under discussion with your committee.'

'And while you're discussing it,' said Clara, 'demolition will continue and the old burial ground will be lost. We've seen it before.'

'I appreciate your concern, Mrs Clifton,' he said with a look which suggested he didn't appreciate it at all. 'But people are never pleased with change. They complain about old buildings then protest when we make way for new ones.'

'But people have lost their homes,' Penny said. 'And the new ones will be too expensive for them.'

'The new buildings will improve the area,' said a man with white whiskers. 'And the burial ground is a dismal place.'

'It can be turned into a park,' said Clara. 'It's the most sensible solution because it's forbidden by law to build on it.'

The man looked at his pocket watch. 'I'm afraid that's all we have time for,' he said.

'But you've only given us five minutes of your time,' said Harry.

'Five minutes is long enough.' He gathered his papers together.

'Have you received a payment from Sir Laurence Mulholland?' Harry asked him.

'I beg your pardon?'

'Did he pay you to have the buildings condemned and sold to him at a low price?'

'That's an outrageous suggestion! How dare you!'

The other men joined in with a chorus of remonstrations. Some pointed angrily at Harry and Emma felt a little sorry for him.

'Order!' Penny called out over the noise.

Her intervention surprised everyone and the room fell quiet again. 'Mr Wright is a journalist,' Penny said. 'And he's entitled to ask challenging questions. Questions which a member of the public would ask you if they had the opportunity. You are all paid from the public purse and are therefore accountable for your actions. If Mulholland and Son is allowed to continue with its activities unchecked, then people will begin to wonder why. They'll wonder why those in authority appear to give Sir Laurence's company preferential treatment. I'm quite sure you wouldn't wish to be scrutinised in that way, would you? As gentlemen devoted to public service, you no doubt wish to ensure your actions are carried out with propriety and rigour for the good of the communities you serve. No one wishes to have scandal attached to his name or a tainted legacy long after he has departed his post.'

The room remained silent.

'I'm merely asking you to examine your consciences,' Penny said softly. 'If you don't wish to, then I fear your actions will come back to haunt you.' She got to her feet. 'Thank you for your time, gentlemen.'

Emma got to her feet too, impressed with Penny's ability to quieten a room.

'Thank you, everyone,' said Harry, also rising. 'I've got everything I need for my article now.'

'Erm... just a moment,' said the florid-faced man. 'I would like an opportunity to put a few points to you.'

'I thought five minutes was long enough for you?' asked Harry raising his eyebrow. 'We need to leave now but do feel free to put your points in a letter to the editor at the *Morning Express*. I'll ask him to publish it in full.'

Emma couldn't resist a smile as she left the room with her friends.

'What a group of miserable men!' said Clara as they waited for the horse tram on Pancras Road. 'It's quite obvious they've accepted money from Sir Laurence to do his bidding. If only we could prove it!'

'They won't get away with it for much longer,' said Harry. 'The first article on Sir Laurence will be published in the *Morning Express* tomorrow. Hopefully it will be the start of his downfall and of those who have conspired with him.'

SEVENTY-ONE

'The newspaper's just been delivered,' said James as he stepped into the dining room with the *Morning Express* in his hand.

'Oh, excellent!' said Penny as she spread marmalade onto a piece of toast for Thomas. She put it on his plate then took the newspaper from James. 'We can finally read what Harry Wright has found out about Sir Laurence Mulholland.'

She pushed her plate to one side. 'It's not on the front cover,' she said, looking over the headlines. 'Possibly page two or three, then.' Penny opened the newspaper and James peered over her shoulder as she looked through the pages.

'I'm not sure why Edgar has decided this report on a parliamentary debate is more important than Sir Laurence's corruption, but let's keep going.'

She began to feel puzzled as she turned through pages four and five, then six and seven. The paper rustled under her increasingly impatient fingers.

'Page eight?' she said, frowning. 'Surely not.'

By the time she reached the classified advertisements, a quiet dread was rising in her chest. She went back to the front page then turned it, more methodically this time.

'Let's start again,' she said. 'Perhaps it's a smaller article than I was expecting.'

James stood back, arms folded. 'I didn't see it at all. Do you think Edgar Fish changed his mind?'

'No. Harry was adamant it would be printed today. Edgar couldn't have changed his mind.'

She scanned the pages again, peering closely at every article. 'It's definitely not here.'

'Perhaps it's been held back for a later edition today?'

'No, the only changes in the later editions are for news which has come out today. Harry's article was finished and ready for publication.'

Once she reached the end for the second time, she folded the newspaper in half and dropped it onto the table. 'This is disappointing. Why hasn't it been printed? It's the only real hope we have of getting people to know what Sir Laurence is up to.'

'Well, Fish clearly made a decision not to print it,' said James. 'Perhaps there wasn't enough space and he's saving it for tomorrow.'

'There was plenty of space,' Penny snapped. 'It was all planned!' She lifted her serviette from her lap and got to her feet.

'What are you planning?' James asked.

'I'm going to speak to Edgar Fish.'

'But Mrs Tuttle isn't in today. You'll have to take the children with you.'

'They'll be fine. They'll enjoy the outing.'

James frowned. 'Enjoy it?'

'Yes. It will be good for them to see where I used to work.'

'They're too young to understand it, Penny.'

'Thomas will like the typewriters and the printing press. I have to go and find out what's happened. Now that Emma and I have been removed from the investigation, Harry is our only hope of discovering what Sir Laurence has been up to. And if he's been silenced...' She bit her lip as she thought for a moment. 'No. I can't imagine anyone silencing Harry.'

'Very well. But before you go, there's something I forgot to mention to you yesterday evening. I realise you're not working on the Archie Mitchell case anymore but Simpson believes the murder weapon has been found.'

'Found? Where?'

'In Rosie Clark's home.'

'Rosie?' Penny stared at him for a moment, trying to comprehend the news. 'That can't be right... Rosie had the murder weapon?'

'It appeared after an intruder broke into their home.'

'I see.' It made sense now. 'So the murderer is trying to frame her.' Penny shook her head. 'What a horrible thing to do. I hope Simpson hasn't fallen for it?'

'No, I think he feels Rosie and her mother are innocent of murder. He does believe, however, that Seamus Byrne could be behind it.'

'Not Johnny Cooper? The man who threatened the witnesses called to the inquest into Harriet Barnes's death?'

'We suspect Cooper murdered Miss Barnes. But it doesn't necessarily follow that he murdered Mr Mitchell too.'

Penny sighed. 'Simpson needs to be investigating both of them.'

'I'm sure he will,' said James. 'And as for Cooper, I don't think his recently found freedom is going to last for very long.'

SEVENTY-TWO

Harry Wright climbed the staircase to the *Morning Express* offices two steps at a time, his body tight with anger. He'd spent countless hours researching and writing the article about Sir Laurence Mulholland and now, at the very last moment, it hadn't even been published.

Worse still, Mr Fish hadn't given him an explanation.

He marched along the corridor towards the editor's office, his breath shallow, his hands trembling. Before he reached the door, he stopped and tried to steady himself. It wouldn't do to burst in there in a rage. He needed to sound calm and measured. Losing his temper would only weaken his case.

He took a long breath, rolled back his shoulders, and tried to push the anger down. But just as he began to feel his composure return, the thought struck him again: all that work. For nothing! The fury surged back, sharp and hot in his chest.

He rapped on the door and entered when he heard the call to come in.

'Ah, Wright,' said Mr Fish, looking up from the papers he was sorting on his desk. 'I was just about to find you.'

'To talk about the article you didn't publish, sir?' Harry's voice trembled despite his best effort to control it.

'Yes, that's right,' said Mr Fish. 'I'm afraid Mr Conway intervened at the last moment last night.'

'Why?'

'His telegram told me he had concerns about the facts in it.'

The words made Harry's stomach twist. He clenched his fists at his sides. 'You have my assurance, Mr Fish, that every single fact in that article was thoroughly checked. I know how to do my job properly.'

'I don't doubt it. But when Conway intervenes like this, I'm afraid I have to listen to him.'

'Of course. He pays our wages,' said Harry bitterly, 'but couldn't you have argued my case?'

'No, he was clearly in one of his moods. I know better than to argue with him when he's like that. His telegram arrived very late and it wasn't the time to start a battle. I thought it best we revisit the article and address his concerns.'

'Revisit it, sir?' Harry gritted his teeth. 'There's nothing in it that needs revisiting. Everything was checked and checked again. It's accurate. Completely accurate. And I promised my sources they'd see their words in print today.'

Mr Fish scratched the back of his neck. 'I understand your frustration. Nobody likes having a story pulled at the last minute. But these things happen. I have every intention of running it in the future.'

'When in the future?' asked Harry. To his ears, that sounded like never.

'I will publish it,' the editor insisted. 'But I need to speak to Mr Conway first.'

'Why did he decide we couldn't run it? Does he know Sir Laurence?'

Mr Fish hesitated. 'I'm afraid I don't know. I'll ask him, though. I'm curious myself.'

'I expect he does,' said Harry. 'And that's exactly why he doesn't want it published. If he's a friend of Mulholland's, he won't want to see anything else I've written either. I've got three more pieces lined up. A full investigation!'

'I know, Wright. And I support you.'

'If you supported me,' said Harry, 'you'd have published my article.'

'It's not quite that simple.' He gave a weary sigh. 'Can't you see I'm caught between the pair of you? My best journalist and the man who owns the newspaper. It's a difficult balance.'

Harry's anger flared again. 'I don't believe a proprietor should control what his paper prints. If he can silence us because he's friendly with the people we expose, then what's the point of any of it, sir? We might as well give up and print society gossip!'

Mr Fish frowned. 'I wouldn't say it's quite that serious, Wright. In all my years here, Conway's rarely interfered. It's not his habit to meddle.'

'Until now,' said Harry. 'Until this. All that work, gone to waste.'

'Now, come on,' said Mr Fish, stepping round the desk and placing a hand on his shoulder. 'It's not wasted. I know you're passionate. You're young, ambitious and full of fight. I was just like you once. But sometimes we have to face the obstacles in our way and find a path round them. We'll get there, Wright.'

Harry looked at him, jaw tight. He wanted to believe him. But as he left the office, his anger hadn't cooled. It had only hardened into resolve.

SEVENTY-THREE

Mr Pugh stepped into Sir Laurence's office with a folded copy of the *Morning Express* in his hand.

'Well?' asked Sir Laurence.

'There's nothing in the paper, sir.'

Sir Laurence exhaled, his shoulders relaxing. 'Good. I'm pleased to hear it. We can't have these newspapers publishing entirely unfounded stories, can we? That's excellent news indeed.' He leaned back in his chair, steepling his fingers. 'And the two women who bothered me the other day? Have they been told they're off the case?'

Pugh gave a polite nod. 'Absolutely. My contact at the Yard says they're no longer permitted to work on it.'

'Good. Well, I think that calls for a celebratory drink!' Sir Laurence got to his feet and gestured for Pugh to sit. 'Hopefully the two women and that young lad from the *Morning Express* will keep their noses out of other people's business. I really would prefer not to resort to... other measures.'

He poured out two glasses of whisky. 'You're proving yourself to be rather good at fixing things, Pugh. Who'd have thought? I employed you to find the locket and you've managed to solve a few problems for me as well.'

'Talking of which, sir. I know where the locket is.'

'You do?' Sir Laurence felt a grin spread across his face. 'Where is it?'

'The girl has it again.'

'I see.' Sir Laurence took a sip of his drink.

'I've been watching her home for a few days, sir, and seen her coming and going. She wears the locket around her neck.'

Finally. The mystery of its whereabouts was solved.

A short silence followed and Pugh cleared his throat. 'I think the best plan of action now is to deal with the girl. As we discussed a few days ago, sir.'

Sir Laurence stepped over to the window and looked down at Portland Place. He didn't wish to dwell too much on the details of what Pugh was suggesting.

'Very well,' he said over his shoulder. 'Just do what needs to be done, Pugh. And let me know when you've done it.'

SEVENTY-FOUR

'Good evening, sir,' said the footman as Sir Laurence Mulholland stepped into the Albion Club on Pall Mall.

The cloakroom attendant took his coat and umbrella and Sir Laurence made his way to his favourite lounge. His shoes sank into the soft carpet as he walked to his usual armchair near the fireplace. A waiter lingered discreetly, awaiting the familiar nod for his drink.

Sir Laurence sank into the chair and surveyed the room. The usual faces were here: city men, barristers, MPs... most of them dull, but useful in the right circumstances.

He didn't have to wait long before Mr Conway, the proprietor of the *Morning Express*, entered. He was a large man who always wore baggy brown tweed. Sir Laurence raised a hand in greeting.

'Ah, Sir Laurence.' Conway adjusted his cravat and joined him. Sir Laurence nodded at the waiter for their drinks.

'I wish to extend my gratitude to you for ensuring the misleading article wasn't published today,' he said. 'I must say, you employ some excellent journalists, Mr Conway. But on this occasion, one of them was clearly misinformed.'

Conway smiled. 'It was no trouble at all. I had a conversation with Mr Fish. He was disappointed, of course. The reporter –

Harry Wright – is apparently quite upset. Fish tells me he's a diligent young man. I've met him myself. He struck me as thorough.'

'Indeed,' said Sir Laurence. 'I don't think he set out to mislead. But I fear he's been... unduly influenced. There are two ladies involved – self-styled private detectives, I believe – who've been spreading rumours. They've rather beguiled Mr Wright, I fear.'

'Two lady detectives?' Conway raised an eyebrow. 'I think I may know one of them. Mrs Penny Blakely, isn't it? She worked for us for more than a decade.'

Sir Laurence paused, caught off guard. 'Did she really? That explains a great deal.'

'She was one of our finest,' said Conway, his tone guarded but proud. 'Tenacious. Smart. And well respected by our readers.'

Sir Laurence shifted in his seat; he didn't want to hear the woman being praised. 'I see. Well, she's now married to a Scotland Yard man and seems reluctant to give up her old career. A shame, really. It may be worth considering whether her judgement has been clouded.'

Conway didn't respond immediately. Instead he lit his pipe. 'I'd be cautious about casting aspersions, sir,' he said at last. 'Mrs Blakely has never given me cause for concern.'

Sir Laurence forced a genial smile. Conway's loyalty to the former reporter clearly ran deeper than expected. 'Of course,' he said. 'I only meant there's been a lot of speculation, and journalism which reports on emotions rather than facts can be damaging. Which is why I wanted to propose something more constructive.'

He leaned forward, lowering his voice. 'I'd like the *Morning Express* to report on my new building in Hackney. The new tenants are very happy in their homes and the area's been transformed. An article about it in your esteemed publication would do a great deal to reassure the public that change isn't something to be feared.'

Conway gave a non-committal nod. 'I'll mention it to Fish.'

'I can supply all the details... interviews, plans, drawings. It would save your reporters the trouble.'

Conway shifted in his chair. 'I appreciate the suggestion, but I believe in letting our reporters do their jobs. We pride ourselves on presenting the facts with balance. If we were to publish anything, it would have to be written by someone independent.'

'But someone who gets the facts right,' said Sir Laurence.

Conway smiled. 'Naturally.'

Their drinks arrived and Sir Laurence took a large sip of his. It seemed Conway wasn't as easily managed as he'd assumed.

SEVENTY-FIVE

Rosie stepped out of the door with her shopping basket and shopping list the following morning. Baby Edward was swaddled against her chest and she pulled her woollen shawl across to keep him warm.

'Don't forget to ask the fishmonger what's cheapest,' her mother called after her. 'He always tries to sell you the catch of the day.'

'Yes, Ma,' replied Rosie, closing the door behind her.

She left the square and made her way to the Ratcliffe Highway. Ignoring the whistles of some passing sailors, she turned left into the street and headed for the fish stall. A young barefoot boy tried to sell her some gingerbread but Rosie ignored him and the other distractions. Whenever she walked along the Highway, she concentrated on her errand and kept to herself.

She walked with one arm across Edward and her shopping basket looped over the other. The encounter with the police inspectors two days previously weighed in her mind. Was there still a chance they didn't believe her? Was it possible she could be arrested for hiding a murder weapon?

She shuddered as she thought of that gun in her home. A place which was supposed to be safe for her son. Rosie longed to live in a better, safer home. Somewhere in the West End where the rich people lived. It was a world she knew but only briefly. Working in service had opened her eyes to how the rich lived. Comfort and security. It was a world Gregory still lived in now.

Her throat tightened as she thought of the life he led with his aristocrat wife in Scotland. They probably lived in a castle with a hundred servants. It was a life she could barely imagine.

Instead, she was trapped in the East End in a house which didn't feel safe. Who had got into her home and put the gun there? She didn't want to believe it had been Seamus but she couldn't think who else it could be. Was it possible he had murdered Archie Mitchell after all?

She heard a shout from behind and the clatter of hooves. A horse had probably startled and knocked into something. She was just turning her head to look when she heard someone shout her name.

'Rosie!'

A person slammed into her and her feet left the ground.

Edward. She had to protect him.

She seemed to be in the air for a while. Long enough to drop her basket and hug both arms tight around her baby. One hand cradling his head.

Then she screwed her eyes shut, waiting for the inevitable impact of hitting the ground.

When the blow came, everything went black.

SEVENTY-SIX

Rosie could hear shouting around her. Someone tugged at her neck then left her alone again. Footsteps running. Someone crying. More horse hooves and the heavy wheels of a cart.

She couldn't move, her head hurt too much.

What about Edward?

She held her breath. Could she feel him?

Then his cry rang out, louder than everything else around her. Her vision began to clear a little and concerned faces peered down at her. Blurry at first but then she could see a lady and two gentlemen.

'She's all right!' one of them cried out in glee.

Hands helped her up and soon she was on her feet with Edward bawling in her arms.

'You're both all right,' said the lady. 'Sit here for a moment.' She guided Rosie to the kerbside.

A man pulled out a hip flask and passed it to her. 'Have a bit of brandy,' he said. 'It will do you good.'

But Rosie's eyes were drawn to the other side of the road. Someone was lying on the ground and people were bent over them.

She saw a man step away, shaking his head. His expression was wrought. The person on the ground wasn't moving.

'What's happened?' Rosie asked.

'That young man in the road saved your life,' said the man with the hip flask. 'He pushed you and your baby out of the way of two bolting horses and a carriage.'

Rosie gasped. 'I didn't even see it!'

'Not many of us did. The horses galloped down here out of nowhere. And now they've gone again. I guess they couldn't be stopped.'

A cold sensation creeped through her and she tried to get to her feet.

'Steady on, not so fast.' He rested a hand on her shoulder. 'You recover yourself before you try going anywhere.'

Rosie could recall now the voice which had called her name shortly before the impact. Her breath quickened and tears sprang to her eyes. 'Seamus!' she called out to the body on the ground. 'Can you hear me? Seamus!'

SEVENTY-SEVEN

'Seamus Byrne is dead,' said Penny. She sat in the parlour with Emma and her two children.

Emma felt a sudden chill run through her. 'What?' She shook her head, trying to push the news away. Surely it couldn't be true? Penny handed the afternoon edition of the *Morning Express* to her. It was folded open at the relevant page. Emma took in a breath and read.

Man Killed by Loose Horses on the Highway

A man was tragically killed this morning on the Ratcliffe Highway by a carriage and pair. It is understood the horses had bolted and were out of control. Witnesses said the carriage travelled at "great speed" in an easterly direction along the street, scattering people in its path.

It has been reported the man was an Irish labourer called Seamus Byrne who was twenty-four years old. Fishmonger Peter Harris said he saw Mr Byrne push a young lady and her baby out of the path of the runaway vehicle. He described Mr Byrne as acting "very bravely and with no regard for his own safety."

The young woman is believed to be Miss Rosie Clark. Mr Harris stated that she was a regular customer of his. She and the child are reported to be unharmed.

The whereabouts of the horses and carriage is currently unknown.

Emma and Penny sat in silence for a moment. Thomas lay back on the settee and hummed a little tune with his fingers in his mouth.

Eventually Emma felt able to speak. 'So Rosie was walking along the Ratcliffe Highway when a pair of bolting horses ran at her. Seamus was there too and he pushed her out of the way and saved her and Edward's life.'

'That appears to be what happened,' said Penny.

'The bolting horses...' said Emma. 'It's not unheard of, but it's unusual. And the last line of the report bothers me, "The whereabouts of the horses and carriage is currently unknown." That suggests the carriage didn't stop, doesn't it?'

Penny nodded. 'It's difficult to stop a bolting horse. Almost impossible, in fact. But you'd have thought the coachman would have returned to the scene once he'd got his horses under control. Why didn't he? It makes you wonder, doesn't it?'

'Yes, it does,' said Emma. 'It makes me think someone drove at Rosie and her child deliberately.'

'I think we need to call on Rosie and find out how she is,' said Penny. 'Let's go tomorrow.'

'Are we allowed to?' said Emma. 'We're not supposed to be working on this case anymore. What will happen if the Yard finds out?'

'I don't know,' said Penny. 'Perhaps they'll take it out on James.'

'But that's not good, he doesn't deserve that!'

'The Yard won't find out that we're calling on Rosie,' said Penny. 'And besides, we're visiting her out of concern. We want to know how she's faring, don't we? We're not investigating the case at all.'

SEVENTY-EIGHT

Sir Laurence read the brief report in the newspaper then folded and tossed it onto his desk. 'The girl and the baby survived,' he said.

Mr Pugh scratched his temple. 'That's right, sir. No one could have predicted a young man would save them from danger by sacrificing his own life. Quite unforeseen.'

'Couldn't there have been a better way, Pugh? It's quite obvious that a runaway carriage on the Highway is going to draw attention to itself. It clearly caught the attention of this young, tragic hero.'

'It was planned to look like an accident, sir. And it seems everyone is treating it as such.'

Sir Laurence sighed. 'But the report here makes a point of saying the whereabouts of the horses and carriage is unknown. In an accident of this severity, the police will wish to speak to the coachman. Where is he now?'

'Hiding, sir. And he's been paid good money to keep quiet. The carriage and horses were hired.'

'Any damage to them? The owners could notice it.'

'Not that I'm aware of.'

Sir Laurence got up from his seat and looked out of the

window. The attempt on the girl's life had been too bold, too obvious. It left him worried. Perhaps he'd put too much trust in the private investigator.

He turned back to Pugh whose shoulders had slumped a little. His demeanour was sheepish, despite him refusing to admit he'd made a mistake.

'So what do you suggest we do now, Pugh? Have another go at her? I'm already concerned about how this has gone. The more we try to solve the problem, the greater the chance we have of drawing attention to ourselves.'

Pugh said nothing and instead reached into his pocket. Then he held out his hand and opened it.

Resting in the centre of his palm was the gold locket.

Sir Laurence let out a gleeful laugh and seized it. 'You got it, Pugh! You found it!'

'The girl was wearing it.'

Sir Laurence paused for a moment, catching his breath. 'Did anyone see you take it?'

'No. Lots of people rushed over to her. In the melee I was able to pull it off.'

Sir Laurence examined the broken chain. 'So you did. Well I hope no one saw. Hopefully there was too much chaos at the time. Thank you, Pugh. All in all, it seems you've done a good job. But there have been mistakes too. We'll have to bide our time and see if any of this comes back to us.'

'I've little doubt something could occur, sir. Perhaps someone may notice damage to the carriage. Perhaps a witness will state they saw a man take the locket from the girl as she lay in the gutter. But none of it is traceable to you, sir. I feel sure you're quite safe.'

'Good,' said Sir Laurence, feeling a little more reassured now. 'That's what I like to hear.'

SEVENTY-NINE

Sarah Lyford sat down beside her mother that evening and pulled out an apron which needed mending out of the sewing basket. The children were asleep and the evening was quiet.

'Thank goodness I don't have to work in the tavern this evening,' Sarah said. She threaded her needle with a long piece of white cotton.

'There's a vacancy at the bakery,' said her mother. 'You would do better working there than at that tavern. You get some rough men in there.'

'And yet, the worst-behaved customer recently was an aristocrat,' said Sarah as she pushed her needle into the apron where the pocket was coming away.

'That's not surprising,' said her mother. 'I've always thought those types of people were the worst behaved.'

Heavy footsteps sounded on the wooden staircase which led to their rooms. Sarah caught her mother's gaze and saw her lip curl. 'Is he out?' she whispered.

'He must be,' replied Sarah as a knock sounded at the door and it swung open. Heaviness shifted in her chest and she took in a slow breath. What did Johnny Cooper want now?

He swaggered into the room, accompanied by the sharp stench of beer and tobacco.

'My darling wife!' He grinned at his joke. Sarah got to her feet and he caught her in a firm squeeze before pressing a kiss to her cheek. She managed a smile as she gently pulled away.

He furrowed his brow. 'Aren't you pleased to see me?'

'Of course.'

He turned to wink at her mother who said nothing.

'So they let you go, then,' said Sarah.

'Oh yes, they let me go all right.' His words slurred a little and he sank into a wooden chair at the table, legs sprawled. 'Three days ago! You would've known that if you'd bothered to call on me. But no... While Johnny's locked away, Sarah will play.'

'You watch your words, young man,' said her mother. 'While you've been sitting in jail, my daughter has been working hard to provide for her family.'

Johnny laughed and Sarah noticed her mother's jaw tense. 'Why don't you check on the children, Ma?' she suggested.

'I'd be honoured to.' She put down her mending work and disappeared into the other room.

'What about some food?' Johnny said. 'I'm starving.'

Sarah wished now she'd never invited him into her life. She'd been charmed by him to begin with. Impressed with his notoriety. For a time, her own status had risen. She was Johnny's girl. And nobody messed with Johnny.

But as she regarded him now, she saw little more than a petulant man who shirked responsibility. He drank too much and cared nothing for the needs of others.

'We don't have anything,' she said. 'Only a bit of bread.'

'Bread?' he spat. 'Bread?'

'Yes.' She got to her feet, irritated. 'And if you're not happy with that then you can show yourself the door.'

She put her hands on her hips, adopting the posture she used with difficult customers in the tavern.

But felt herself tremble as something passed across Johnny's face like a dark veil. Slowly, he got to his feet. His movements were measured now, no longer drunken and uncoordinated.

His voice, when it came, was low. 'Say that to me again.'

She didn't dare. He would use it as an excuse to hit her. The palms of her hands felt damp and her heart was racing. But she felt determined not to show fear.

'You heard what I said,' she replied trying to keep her voice steady.

He bared his teeth. 'No one speaks to me like that, especially not my woman!'

He lunged at her like a wild animal. She closed her eyes and tried to duck out of the way. But he'd slammed her back against the wall and there was pressure on her neck.

Too much pressure.

She kept her eyes shut, concentrating only on her breath. But she couldn't catch it. It wouldn't come. A part of her brain screamed for air and she could feel a spasm in her arms.

Was this how her life was going to end? At the hands of Johnny Cooper?

A deafening crash came, along with shouts.

Suddenly Johnny's grip was gone and she collapsed to the floor, gasping for air.

He stepped towards the back room where Sarah's mother was with the children.

She tried to cry out but no sound came. Her throat was too choked. Not her children. She'd rather he beat her black and blue than lay a finger on them.

'No!' The sound tore itself from her but she could tell it was useless. She tried to push herself up but her head swam and the room tilted violently beneath her.

'Get away!' Her mother's voice sounded from the doorway. Sarah prayed she'd armed herself with something. A poker or a broom. But her stomach filled with dread. She'd never forgive herself if Johnny harmed her.

'Get off!' There was the scuffle of a struggle. Johnny must have lost his mind. She could feel her mind clearing with each breath and now she was able to get to her feet.

Suddenly the room was filled with men. They wore uniforms. She saw Johnny pushing her mother just before the men pounced on him.

Sarah lunged over to her as three policemen pulled Johnny away.

'Are you all right?'

Her mother nodded in reply, her gaze fixed on Johnny. Her expression was filled with hatred.

'Mr Cooper, you're being arrested on suspicion of the murder of Harriet Barnes,' barked a constable. 'And we witnessed you assaulting these two ladies as we arrived, so we're also arresting you for occasioning actual bodily harm.'

Sarah put her arms around her mother, trying to choke back the sobs wracking her body. The children ran over to them both and she held them tightly to her. They remained where they were until they could be sure Johnny had gone for good.

'Don't worry, love,' said her mother once silence had descended. 'He's gone now.'

EIGHTY

'Rosie,' said her mother the following morning. 'There's someone at the door for you. A gentleman.'

A gentleman? Rosie didn't know any gentlemen. And besides, her head ached too much to speak to anyone. She wanted to be left alone.

'Rosie?'

'Just show him in,' she called back, her voice weak. 'I don't want to get up.'

It hurt to move. Every bone in her body felt bruised.

Edward, however, seemed remarkably unbothered by the accident. Somehow she'd managed to keep him unharmed.

But both of them owed their lives to Seamus.

Tears welled in her eyes as she thought of him again and his final selfless act.

Perhaps it could have been different. If she'd told him about Edward at the very beginning, perhaps he wouldn't have minded so much. It was the secrecy he hadn't liked.

She wanted to tell him how fond she'd been of him. But it was too late now.

Had he died feeling let down by her? She wished there was a

way to make it all better again. To have Seamus back again. But yesterday had torn a rip in her life which could never be repaired.

Life was different now. Very different.

'Rosie?'

She'd been so lost in her tears that she'd barely noticed the gentleman walk into the room.

She hadn't seen him since they'd met a year ago in Regent's Park and discussed the baby she was expecting. He'd been sent away to Scotland the following day after his father had found out about their love affair.

'Gregory?' For a moment, she couldn't be sure. Was it really him?

He nodded and smiled. Still as handsome as he'd ever been.

A warmth surged through her and she gave a gasping laugh. 'What are you doing here? I thought you were in Scotland!'

'I read what had happened in the newspaper and I took the overnight train from Edinburgh,' he said. 'I've told my family it's an urgent business trip. I wanted to make sure you... both of you...' He pushed his lips together as he glanced at the baby in her arms. For a moment, it seemed he was unable to say anything more. But eventually he recovered himself. 'I wanted to make sure you were both all right.'

'We are.' She smiled, fresh tears coming to her eyes. 'The man who saved us died, though. He was a good friend of mine...' Her voice choked and she couldn't speak anymore.

Gregory crouched beside her chair and rested a hand on her arm.

Rosie wiped her eyes with the back of her hand and lifted the baby so Gregory could see his face better. 'Here's your son,' she said. 'Edward. I never thought you would get to see him.'

<h1 style="text-align:center">EIGHTY-ONE</h1>

Emma and Penny arrived at Prince's Square and noticed a smart carriage and pair pulling away.

'Was that just parked outside Rosie Clark's home?' Emma asked.

'It looked like it, didn't it?' said Penny. 'Let's go and find out.'

'Rosie's a bit tired,' said her mother. 'She's had an awful few days. We both have.'

'We're so sorry about what happened,' said Penny. 'She must be very upset about Seamus.'

Mrs Clark gave a sad nod. 'I never used to think anything good of him,' she said. 'And I feel bad about that now. Because he saved them.' She pushed her lips together and her eyes grew damp. 'Come on in, anyway. I know she'll want to see you but it can't be for long.'

Emma and Penny followed her into the room where Rosie and Edward sat in the old armchair.

Rosie looked pale and drawn, but she smiled as soon as she saw them. 'Thank you for coming to see me,' she said.

Mrs Clark made some tea and Emma and Penny sat on the floor as Rosie told them about the accident.

'That sounds like it was terrifying,' said Emma, once she'd finished. 'And thank goodness you're all right.'

'All they need to do now is catch the coachman who lost control of his horses,' said Mrs Clark. 'There's no sign of him. Caused carnage on the Highway and left.' She shook her head.

It seemed Rosie and her mother thought it had been an accident, but Emma and Penny had another theory in mind.

'Seamus shouldn't have died,' said Rosie. 'He was very brave. People tried to help him but there was nothing they could do. They helped me too. There are some nice people around. Although...' She reached for her neck where Emma could see an angry red line. 'Someone snatched the locket from me.'

'Someone took it?' said Penny. 'Who?'

'I didn't see. When it happened I wasn't even sure if Edward and I were going to be all right.'

Emma felt nauseous. The thought of someone snatching the locket from Rosie as she and her baby lay in the road was shocking.

Penny cleared her throat, as if to speak. But then she seemed to change her mind.

Emma understood what she was thinking. Rosie was trying to recover from a horrible accident and the death of a friend. Telling her that someone had driven the carriage at her deliberately to end her life and take the locket would be much too upsetting for her at this time.

'I'm sure the coachman will be found,' said Penny, eventually. 'He will be asked to explain his actions.'

'I don't mind about the locket,' said Rosie. 'Because the man who gave it to me has just called on me.'

'Gregory Mulholland?' Emma felt her eyebrows raise. 'That was who we saw departing just now?'

Rosie gave a happy nod. 'He read about what happened and came all the way from Scotland to see me. And he met Edward.' She glanced down at her baby and stroked his head.

'That's wonderful,' said Penny, her voice choked with emotion.

'He says he's going to send you a little money when he can, isn't that right, Rosie?' added her mother.

Rosie nodded again. 'He says he'll help us. Quietly, of course. He's married now and he doesn't want his father to find out he's helping me. But he says he'll do what he can. And I believe him.'

Emma hoped Gregory Mulholland could be trusted; if he took after his father then Rosie's faith in him was worrying.

'We heard about the intruder,' said Penny. 'And the revolver they left here.'

'We don't know who it was,' said Mrs Clark. 'The police wanted to blame Seamus but now... well, it wouldn't do to accuse him. We shouldn't speak ill of the dead.'

'I always said Seamus didn't leave the gun here,' said Rosie. 'Someone else did. And they need to find out who it was.'

'Hopefully Rosie and her family will be all right,' said Penny once she and Emma had left the house. 'And Gregory Mulholland had better keep to his word.'

'It seems he cares enough about her to travel down from Scotland so quickly,' said Emma. 'That's a good sign.'

'It is. And now we need to call on his father.'

'Now?'

'Yes. Isn't it obvious Sir Laurence had the carriage driven at Rosie and her baby? And had the locket taken from her? I should think he sent the intruder who left the revolver in Rosie's home too. Just so someone else could be blamed for Archie Mitchell's murder.' She sighed. 'I'm tired of Sir Laurence getting away with everything! He thinks he can bribe and murder people at whim, just to get what he wants! The man's despicable and I've had enough.'

'But we're not allowed to! And he'll refuse to see us, Penny.'

'I don't care. I'm going to his house now and I'm going to create such a scene that someone will have to do something about him!'

She marched on ahead and Emma jogged to catch up with her. 'I don't think you should do this while you're angry, Penny. I think it's best to calm down first—'

'You don't have to come with me, Emma.'

'No, I'll come with you,' she said, keeping step with Penny's pace now. She didn't want to accompany her to Sir Laurence's home. But neither did she like the idea of Penny going there alone.

EIGHTY-TWO

Jane Fielding walked up Portland Place until she reached number thirty-three. She paused for a moment outside, looking at the house which had been her home for twelve years. She'd lived above the coach house in the mews at the back with her husband.

Everything had changed after he died. The Mulhollands had treated her differently. She'd been given more menial work to do – chores which were below her station.

It hadn't mattered too much to her at the time because she'd formed a plan. And for a few months, the plan had worked. Running a lodging house had been enjoyable. Until the money had run out.

Or been stolen.

It had taken her some time to muster up the courage to come here. In her bag was the letter Sir Laurence had sent her nine days previously. She was finally here and ready to talk to him.

Her heart thudded heavily in her chest as she walked up to the front door and knocked.

Sir Laurence was at home and Mrs King the housekeeper walked with her to his study.

'How have you been keeping?' asked the housekeeper.

'Well, thank you.' Jane had never liked Mrs King. 'And you?'

'Very well.'

Moments later she faced Sir Laurence in his study. He didn't get up from his seat behind the desk. Nor did he invite her to sit.

'Mrs Fielding,' he said. 'So you're alive, after all.'

'Yes.' She gripped her bag with both hands, holding it in front of her as a small barrier. 'Why wouldn't I have been?'

He leaned forward on his desk. 'I called on you a number of times but there was no answer. I was quite worried about you.'

'I doubt you were.'

'Did you receive my letter?' His dark brown eyes rested on her, unblinking.

'Yes. That's why I'm here.'

He sat back. 'You took your time.'

'Yes. That's because I had to deal with a burglary at my home.' She felt herself growing flustered and she stammered a little as she continued. 'I'm here because I've...' She took in a breath. 'I've come to demand back what is mine.'

A pause followed and a bemused smile spread across his face. 'Yours, Mrs Fielding?'

'Yes. You sent some men to take my money. I saw them running away with it.'

He shook his head. 'Why would I do something like that?'

'To make me suffer!'

He laughed. 'You don't think you brought it on yourself, then?'

Her grip tightened on the handles of her bag. 'I've only ever tried to do what was right! You and Lady Mulholland pushed me away after my husband died.'

He laughed. 'We did nothing of the sort. Stephen Fielding was a good man and we always gave you – his widow – the utmost respect. Your job changed after he died but we always thought you were happy with it. Anyway...' He picked up a silver letter opener and turned it in his hand. 'There's no use in discussing all that now. It's history. The truth is, I no longer need you, Mrs Fielding. Since

I tried calling on you and wrote you that letter, everything has changed.'

She felt a bitter taste in her mouth. 'What do you mean?'

'I mean what I say. Now all I have to do is decide what to do with these...' He opened a drawer in his desk and pulled out a bundle of papers tied neatly with a piece of ribbon.

Jane felt her jaw tense.

'You probably thought I destroyed them, didn't you? But no. I like to keep a record of everything. Now get out.' He pointed at the door. 'Don't ever come here again.'

She felt her face crumple, but she blinked back the tears. 'My money...' she said. 'I need it.'

'Your money, Mrs Fielding?' He shook his head. 'You really do have a warped sense of right and wrong. Leave now. Before I call the police.'

She turned to go, but the bundle of papers was close by. Just six feet, she estimated.

She glanced back at Sir Laurence and he was already occupied with some other papers on his desk. In a swift movement, she stepped over to the desk, seized the bundle of papers and headed for the door.

'Oi!' Sir Laurence leapt up from his seat.

Her hand fumbled on the door handle, but eventually it turned and soon she was out – running along the corridor she had once had to dust and sweep.

'Mrs Fielding?' The housekeeper loomed into view at the end of the corridor, her mouth agape.

Jane pushed past her and headed for the door.

'Stop her!' came Sir Laurence's voice from behind.

Dashing through the entrance hall, Jane's feet slipped a little on the tiles. But she made it to the door before anyone could get in front of her. Wrenching it open, she ran through and out onto Portland Place.

EIGHTY-THREE

As Emma and Penny were getting out of the cab on Portland Place, they caught sight of a slight woman running towards them. Her arms flailed and her skirts flapped, she appeared to be running too fast to control herself. A look of fear was etched on her face.

A face which was familiar.

'Good grief,' said Penny. 'Isn't that Jane Fielding? Archie Mitchell's landlady?'

She was heading straight for them, but a coal delivery boy was in the way. Mrs Fielding ran around him and misjudged her step. She bumped into a lamp post and dropped a bundle of papers which had been in her hand.

She let out a cry as they scattered across the pavement. 'Oh my letters! My husband's letters!'

She dropped to the ground to retrieve them. The coal boy helped and Emma and Penny stooped down to do the same.

'Mrs Fielding,' said Penny. 'What are you running from?'

'Him! That's who!' She snatched the letters from the three of them and bundled them into her bag.

'Sir Laurence?' said Emma.

But Mrs Fielding had already run on. Emma and Penny ran after her.

The landlady turned right into Cavendish Street, then left into Mansfield Street. They were smart residential streets with pleasant homes and expensive-looking shops.

'Mrs Fielding!' Penny called out. 'Can we help you with something?'

The landlady's pace was slowing as they turned right into Queen Anne Street and they caught up with her as she turned left towards Cavendish Square.

'Is anyone following us?' asked Mrs Fielding, panting.

Emma looked behind. 'I can't see anyone.'

'Good.'

'You need a rest,' said Penny, taking her arm. 'There's a nice coffee room in the Langham Hotel.'

A short while later, Emma and Penny sat with Jane Fielding in some velvet chairs arranged around a low table. A waiter brought a pot of coffee and three delicate china cups and saucers.

Mrs Fielding didn't say much. Her flight from Sir Laurence's home had clearly taken its toll on her. She pressed a serviette to her pale, damp face and muttered breathless words which Emma struggled to understand.

Penny poured out the coffee and handed Mrs Fielding a cup. 'You'll need a biscuit too,' she said, holding out a plate with an assortment of flavours.

The landlady helped herself and – after a few minutes – some colour began returning to her face.

'When we last spoke with you,' said Penny, 'you told us you didn't know Sir Laurence very well. And yet you called on him today?'

'Yes, that's right.' She took a sip of coffee. 'I wanted my husband's letters back.'

'So how well do you know Sir Laurence?'

'As I told you. Not very well.'

'Your husband was his coachman.'

'Yes, that's right.'

'For how long?'

'Twelve years.'

'And did the pair of you live at the house?'

'In the mews.'

Penny frowned a little. 'So you must have known the Mulholland family reasonably well if you lived there for twelve years.'

'A little. But we were servants. So we didn't know them as someone would know a friend. I barely saw Sir Laurence and his wife.'

Emma found Mrs Fielding's answers a little strange; she seemed determined to deny she'd ever known him well. Although Emma could understand why she wanted little to do with the man, her explanation felt unsatisfying.

'And what was Sir Laurence doing with your husband's letters?' Penny asked.

'He kept them after Stephen died last year. I've been asking for them for a long time and today I finally... well, I snatched them.'

'So that's why you were running away so fast,' said Penny.

The landlady nodded. 'It was all I could do. I had to grab them and get out of there. Sir Laurence was angry, of course, but thank goodness he didn't chase me down the street.'

'He's probably too proud to do that,' said Emma.

Mrs Fielding sighed and appeared to relax a little. 'I'm sorry if my explanation seems confusing. I just became... very emotional when I was in Sir Laurence's home. Going back there isn't easy. It reminds me too much of my late husband.'

'I'm sorry to hear it,' said Penny.

'Everything changed after Stephen died,' continued Mrs Fielding. 'I lost the heart for service. And that's when I decided to take on the lodging house. My aunt ran it before me but she retired to the coast. The opportunity came at just the right time. I needed something steady. Something quieter.' She paused for another sip of coffee. 'Most of the lodgers are decent enough and I enjoy my work. Hopefully now that I've got my husband's letters back, I can get on with things in peace.'

'Why did Sir Laurence have them?' Emma asked.

'They say...' She leaned in closer. 'Disparaging things about him.'

'What sort of disparaging things?'

'Lots of things. Sir Laurence is very good at burying his scandals. Anyone who knows him well will tell you that.'

'So the letters contain details of his scandals?' asked Emma.

'That's right.'

'Such as what?'

'It's not my place to say.' She rested a hand on her bag. 'When I get home I will destroy these letters. Otherwise Sir Laurence will merely try to take them from me again.'

Penny took a sip of her coffee and Emma could tell from her expression that she felt rather puzzled about what Mrs Fielding was telling them. 'Talking of scandal,' Penny said once she'd put her cup back in its saucer. 'Did you know Rosie Clark?'

Mrs Fielding's expression turned to disapproval. 'The maid? Yes I remember her. She left in a hurry.'

'Do you know why?'

'She was in the family way.' She shrugged. 'It's always happened and it always will.'

'A precious locket was stolen from her while she was working at the house,' said Penny. 'Did you hear about that at the time?'

She shook her head. 'No.'

'It was the same locket which Archie Mitchell was in possession of.'

'Oh, that locket. I remember you mentioning it to me. I never saw it. How did Archie end up with Rosie's locket?'

'It's something we've tried to fathom for a while,' said Penny. 'But it's in the hands of Sir Laurence now.'

'Is that so? Well...' Her gaze fell into the middle distance as she thought. 'I see. That explains a few things.'

'Explains what?' asked Penny.

Mrs Fielding shook her head, as if waking herself from a brief daydream. 'Well, nothing really. It explains nothing.' She got to her feet. 'Thank you very much for coffee, ladies. It was lovely seeing you again.'

'Will you be all right now?' Penny asked.

'Of course.' Mrs Fielding smiled. 'I have my husband's letters again and all is well with the world.' She bid them goodbye and left.

'What a strange lady,' said Penny as they watched Mrs Fielding leave.

'Husband's letters…' mused Emma. 'Containing scandal? But she didn't wish to tell us what the scandal was.'

'I'm even more confused than I was before,' said Penny. 'An hour ago, all I wanted to do was confront Sir Laurence.'

'Well, let's see what Mr Fielding's letters say first, shall we?'

'How?'

Emma reached into her coat pocket and pulled out two sheets of paper. 'I kept hold of a couple which I picked up from the ground.'

Penny's eyes widened. 'You kept some?'

Emma edged closer to her and opened out the first letter. 'Let's see what Mr Fielding had to say about Sir Laurence.'

EIGHTY-FOUR

It was only a short walk from the Langham Hotel to Sir Laurence's home on Portland Place.

'He'll refuse to see us,' said Emma.

'Not when we tell him what we've learned from these letters,' said Penny. 'Letters which we now realise weren't written by Mr Fielding at all.' The two which Emma had managed to keep hold of had been written by Mrs Fielding instead. 'He won't be able to turn us away when we confront him.'

'And if he denies things again? Lies to us? What then?'

'Let's see how the conversation goes,' said Penny. 'We have to remain hopeful.'

As Emma feared, the housekeeper told them Sir Laurence didn't wish to see them. 'He's told me to tell you he's busy,' she said curtly.

'Then please tell him we know why Mrs Fielding ran off with the letters. In fact, we have a couple which can be returned to him.'

The housekeeper frowned. 'I'm not sure what you're talking about.'

'No, I'm sure you're not. But Sir Laurence knows what we're

talking about so it would be much easier if we could explain everything to him directly. After all, didn't Mrs Fielding run out of here half an hour ago with a bundle of letters?'

The housekeeper nodded. 'She did. I'll tell him it's regarding Mrs Fielding, shall I?'

'Please do. I think he'd be grateful to hear what we have to say.'

Penny's perseverance worked. A few moments later, they found themselves in Sir Laurence's office. But this time, he wasn't settled behind his desk. He was pacing the floor.

Emma recalled how nervous she'd been the last time they were here. She didn't feel much more confident now. But this time she was determined to show he didn't intimidate her. She straightened her shoulders, lifted her chin and glared at him. The man was a bully.

A killer.

'Mrs King tells me you know something about Fielding and her letters,' he snapped. 'What is it?'

'She dropped them in the street while she was running from you earlier,' said Penny. 'We kept a few.'

He paused and one corner of his mouth lifted a little, as if he approved of the action. 'And?'

'We read the letters we found and we know now she was blackmailing you.'

'I see.' He continued to pace the floor but there was an obvious hint of a smile in his expression now. 'So she's finally been found out. I've been waiting for this moment for some time.'

He stopped and turned to face them. 'She had the locket,' he said. 'She stole it from that girl...'

'The girl has a name,' said Penny. 'Rosie Clark.'

'I'd forgotten the name. Anyway... Mrs Fielding took the locket and left her job. I wasn't sorry to see her go. Her husband was a good man, but she...' He shook his head. 'I never warmed to her. I didn't realise when she left that she had the locket. I'd heard it was missing and I'd hoped my son Gregory had taken it after making the mistake of giving it to the maid... The maid left shortly after that because she... well, you know. I sent Gregory up to Scotland and got him married into a proper family. He was still a little too young for all that but I needed him out of the way.'

He wandered over to the window. 'Fielding left, the girl left, Gregory left... although not for good. For a brief spell, I thought everything was under control.' He turned back to them. 'But then the letters came from Mrs Fielding. Demanding money, of course. What else would you expect from her? I had to go along with it initially and give her some money. I didn't want word getting out.'

'She threatened to spread the news of your son's indiscretion.'

'Exactly. And the locket was her evidence. With his photograph in it! The fool...'

'You needed the locket back,' said Emma.

'Yes, I did. I tried asking for it nicely but that didn't work as you can probably imagine. So I watched the house for a few days, familiarising myself with the lodgers staying there. Eventually I noticed one I could approach.'

Emma felt her heartbeat quicken. Things were beginning to make sense now. 'Archie Mitchell,' she said. 'You asked him to find the locket.'

'And you gave him your calling card,' said Penny. 'And probably offered him a sum of money too.'

'Absolutely. If you want to get things done then you've got to pay people.'

'And Archie managed to get hold of the locket,' said Penny. 'But he didn't give it to you?'

'No! That's where the plan went wrong. I never heard from him again. Even after I paid him good money to find it. In fact, the first I knew Archie had ever got hold of it was when my private investigator, Pugh, discovered he'd hidden it in a run-down tavern by the Tower of London.'

'You visited The Tiger Tavern and broke the seat looking for it,' said Penny. 'Although you denied it to us.'

He gave a sniff and said nothing.

'And before then, you confronted Archie Mitchell didn't you?' said Penny.

'No. As I told you, I never saw him again after I asked him to find the locket.'

'You found out he was a regular at The Tiger Tavern and you waited for him one night.'

'No, that's not true.' His voice grew agitated.

'You took a revolver with you and walked with him along the riverside path. You shot him because he wouldn't tell you where the locket was.'

Sir Laurence shook his head. 'Not true at all. I may be many things, Mrs Blakely, but I'm not a murderer.'

Penny laughed. 'Not a murderer? You arranged for two horses and a carriage to be driven at Rosie Clark so you could be rid of her and your grandchild.'

He glowered and stood very still.

'And you took the locket from her as she lay in the road with her child. And you killed Seamus Byrne – the young man who saved her.'

'I don't know where you're getting all this nonsense from, Mrs Blakely.' His voice was very low and quiet. Emma felt an uncomfortable prickle on the back of her neck.

'You have the locket again, don't you? If the police find it in your possession then I'll know that what I say is true.'

He raised his chin. 'I advise you both to leave now, before I do something I might regret.'

Emma felt happy to oblige. She took a step towards the door but Penny remained where she was. 'And what might that be, Sir Laurence?' she asked.

The door opened behind them and Emma's heart plummeted. Someone was here to help Sir Laurence. Possibly more than one person.

How were she and Penny going to escape?

EIGHTY-FIVE

A young, dark-haired gentleman walked into the room. He was handsome with a softness to his features which Emma found faintly reassuring.

'Good afternoon, ladies.' Then he nodded at Sir Laurence. 'Father,' he said coolly.

'Get out, Gregory. I'm busy.'

Emma felt her shoulders relax. This was Gregory Mulholland, the man Rosie had fallen in love with. And Emma could understand why. Although he bore some resemblance to his father, there was nothing similar in his demeanour and tone.

'I think I should stay,' Gregory replied. 'You sound angry with these two ladies and I know what you're like when you're angry.'

'What's that supposed to mean?'

Gregory strolled over to his father's desk. 'I told you to get out of here!' snapped Sir Laurence. 'What are you doing?'

Gregory had begun pulling open the drawers. 'Looking for something which doesn't belong to you.'

Sir Laurence turned back to glare at Emma and Penny, then turned back again to his son. He didn't seem to know which problem to address first.

Penny remained silent, clearly happy to allow the scene to play out. There was little doubt that Gregory's arrival had thrown Sir Laurence into a spin.

He stepped over to the desk. 'You're forbidden to look through my drawers!'

'Am I? Well that's a shame. I'll be on my way.' Emma noticed him slip something into his pocket.

'Get out,' hissed Sir Laurence. 'I'll deal with you later.'

Gregory moved towards the door. 'I do apologise for my father's mood, ladies.'

His calm demeanour was impressive, but Emma could tell he was working hard to maintain it. There was a tightness between his brows and he blinked rapidly. 'My father often allows his temper to get the better of him,' he continued. 'And when it does, who knows what he's capable of?' He paused for a moment, glancing away. 'Ordering the murder of an innocent young woman and her child, perhaps. Or killing anyone else who gets in his way.' He shook his head, clearly dismayed.

Emma gasped. Gregory knew what his father had done.

'There's no way out of this now, Sir Laurence,' said Penny. 'Even your own son knows what you've done. When we suspected you were bribing an official at the Metropolitan Board of Works, we thought that was scandal enough. But you're more evil than we ever imagined. Even your own family has turned against you.'

'Benedict Pugh,' spat Sir Laurence. 'He's the man behind all this. And I only found out about it this morning.' He shook his head. 'A dreadful business.'

'There's no need to explain it all to us,' said Gregory. 'Save your words for the police. They will have arrived by now so I'll show them in.'

Sir Laurence paled. 'The police? You've colluded with them?'

'I need to go now,' said Gregory. 'I need to return this locket to Rosie Clark.' He pulled it from his pocket. 'And before I do that, I'll show it to the police and explain I just found it in your drawer.' He turned to Emma and Penny. 'You witnessed me do that, didn't you, ladies?'

Emma smiled. 'We certainly did.'

They left with Gregory and encountered Detective Inspector Simpson on the other side of the door. His brow furrowed when he saw them. 'What are you doing here?'

'We're trying to understand Sir Laurence's lies,' said Penny. 'But you can do that now. You're arresting him for murdering Archie Mitchell and Seamus Byrne? And attempting to murder Rosie Clark and Edward Clark?'

'Yes, but not Mitchell I'm afraid. What makes you think he was responsible for that one?'

'He had motivation; he wanted to know where the locket was which Archie had hidden, and Archie refused to tell him.'

'Any evidence?'

'No,' said Penny through gritted teeth. 'But we'll find it.'

EIGHTY-SIX

'All I ever wanted was to protect you!' said Sir Laurence to his son. 'And this is how you choose to repay me?'

His heart ached as Gregory turned his face away.

'We're talking about murder, Father,' he responded quietly. 'Whatever your motives were, it was unforgivable.'

Gregory couldn't meet his eye. How had it come to this?

In the past year, Sir Laurence had done everything in his power to shield the family name from scandal. He had worked tirelessly to ensure that the affair would never come to light. He had removed the girl from their lives, seen Gregory married into a respectable family in Scotland, and kept him away from London and the poisonous gossip. He had even searched for that infernal locket, the one which proved his son's relationship with the servant girl. But now, after everything, his own son had turned against him.

Gregory stepped towards the door and ushered in the detective from Scotland Yard. The sombre man had a long face with steel-grey whiskers.

Sir Laurence drew himself up, shoulders squared and chest out. He would not cower before a petty official from the Yard. A man inflated by his own importance.

'Here is the locket,' said Gregory, handing it to the inspector. 'It was in the drawer of my father's desk.'

Sir Laurence watched in silence as the inspector examined it.

'This is the same locket that was taken from the young woman who was almost struck by the horses and carriage on the Ratcliffe Highway,' said the inspector. He turned towards Sir Laurence. 'Where did you get this, sir?'

'I have no idea, Inspector.'

'A denial is to be expected, I suppose,' the man said coolly. He slipped the locket into his pocket. 'I'm taking you into custody, Sir Laurence. I believe you arranged for the horses and carriage to be deliberately driven at Miss Rosie Clark and her infant son. Although they both survived, a young man died protecting them. I have reason to believe you were responsible for that, Sir Laurence.'

'Pugh,' he said. 'He's the man you need. This has nothing to do with me.'

Before the inspector could reply, the door flung open and Eugenia burst in.

'Good grief!' she exclaimed. 'What on earth is happening?' Her expression was one of horror, her eyes and mouth wide.

Gregory moved quickly to her side. 'Please, Mother... keep calm. This has to be done.'

'What has to be done? Why are the police here?'

'Everything will be explained to you in due course, Lady Mulholland,' said Detective Inspector Simpson, his voice grave. 'But for the time being, I'm afraid I must arrest your husband.'

'No!' cried Eugenia. 'There must be some dreadful mistake!'

'Please remain calm, my dear,' said Sir Laurence. 'This is a mistake, and we shall have it cleared up soon enough. Gregory, perhaps you'd escort your mother to the morning room.'

Gregory took his mother gently by the arm and led her away. Her wide, terrified eyes remained fixed on her husband until she disappeared through the door.

Sir Laurence turned back to the inspector, lowering his voice. 'You have no evidence. And if you take me into custody now, I assure you the commissioner of Scotland Yard will not be happy about it.'

'I'm aware you are on good terms with the commissioner, sir,' said Simpson. 'Before coming here today, I discussed the case with him. He was, of course, deeply disappointed to hear that you could be implicated. But he agrees that the wheels of justice must turn, regardless of personal friendship.' He paused, then added, 'There's a Black Maria waiting outside.'

Sir Laurence felt a sickening lurch in his stomach. 'A Black Maria?' The police van would be parked in full view of every passer-by, neighbour and curious maid or butler peering out of the window. He could already picture the whispers spreading across the street, the smug faces of those who had always envied him.

And the commissioner had already known about the plans for his arrest? Why hadn't his old friend warned him?

Sir Laurence scratched at a nagging itch at the back of his neck. This situation was worse than he'd realised. People he'd once trusted were turning against him.

'Let's make this quick and quiet, shall we, Sir Laurence?' said the inspector. 'I'm sure you don't want the Black Maria waiting out there for too long.'

Sir Laurence drew himself up once more and set his jaw. If he was to be paraded before the world, then he would meet it with his head held high.

EIGHTY-SEVEN

Emma and Penny paused for a moment by the Black Maria waiting outside Sir Laurence's home. Emma shuddered a little, she couldn't bear the thought of being transported in a dark, miserable box. It was a shiny black van, windowless except for a small, barred window in the door at the back. Long slots for ventilation ran along the top of each side. The door stood open and a flight of steps had been lowered, ready for the prisoner to climb inside. Two black horses and the uniformed coachman waited patiently.

'Hopefully Sir Laurence will receive the punishment he deserves,' said Penny. They both walked on.

'Where are we going to find the evidence that he murdered Archie Mitchell?' Emma asked Penny as they walked along Great Portland Street.

'I don't know. And perhaps there isn't any. Perhaps it happened too long ago now.'

Emma thought for a moment. 'That's not true. You and James managed to prove Johnny Cooper had lied about Harriet Barnes's death. And that happened before Archie was murdered.' They were now walking along the stretch of street where Mrs Fielding had bumped into the lamp post. 'Let's go back to the Tower and the place where Archie was attacked,' said Emma. 'I feel it would help us.'

They travelled by cab to Tower Hill then walked down to The Tiger Tavern. The clouds parted and late afternoon sunshine bathed the walls of the Tower of London.

'So there was a fight outside here that night,' said Penny. 'And Sarah Lyford was sluicing the pavement when she heard the gunshot. Who did she see out here that night? An old singing soldier and some women who were waiting for their husbands.'

'But she said there was no one when she was washing the pavement,' said Emma.

'True. She saw them earlier that evening, didn't she? Let's walk up to the place where he was found.'

They went on their way and the new bridge loomed into view. The platform bridging the top of the two towers was almost complete now.

'They're making good progress,' said Penny. 'Quite a lot can happen in just a few weeks, can't it?'

'It certainly can.' Emma stopped, once again imagining what Archie Mitchell's last moments had been like.

'He left The Tiger Tavern that night,' she said. 'But he didn't go to the Tower Subway entrance to walk home as he usually did. Instead, he walked along here. He must have arranged to meet someone. Or maybe they met him and asked him to join them for a walk?'

Penny nodded. 'I think so.'

'It was someone who knew he was in The Tiger Tavern,' said Emma. 'But more importantly, it was someone who knew he had the locket. We think that whoever shot him that night wanted the locket.'

'Sir Laurence.'

'And other people too. It was valuable to Rosie. It was valuable to Gregory. And we've learned it was valuable to Mrs Fielding too.'

A cawing sound interrupted her. She looked up at the Tower

walls to see two ravens sitting there – black silhouettes against the sky.

'I don't like those birds,' she said with a shiver. 'They prophesise death.'

'But they're also clever,' said Penny. 'And some say they can provide insight into things we don't always understand. The mind of a murderer, perhaps?'

Emma nodded. 'Perhaps that's why I always feel an uneasy chill when we're here. Are the birds trying to tell us something?'

Penny laughed. 'If you want to believe so, then yes.'

'Then I know where we need to go next. Someone must have seen Archie's murderer that night and I think I know who.'

EIGHTY-EIGHT

'Not you two again,' said Sarah Lyford as Emma and Penny approached the bar in The Tiger Tavern.

However, there was a lightness in her voice, as though she were secretly pleased to see them. Emma noticed a change in her appearance too. She looked less wary, her face a little fuller, her eyes brighter. She seemed younger somehow. 'How are you getting on with the investigation?' she asked, wiping her hands on her apron.

'Well, quite a lot's happened since we last saw you,' said Penny. 'And we think we're getting closer to the truth now. You'll be pleased to hear that Sir Laurence Mulholland, the gentleman who caused the damage here that night, has been arrested.'

'Good,' said Sarah. 'I can't say I liked that man when he came in. Is he the one who murdered Archie Mitchell?'

'We don't think so,' said Emma. 'And that's why we're here again, I'm afraid. We've just got a few more questions, and we really hope you can help us.'

Sarah sighed. 'I've honestly told you everything I know. I really don't know what more there is to say. Except... Sir Laurence isn't the only one who's been arrested. Johnny Cooper has been too.'

Penny smiled. 'Johnny Cooper?'

Sarah nodded firmly. 'The police think he pushed Harriet Barnes off the bridge that night. He's been arrested for her murder. And arrested for assaulting me and my mother too.'

'Assaulting you both?' said Penny. 'That's awful!'

'Well, he can't do it anymore, can he? Until they took him away, I hadn't realised how frightened I'd been of him. It's strange, isn't it? The way men like that work. Slow and careful, so you don't even see it happening. But now he's gone...' She smiled. 'I can finally breathe again. My ma and my children can too.'

Emma felt a warmth rise in her chest, her throat tightening with emotion. She blinked quickly, embarrassed by the sting of tears. 'That's wonderful news, Sarah,' she said. 'I'm so pleased he's been arrested for Harriet's murder. It's what should have happened long ago.'

Sarah gave a small nod. 'If it had, I'd never have got mixed up with him. I made the mistake of thinking he'd protect us. He did, at first. But then he turned nasty. Men like him always do.'

'At least justice has been done,' said Penny gently. 'Now all we need to do is find out who killed Archie Mitchell.'

'For all I know, Johnny could've done that too,' said Sarah. 'Archie was on the bridge that night when Johnny pushed Harriet. Johnny probably wanted him to keep quiet.'

'It's certainly a possibility Johnny murdered Archie too,' said Penny. 'But if he had done, I think someone would have seen him around here that night. We think someone saw Archie's murderer. And we think it might have been you, Sarah.'

'Me?' Sarah's brows raised. 'I've told you... I didn't see anyone.'

'The women waiting outside the tavern for their husbands that night,' said Penny. 'Did you recognise any of them?'

Sarah frowned. 'Maybe one or two. I didn't look too closely. I suppose a few might have looked familiar.'

'Did any of them look unfamiliar?' asked Emma.

'Yes, one did.'

EIGHTY-NINE

The sun was setting as Emma and Penny arrived in Shand Street. Once again, their route had taken them through the damp and dingy Tower Subway – the route Archie Mitchell would otherwise have taken on the night he died.

Mrs Fielding opened the door a crack and gave them a cautious glance.

'We found two of your husband's letters lying in the street,' said Emma. She waved them at Mrs Fielding.

The landlady pushed her hand through the gap and held it out for them.

'Can we come in?' Penny asked. 'We think you'll be interested in hearing what's happened to Sir Laurence Mulholland.'

'What's happened to him?' Mrs Fielding asked, her eyebrows raised.

'Let us in and we'll tell you everything,' said Penny.

'Very well.'

They joined Mrs Fielding in her parlour.

'You didn't read the letters, did you?' she asked, holding out her hand for them.

'We did actually,' said Penny as Emma passed the letters to her. The landlady snatched them from her and folded them up small.

'He sometimes wrote some strange letters. My husband that is. He wasn't always thinking straight. His nerves got the better of him sometimes.'

'He didn't write the letters, did he?' said Penny. 'You wrote them and sent them to Sir Laurence. You were in possession of the locket at the time and you were blackmailing him.'

Mrs Fielding's lower lip wobbled a little. 'I may have been. But he's a bad man. You know that yourselves.'

'Yes, we do,' said Penny. 'Tell us about the locket you stole from Rosie Clark's room. Without the locket, you wouldn't have been able to blackmail him.'

'I didn't take it... I just saw it there.' Her fingers fidgeted with the letters, folding and unfolding them.

'Just lying around?' said Penny. 'That's hard to believe. Rosie says she kept it in her pillowcase.'

'Well, it must have fallen out.' She looked away, still fidgeting with the letters.

'When did you realise Archie had it?' Emma asked.

'When it went missing! I kept it in my nightstand. And one day I saw it was gone. I didn't realise Archie had it. Not to begin with, anyway. So I asked my lodgers and they all told me they hadn't seen it. That's what Archie said too. But unfortunately for him, he was a bad liar.' She pointed a finger at them. 'I can always spot a liar.'

'Where were you on the night Archie died?' Penny asked.

'I was here. Where else would I have been?'

'You weren't waiting outside The Tiger Tavern for him?'

'No!'

'It's not far from here, is it? Just a quick walk under the river through the Tower Subway.'

'I don't like walking through that subway.' She folded her arms around her protectively. 'I won't do it. And I wasn't there that night. I was here!'

'Who saw you here?'

She scowled. 'My lodgers!'

'Well, I suppose that's easily checked,' said Penny. 'However, on our way here we called in at The Tiger Tavern. We know a barmaid there, Sarah Lyford. We asked her if she saw a lady matching your description that night. It took her a moment to think about it but she thinks she saw you loitering outside the tavern a few times.'

Mrs Fielding twisted her lip. 'I don't loiter!'

'Well, you did that night because you waited for Archie Mitchell outside The Tiger Tavern.'

'I hate the dark! I'd never do that!'

'You must have confronted Archie a few times about the locket before that night,' Penny continued. 'And you must have grown frustrated he wouldn't tell you where it was. That's why he hid it in The Tiger Tavern, isn't it? If he'd hidden it in his room you'd have got hold of it. Why do you think he kept hold of it?'

'I don't know.' She shrugged. 'He probably had his own ideas about blackmailing Sir Laurence. Saw a way to make a bit of money for himself.'

'By the time you met him that night, you'd had enough,' said Penny. 'You needed him to talk so you threatened him. And to threaten him, you needed a weapon.'

'I've never touched a gun in my life!'

'We don't believe that's true,' said Emma. 'But there is something we believe... we don't think you intended to kill Archie Mitchell that night.'

Mrs Fielding gave a start and stared at her. 'I didn't,' she said, eventually. 'I never wanted to kill him!'

Unintentionally, the landlady was almost admitting she'd fired the shot.

'You shot him in the leg because you wanted him to tell you where the locket was,' Emma continued. 'You thought it would be an injury he would recover from. But he died because he knocked his head on the ground when he fell.'

'When he was in hospital you must have been hopeful he

would recover,' added Penny. 'But then again, maybe not. Because he'd have been able to tell people who'd shot him, wouldn't he?'

'He'd have been too scared to,' she said. 'Because then people would know he had the locket. Sir Laurence wanted that locket and he couldn't risk Sir Laurence finding out.'

'But then we made a mistake,' said Emma.

'What mistake?' asked the landlady.

'When you asked if the Mulholland family had the locket, we told you it was with its rightful owner. And you knew who the rightful owner was, didn't you? Rosie Clark.'

Mrs Fielding gave a shrug. 'I don't remember that conversation,' she said.

'I think you do,' said Penny. 'Because two days later, someone broke into Miss Clark's home and ransacked the place. Not only were they looking for the locket but they also placed the murder weapon there so the police would suspect Rosie Clark and Seamus Byrne. That intruder was you.'

The landlady folded her arms. 'If only I was that clever,' she said.

'You are that clever,' said Penny. 'And you have fooled the police for a long time.'

Emma couldn't be certain, but she thought Jane Fielding seemed a little proud of her achievement.

'It sounds like a good story,' said the landlady. 'But you can't prove anything.' She unfolded her arms and rubbed her palms together. 'Does it feel cold in here to you?'

'Not particularly,' said Penny.

'Well, I'm cold. I'm going to light the fire.'

She got up, took a matchbox from the mantelpiece and bent down to light the kindling which was laid ready in the fireplace.

'I need a drink too,' she muttered. 'Brandy should do it.' She bent down to open a little cupboard, then took out a bottle.

Emma heard something fall over. 'Oh dear,' said Mrs Fielding. 'The lid wasn't on properly and it's spilled all over this rug. Oh dear.'

'Do you need a hand with something?' asked Penny.

'No, I'm quite all right.'

Emma felt her scalp crawl. Mrs Fielding was behaving very oddly indeed.

The landlady stepped over to the door and locked it.

Penny gave Emma a concerned glance and got to her feet. 'What are you doing?'

'Oh nothing.' The landlady pulled the key out of the lock and tossed it into the flames.

Penny gave Emma another worried glance and their gaze went to the narrow window. Was it to be their only way out?

'Oh dear,' said Mrs Fielding again.

The brandy on the rug went up in flames.

'No!' Penny pulled the lace tablecloth off the table and tried to smother the flame.

But lace was no good.

'Oh dear!' said the landlady. The hem of her skirt had caught fire.

'Good grief!' Penny cried out. She tugged at the curtain by the window and eventually managed to pull it off the curtain pole.

The heat in the room was intensifying. Emma glanced around looking for something she could use to put out the flames.

Penny launched herself at the landlady, trying to smother her with the curtain. The woman let out a strange cackle. It was a dreadful sound which chilled Emma's blood.

She ran to the window and fumbled with the clip which kept it closed. It moved, but when she tried to pull up the sash it wouldn't budge.

Choking smoke was filling the room and Emma's eyes watered. She could see the landlady on the floor with the curtain over her. The curtain was alight too and Penny was now having to stand back helplessly.

Her cackle turned to a scream. One that became so loud that Emma couldn't bear it a moment longer.

Coughing hard from the smoke, she picked up one of the dining chairs and aimed one of its legs at the window.

The glass was tough but she kept trying. They had to get out. They had to escape the flames.

Eventually the glass shattered. The gap was small but it was possible they could squeeze through it.

'You go!' Penny called out. 'I'll follow!'

'No! You first!' said Emma. 'You have children waiting at home for you.'

Penny stared at her for a moment, her face becoming lost in the smoke. 'Go!' shouted Emma. 'Go now!'

NINETY

The smoke. The heat. The screams of the landlady as the flames engulfed her.

The memories were seared in Emma's mind as she drifted in and out of a fitful sleep. Time passed and she had no idea whether it was night or day. Each breath felt shallow and rasping, as if the smoke still lingered somewhere inside her.

The world around her seemed muffled, as though wrapped in fog. She could taste the acrid bitterness of the fire still clinging to her tongue, could smell it faintly in her hair and on her skin no matter how carefully the nurse had washed her.

Once she felt well enough, Penny visited.

They said little to begin with. Penny held her hand and Emma could feel the roughness of the bandage wrapped around her injured palm.

'Thank you,' said Penny.

'For what?' Emma could barely find her voice. It hurt to speak. Her throat was raw and her chest ached.

'For telling me to leave,' said Penny. 'For saving me. You did it for my children.'

Emma managed a smile. She tried to speak again but Penny stopped her. 'You don't have to say anything,' she said. 'You can do that when you start to feel better. And there's a lot to talk about when you're ready.'

Penny returned the following day. This time Emma managed to prop herself up on her pillows but a dull pounding filled her temples. She felt fragile, as if the smallest movement might cause her to shatter.

But she was alive. And so was Penny.

'I keep seeing her,' Emma said, gripping Penny's hand. 'How do I stop seeing her?'

'Don't try to stop it,' replied her friend. 'The harder you try, the more she'll stay with you. Eventually she'll fade, I promise. And when you get out of hospital and gradually resume your everyday life again, she will fade even more. You'll create new memories. Good memories. Ones that you'll happily remember while the unwanted ones drift away. But for now... it will be difficult. I find it difficult too.'

She looked down at the bedclothes, her face sombre.

'Why did she choose to die like that?' Emma said. 'She could have cooperated with the police and her arrest could have been calm. She may even have been shown mercy at the trial because she never intended to kill Archie Mitchell. Or so she claimed.'

Penny sighed. 'Perhaps it seemed to her like the easiest escape at the time. Although it wasn't, was it? She suffered.'

Emma nodded, closing her eyes for a moment. 'She did.'

Penny squeezed her hand. 'But you're getting better every day, Emma. The nurses told me earlier how pleased they are with your progress. You're going to be all right.'

Emma opened her eyes again and smiled. 'Thank you, Penny. I think we'll both be all right. Eventually.'

NINETY-ONE

'The first item on the agenda this evening,' said Mr Curtis, chairman of the Metropolitan Public Gardens Committee, 'is the arrest of Sir Laurence Mulholland. His sudden downfall has come as a great shock to many of us.'

'A shock?' said Clara before she could stop herself. Every face in the room turned towards her. She felt obliged to continue, 'I can't say I'm surprised at all. It's been quite apparent for some time that he was up to no good.'

'Thank you, Mrs Clifton,' said the chairman. 'I shall continue.' He adjusted his spectacles and glanced at his notes. 'I also read in the newspaper that the distinguished Mr Oscar Garland, recently retired from the Metropolitan Board of Works, was arrested two days ago on charges of corruption.'

Mr Sturgeon shook his head. 'It's an outrage,' he said. 'I spoke to Mr Garland's wife yesterday and she's terribly upset.'

Clara held her tongue. It was hardly surprising Mrs Garland was upset. She'd likely grown accustomed to a comfortable life without asking too many questions about where the money came from.

'All of this,' said the chairman, 'appears to have come to light after the publication of a series of articles in the *Morning Express* concerning Sir Laurence Mulholland's business dealings. The investigation revealed that Mulholland paid bribes to Mr Garland.' He shook his head. 'Quite disgraceful.'

'The police will look into it all, of course,' said Mr Sturgeon. 'You can't always trust these journalists.'

Clara smiled faintly to herself. The discovery of Oscar Garland's signature on so many of the documents she'd found in the archives had proved very useful indeed.

'I should add,' said Mr Curtis, lowering his voice slightly, 'that Sir Laurence hasn't merely been arrested for corruption. There are dreadful rumours – so awful I hesitate to repeat them – but they must be acknowledged, nonetheless. It's said that he was involved in the death of a young man on the Ratcliffe Highway. The young man died protecting a lady and her child whom Sir Laurence had wished to harm.'

'That's awful!' cried Mr Wheeler, the committee secretary.

'Yes, quite. The story goes that a carriage and pair was deliberately driven at the woman. But that's only what I've heard. I expect the details will appear in the papers soon enough. Don't minute any of this, please, Wheeler.' He gave the secretary a pointed look. 'In fact, there's quite a lot of this discussion I don't wish to have recorded. But I'm informing you all because the arrest of Sir Laurence naturally has implications for the St Pancras development.'

He paused, adjusted his papers and continued. 'I understand the company will now be run by Sir Laurence's son, Gregory Mulholland. From what I hear, he intends to take a very different approach to his father. He's already paused the plans for the St Pancras project and has been visiting the site to assess what his father was doing there.'

This news pleased Clara. 'So he'll save the disused graveyard?' she asked. 'And consider our proposal to turn it into a public garden?'

'Yes, I sincerely hope so,' said Mr Curtis. 'From what I hear, the young man is quite unlike his father. In fact, there's word that he was the one who betrayed him to the authorities.'

'Goodness,' said Mr Sturgeon. 'Did father and son fall out, then?'

'It appears so,' said Mr Curtis. 'In any case, it's promising news for our plans for the St Pancras burial ground. I propose we write to Mr Gregory Mulholland, expressing our interest in the site and suggesting a meeting to discuss our proposal. How does that sound?'

He glanced around the table. To Clara's satisfaction, heads nodded in agreement.

'I think it's an excellent idea,' said Clara with a grin.

NINETY-TWO

'I've decided to return to London,' said Gregory to Rosie. They sat together in the front room. Edward slept in her arms while her mother boiled the kettle on the stove. 'I'm going to be taking over the family company because Father can't be in charge anymore.'

'Because he's been arrested?' said Rosie.

'That's right.'

'What are the charges?'

'Oh, there's a great long list of them. I'll explain them all to you another time. Don't worry about them for now, you need to feel better first.' He paused for a moment, running his hand through his hair. 'I shall move my family down too. My wife... she's expecting our child in September.'

Rosie smiled. 'That's lovely.'

'Yes, it's... She doesn't know about you. Or Edward.' He glanced down at the baby in her arms. 'Unfortunately it may have to stay that way.'

'I understand.' It wasn't easy to accept, but Rosie knew she had no choice.

'But I would like to call on you both, if that's all right? As a friend... It sounds odd saying it, but I'm married now.'

'To a lucky lady.' She meant it.

His expression fell. 'I'm so sorry, Rosie. I wanted this to be different. You know I did.'

'I know.'

'So I shall do what I can. I'll pay your rent for a nicer place and I'll make sure you're looked after.'

'We're not a charity case!' piped up Rosie's mother.

'No, I realise that. You're proud people too. You don't want to be reliant on anyone's money. I just want to help so you're not living in a place like this. And I would like to...' He looked down at Edward again. 'See this little chap grow up.'

Rosie wiped a tear from her eye. Gregory's return was more than she'd ever dreamed of.

'It's important you look after your own family first,' she said. 'But if you want to call on us from time to time, then we'll always be here, won't we, Ma?'

'Oh yes,' said her mother with a roll of her eyes. 'We'll always be about. You won't get rid of us quite so easily again, Mr Mulholland.'

A few days later, Emma glanced at the line of visitors arriving in the ward. It was visiting time and she hoped she'd catch sight of a familiar face soon.

Penny was first. There was a spring to her step as she approached Emma's bed with a broad smile on her face. 'You're looking so much better today!'

'Am I?' croaked Emma.

'I brought you these.' Penny held up a box of biscuits then put it on the nightstand next to Emma's bed.

'Here comes Mrs Solomon,' said Penny. 'Is that a new hat she's wearing?'

Emma took in the enormous bonnet which was decorated with feathers. 'Gosh,' she said. 'It must be.'

'How lovely to see you looking so well, Mrs Langley,' said her landlady. 'Have they told you when you're going to be out of here yet?'

'Not yet. I don't really need to be in here.'

'Oh but you do! The fireman said he didn't know how long you were out cold on the floor for. It's an absolute miracle the flames didn't reach you.'

'Yes,' said Penny. 'A miracle.' Her voice was sombre. 'I'll never forget that moment when I feared the very worst. Even when they carried you out, you looked...'

'Dead,' said Mrs Solomon.

'I wasn't quite going to say that!' said Penny, a little horrified.

'It's true though isn't it?' said the landlady. 'Just awful. And yet here you are, Mrs Langley, looking like a picture of health. It's restored my faith in the Lord almighty.' She lifted her eyes upwards.

Clara Clifton approached, smiling broadly. 'I've brought you biscuits today!' Then her gaze fell on the nightstand. 'Oh. You already have some.'

'I can never have too many biscuits,' said Emma, wincing at the hoarseness in her voice. 'Perhaps we can all share some now?'

'That's an excellent idea,' said Mrs Solomon.

'What's happened to the burial ground?' Emma rasped at Clara. 'Have you managed to save it?'

'Yes.' Clara grinned. 'The Metropolitan Public Gardens Committee has managed to step in now. The new director of Mulholland and Son, Gregory Mulholland, has agreed we can create a little park there. And demolition work on the rest of the site has been halted for the time being while he decides what to do.'

Penny sighed. 'He's got a lot of work to do. But he seems sensible so let's hope he can banish the legacy of his father.'

Emma's heart gave a skip as she saw Harry Wright walking towards them with a bouquet of roses and tulips in varying shades of cheerful pink.

'Oh, goodness me,' said Penny. 'These look pretty.'

Harry looked bashful as he approached. 'I didn't realise there'd be so many people here already.'

'There are only three of us,' said Mrs Solomon, opening a packet of biscuits.

'I think Harry might be embarrassed that we've all seen him arrive with flowers,' said Penny.

He blushed. 'Actually, I've been celebrating,' he said. 'Have you seen my articles in the paper? Three of them have been published now and Oscar Garland, formerly of the Metropolitan Board of Works, has been arrested for accepting bribes from Sir Laurence Mulholland.'

'That's wonderful news!' said Penny.

'I've interviewed Gregory Mulholland who is taking over the business,' continued Harry. 'And he's promised to house all the people his father evicted. Unfortunately demolition has already begun on the buildings, but the young Mulholland says he'll ensure they're rebuilt quickly and the residents will be able to return.'

'Thank goodness,' said Emma.

'And there's more to come,' he added. 'Sir Laurence's trial for murder and attempted murder. And Johnny Cooper's trial for murder and assault too.' He pulled a grimace. 'It's at times like this when we need to remind ourselves that most people are nice, pleasant people, aren't they? Only a few people are as evil as those two men.'

'But unfortunately they cause a lot of damage,' said Mrs Solomon. 'So we hear a lot about them. What about the woman who died, she was a murderer too, wasn't she?'

'Mrs Fielding?' said Penny. 'Yes, the police are certain she murdered Archie Mitchell. The Bull Dog pistol which she left in Rosie Clark's home was one of three which had been owned by her husband. And Sarah Lyford is certain she saw her waiting outside The Tiger Tavern on the night of Archie Mitchell's death. She'd assumed she was one of the women waiting for their husbands, but when we described Jane Fielding she realised she had seen her. She was a short, distinctive-looking lady.'

'Very sad,' said Mrs Solomon, biting into a biscuit. 'But... as you've reminded us, Mr Wright – most people are very nice indeed. And so are these biscuits.'

A nurse approached. 'What is this?' she asked. 'A party?'

'No,' said Mrs Solomon. 'We're just visiting our dear friend.'

'A maximum of two visitors per bed,' scolded the nurse. 'Two of you will have to leave now.'

'I'll go,' said Penny. 'James is waiting outside with the children and I told him I wouldn't be long.'

'I'll come with you, Penny,' said Clara. They both said goodbye to Emma.

'I'll see you tomorrow,' added Penny.

Harry remained with Mrs Solomon who was quietly enjoying the box of biscuits.

'Thank you for the flowers,' said Emma. 'They're beautiful.'

'Are they? Oh good. I don't know much about flowers. But I'm glad you like them. They're colourful, aren't they?' He glanced around the ward. 'Hospitals aren't very colourful places. Do you suppose a nurse will put the flowers in a vase for you? She seemed a little bit grumpy, that nurse who spoke to us just now. I might find another and ask her. In a while.'

'Thank you,' said Emma.

They held each other's gaze for a moment and Harry fidgeted with the brim of his hat in his hand.

'Oh!' Mrs Solomon startled. 'Have Penny and Clara gone?'

Emma nodded.

'It's just us three? Oh... Well, I should be polite and leave you to it.'

'You don't have to go,' said Emma.

'No, it's fine. I shall.' She licked some biscuit crumbs from her fingers. 'There are still a few left in there. I shall see you tomorrow, Mrs Langley.'

'I feel bad,' said Harry. 'She left so she could leave us alone.'

'Don't feel bad,' said Emma. 'I like you being here.'

'You do?'

'Yes.'

He adjusted his tie. 'Good. That's erm... good, I suppose.' He gave an awkward laugh then paused for a moment. 'When you're better again and out of hospital... would you like to do, erm... do something?'

'Yes,' said Emma. 'I would love to do something.'

'Good,' said Harry. 'I've got that to look forward to. And I've got a bit of time to think about what the something could be. Have you got any ideas?'

'I'm happy for you to choose.'

'Wonderful. Well I... I shall give it some thought.'

NINETY-FOUR

'Well, I never, isn't it lovely?' said Rosie's mother as they stepped into the hallway of their new home. 'A proper house!'

Rosie carried Edward on her hip as she followed her mother from room to room. There was a parlour, a dining room, a separate kitchen and even a scullery. Upstairs were three bedrooms.

Rosie didn't know what to say. It didn't seem real. Her mother moved about with excitement, going up and down the stairs, peering through the windows, her voice full of wonder. 'It's such a lovely location, isn't it?' she said. 'We've got Regent's Park nearby and all the shops within walking distance. And I can't even smell any damp. Can you?'

'No,' said Rosie. 'I can't.'

The house felt dry and welcoming. The paintwork was fresh, and the wallpaper still held a faint scent of paste. She imagined how quickly it would warm once the fires were lit and the curtains drawn.

'It's much bigger than what I'm used to,' said her mother. 'But not too big. Otherwise we'd be needing servants of our own.' She laughed. 'Wouldn't that be funny, Rosie? I can't imagine such a thing.'

A knock at the door interrupted her. The carriage had arrived with the packing crates containing their few belongings. Rosie's mother directed the delivery men to leave the cases in the parlour.

'That's everything,' she said once they'd gone. 'Though these old things are going to look miserable in a house like this, aren't they?'

'Gregory said he can give us a little money for new furniture,' said Rosie.

'Well, I've already told him we're not a charity,' said her mother briskly. 'Perhaps we can accept a few things, but we don't want to take too much. We can look after ourselves, can't we, Rosie?'

Rosie smiled. 'I think so.'

'Of course we can. This is a lovely start for the three of us, and no more than you deserve. It's a stroke of luck that Gregory turned out nothing like his father, isn't it?'

'It is indeed,' said Rosie.

Her mother busied herself with unpacking while Rosie wandered through the house again, trying to comprehend that everything here was now hers. Gratitude swelled in her chest. Gregory had done so much for them, far more than she ever expected, especially after she'd once believed she would never see him again.

He had visited her a few times since his return to London. She enjoyed those visits, although she had to remind herself that he came for Edward's sake, not hers. She wished she could teach herself to feel less for him, it would make things easier. He was kind, generous and handsome. The fact he was married made it difficult, especially when he spoke of his wife.

But the new house was a new beginning. Perhaps, in time, she might make herself respectable again. Perhaps she might even become someone's wife one day.

She looked down at Edward, who was gazing wide-eyed around the unfamiliar room. Rosie pressed a kiss to his forehead. 'Come on, my love,' she whispered. 'Let's go and see what Grandma's up to.'

NINETY-FIVE

Emma smiled once she'd finished reading the letter which Rosie Clark had sent to Penny.

'It was nice of her to write to you and let you know how she's getting on,' she said, handing the letter back to her. She and Penny sat with Clara in the sitting room of Emma's home. 'And it's good to know that she and her son are being looked after,' she added. 'Gregory Mulholland seems to be doing what he can for them. But I can't help wondering how much his wife truly knows.'

'Perhaps nothing at all,' said Penny. 'Still, it's a better situation than before. And the boy will have more opportunities than Rosie ever did.'

'Gregory Mulholland attended our committee meeting the other evening,' said Clara. 'We discussed the St Pancras project and he's promised that the new homes will be offered first to those who were evicted. The burial ground will stay untouched and he's agreed to help us turn it into a small public garden.'

'That's excellent news!' said Penny. 'And a testament to your persistence, Clara. I've no doubt Harry Wright's articles helped too. Public scrutiny keeps men like Mulholland honest.'

'Gregory told us he was always meant to take over the company from his father. But he was sent away to Scotland and knew little of the business. He didn't tell us why he ended up there...' She gave a knowing smile. 'However, he seems determined to make amends now. We'll have to see if he keeps his word.'

Emma gave a little cough and winced from the slight pain it brought with it. Although she was recovering well, some pain and fatigue lingered. Despite the good outcome for Rosie and her family, she couldn't help feeling saddened about the recent events. 'It's heartening that some good has come of it,' she said. 'But nothing will bring back Archie Mitchell or Seamus Byrne. They were two young labourers just trying to earn a living. Unfortunately for Archie, he found himself caught up in something too big for him to understand.'

'And Jane Fielding too,' said Penny. 'For her, the locket became an obsession. The ticket to an endless supply of money. Greed got the better of her in the end and taking on a man like Sir Laurence was always bound to end in tragedy sooner or later.'

'A lot of people fall victim to the ambitions of powerful men,' said Emma. 'Sir Laurence will stand trial, but how many others like him go on untouched?'

'Too many,' said Penny sadly. Then her face brightened. 'But remember what Harry achieved. Newspapers have a great deal of power these days. They present an opportunity for ordinary people to have a voice and learn about the activities of powerful and corrupt people too. When the truth is printed for all to see, even the most influential can find themselves without a defence.'

'The power of a good reporter,' said Clara, smiling. 'You still miss that work, don't you, Penny?'

Penny gave a small laugh. 'Yes, I do. I'm enjoying writing about my reporter days in my new column, Musings of a Lady Detective. In the next instalment, I'm going to describe my investigation into the murders in St Giles Rookery.'

Clara gave a shudder. 'I remember those. It was a worrying time.'

'Yes, it was. It will be interesting to remind myself of what happened during those days. But I don't want to dwell on the past too much. One day I'll look back on these days and miss them too. I think it's important we make the most of the time we're in.'

Emma nodded. 'I couldn't agree more.'

Mrs Solomon entered the sitting room with the tea tray. 'I hope you ladies aren't still talking about that dreadful case,' she said, setting it down with a decisive clatter. 'It's all over now, and you did a good job. But at a cost.' She turned to Emma with a frown. 'You're still not well, Mrs Langley. You've been through an awful ordeal, and if you ask me, it ought to be a lesson to you. Not to get mixed up in these things again.'

Emma smiled faintly. 'Thank you for the tea, Mrs Solomon.'

'Well, that's no trouble at all.' She straightened the tea cosy. 'And I've brought plenty of biscuits too.'

'More biscuits,' said Emma, exchanging a smile with Penny and Clara.

The shaggy cat padded into the room and stared at Emma who was sitting in his usual comfortable chair.

'You can sit on my lap if you like,' she said to him. He turned away from her, as if dreadfully offended by the suggestion.

Penny poured the tea and the three women fell into a companionable silence for a moment. The fire crackled softly and Emma felt grateful that peace could still be found in moments like this. If only for a while.

A LETTER FROM THE AUTHOR

Thank you for reading this Emma Langley mystery. I hope you enjoyed it!

Would you like to know when I release new books? Here are some ways to stay updated:

Sign up here to be the first to know about my latest releases with Storm!

www.stormpublishing.co/emily-organ

Join my mailing list and receive a free short mystery, *The Belgrave Square Murder*.

emilyorgan.com/the-belgrave-square-murder

And if you have a moment, I would be very grateful if you would leave a quick review of my books online. Honest reviews of my books help other readers discover them too.

emilyorgan.com

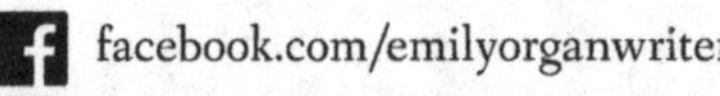

facebook.com/emilyorganwriter

goodreads.com/emily_organ

bookbub.com/authors/emily-organ

HISTORICAL NOTE

Tower Bridge is one of London's most recognisable landmarks. It took eight years to build – from 1886 to 1894. A competition was held to choose its design and the winner was architect Sir Horace Jones who sadly died before the bridge was completed. It's worth looking up the other submissions to the competition – there are some quirky ones among them!

Jones came up with a neo-Gothic design with turrets, arches and ornate stonework. The intention was to harmonise the bridge with the nearby Tower of London. The elaborate exterior is merely cladding and the bridge's true structure is a steel framework.

Along with the two turreted towers, the bridge's other famous feature is the road which is split in two so it can lift to let ships pass through. This was a necessity in the late nineteenth century when London's docks, warehouses and factories depended on river access. In its opening year, the bridge lifted on average seventeen times a day. Today, with heavy industry long gone from central London, it opens only around twice daily – mostly for pleasure craft and special events.

Beneath the river, the foundations for the towers were sunk using massive iron caissons, lowered onto the riverbed and excavated from within. Divers played a crucial and dangerous role, working in heavy, cumbersome suits to assist with positioning the caissons and inspecting the underwater works. Their job required immense strength and nerve; river conditions were murky, unpredictable, and often hazardous.

In 1977, the steel elements of Tower Bridge were repainted in the now-familiar red, white and blue to mark the Silver Jubilee of Queen Elizabeth II, a colour scheme that has remained ever since. Maintenance of the bridge – like all the Thames crossings in central London – is overseen by the ancient Bridge House Estates, a charitable trust founded in 1282.

Before Tower Bridge was built, people crossed the Thames at this point by rowboat ferry or the Tower Subway. The subway was a large iron tube beneath the river and opened in 1870. It was initially fitted with a small cable-hauled carriage which people travelled in, but the service proved unprofitable. The tunnel was converted into a pedestrian route with a halfpenny toll. Contemporary accounts describe the walk as a damp, echoing and claustrophobic experience. Once Tower Bridge opened, the subway quickly fell out of use and closed to the public in 1898. The tunnel itself, however, still survives and serves a more practical purpose as a conduit for water mains and data cables.

The Tower of London has stood on the banks of the Thames for nearly a thousand years, its origins rooted in the White Tower built by William the Conqueror in 1078. Over the centuries the complex expanded and served many roles: royal residence, armoury, prison, the Royal Mint and even a royal menagerie for six hundred years. Animals housed here included lions, leopards, cheetahs, monkeys, a polar bear and an elephant.

The Tower's darker history includes the imprisonment of figures such as Richard II, James I of Scotland, Henry VI, Anne Boleyn, Elizabeth I and Sir Walter Raleigh. The Tower continued as a place of confinement into the modern era, holding prisoners during both World Wars, and even the Kray twins, who spent a brief spell there in 1952 after refusing to carry out national service and assaulting a corporal. Traitors' Gate was built in the late thirteenth century and allowed prisoners to be brought into the Tower via the river.

Legend has it that ravens have lived at the Tower since the seventeenth century. The birds are considered to be the building's guardians and Charles II was apparently warned that if they ever left, both the Crown and the Tower would fall. There's debate about the truth of this, and some say the ravens were a Victorian addition to the Tower.

The Victorians were intrigued by ravens, believing they were guardians but also birds of ill omen. Ravens are intelligent birds and have been known to work with wolves – another animal which humans have an uneasy relationship with. Apparently ravens help wolves find food and receive some of the spoils in return for their help. The birds have been mythologised in Celtic, Norse and Native American cultures. They are also mentioned in the legend of King Arthur and the Old Testament. The Victorians were known for their superstition so it's no surprise they were fascinated by ravens too. Today, eight ravens live at the Tower and are looked after by a Ravenmaster. According to the Tower of London website, the ravens' names are Harris, Jubilee, Poppy, Edgar, Georgie, Chaos, Henry and Poe.

The Tiger Tavern on Tower Hill was believed to have been established in the early sixteenth century. Over the years, it underwent numerous alterations and rebuilds. It survived the Great Fire of London and the Blitz bombings until 1965 when it was demolished. The tavern attracted several colourful legends, including the claim that it once displayed the mummified remains of a cat said to have been stroked by Princess Elizabeth – later Queen Elizabeth I – during her imprisonment in the Tower. Another rumour suggested a secret tunnel once linked the tavern directly to the Tower.

The Ratcliffe Highway in East London is one of the city's oldest thoroughfares and was known for its unruly reputation. Its proximity to the docks made it a natural gathering place for sailors from around the world, and by the eighteenth and nineteenth centuries it was crowded with lodging houses, taverns, music halls and less reputable establishments offering every form of entertainment. Various attempts were made in the later nineteenth century to improve the area's image, and parts of the Highway were even renamed in an effort to distance them from the notoriety attached to the original name. Although these measures had some success, the street's distinctive character was ultimately erased not by reformers but by World War Two – large stretches were devastated during the Blitz. Today's highway still traces the same ancient route, but almost everything along it has been rebuilt.